NOVELS

The Demise of the Soccer Moms

Buried by Debt

The Suburban Abyss

The Hallelujah Horror Show

Getting Ahead

Faceless

An Affair With God

THE HAUNTED SHIP TRILOGY

Alone On the Beach

Slipping Away From the Beach

Haunting the Beach

NOVELLAS

Madison Keith Ghost Story Series

Chances Are

SHORT STORIES

Reduction in Force

Maternal Instinct

Flash Fiction For the Cocktail Hour

Cathryn Grant

Getting Ahead

A Novel

D2C Perspectives

For my Father

Who taught me that getting ahead in your career is not

the most important thing in the world.

Richard E. Mach

November 15, 1933 — September 21, 2013

One

VANESSA KNEW SHE was considered eye candy. Sure, she looked good — long red hair, thick bangs covering her brow, the rest cut in layers so it spilled around her shoulders and tumbled down her back like a waterfall. Jazz classes twice a week kept her body lean but definitely female, and she wasn't going to hide it under jackets and shapeless cotton *business* shirts. It was unfair that her co-workers, not all, but most, didn't recognize the skill required to do her job well. Just because she didn't have a college degree didn't mean she wasn't smart or didn't understand business. Her boss said she was smarter than they gave her credit for. He was right. Besides, she shouldn't let their opinions bother her — being underestimated had always been to her advantage.

The things they said stung. Only a few days ago, Laura and Janelle had been standing near Vanessa's cubicle waiting to meet with Hank. Laura had announced that she disagreed with the plan to trim pricing. "Customers are very willing to pay for systems that store data they consider crucial to their business operations — willing to pay a lot," she said.

Janelle shook her head. Fluffy hair swept across her face and her pink beaded earrings danced as if they had lives of their own.

"I agree with Laura," Vanessa said. "No one thinks the cheapest thing out there is the best. And it doesn't always mean more people will buy your products. Sometimes it's the opposite. Look how many people shop at Bloomingdales."

Laura turned. She folded her arms and raised her eyebrows slightly. Her voice was low, the edges of her words hard, "We're discussing business strategy, not fashion."

"I know. I'm agreeing with you."

Laura smiled. "You're cute." She took a few steps away from Vanessa's cube and turned her back. Her next words were spoken so quietly, Vanessa couldn't hear, even though Laura was only five or six feet away.

Now, rain pounded the windows and ran down the glass in sheets. The sitting area outside Hank's office had a gray cast despite the florescent lights. The halls were silent, as if she were alone in the three-story building that overlooked the southwest tip of the San Francisco bay. The others were in Hank's weekly staff meeting. She picked up a mug with the *Avalon Systems* logo — a silver sword with a black grip, red and gold embossing on the guard, purporting to look like King Arthur's Excalibur. She wheeled her chair away from the desk. She pointed her toes and looked at her feet — nude patent leather Michael Kors with four-inch heels. She stood and adjusted the waist of her skinny jeans. The balled up foil wrapper from a chocolate kiss was lying on the corner of the counter. She picked it up and tossed it in the trash.

As she walked toward the break room, the hiss of the espresso machine rushed down the hallway. She slowed her pace. The staff meeting should have started by now. She thought she'd have the espresso machine to herself. She'd thought she could take half a donut from the plate on the counter without being observed. She liked doing things without being observed. She paused near the doors to the restrooms.

"Who told you that?" Janelle's voice was sharp, trying to sound authoritative but falling short.

"I thought everyone knew." Laura's voice was laced with a false surprise.

"Who's everyone?" Janelle said.

"I honestly don't remember. But it makes sense. She's in his office every day with the door closed. Most of the time when I leave, both their cars are still in the parking lot. Sometimes, even at seven." The espresso machine made a spitting sound and stopped.

Janelle laughed. "You think they're doing it on the office floor? Come on."

"Maybe not actually fucking, but you know."

"Oh God."

A paper coffee cup tapped the counter. Water rushed into

the sink between the espresso machine and the refrigerator.

"What do you think we should do about it?" Laura said.

"It's just gossip. Stop repeating it and it'll die."

"I'm not repeating it. I assumed you already knew."

"Well I didn't, and I'm planning to forget I heard anything. It's icky."

"You don't think I should go to HR?"

"Why?"

"You see the stuff she wears . . . how he's always staring at her."

The break room was silent for several seconds.

"That doesn't mean anything," Janelle said.

"It's inappropriate."

"It's not hurting you. Or anyone else."

"He thinks he's hiding it, but it's embarrassing," Laura said.

"Well lots of men stare at her. She's hot."

"Exactly. And she's inviting it. Look how she walks."

Vanessa sidled further away from the break room until she was at the corner, easy enough to slip out of sight if they suddenly stepped into the hallway, but still able to hear. They weren't doing anything to keep their voices down. The machine fired up again and she couldn't make out their words. She waited. The machine hissed and went silent.

"If they do have something going, which I think they do, it's interfering with the business," Laura said. "I don't like how she controls access to him."

"It's her job to manage his schedule."

"Not like that. I've been trying to meet with him for a week. About the Ops Director job. And she says he doesn't have time. No openings? Not ten minutes? Ever?"

"Send him an email."

"I did, but he hasn't answered yet. You know how he is with email sometimes."

"Maybe he's re-defining the role."

"She acts like she knows things."

"Don't get distracted by slimy stories."

"I'm not distracted. I'm tired of the private meetings at the end of the day, tired of the twosome lunches, tired of her acting smug, like she sees our performance reviews and knows how much money we make. She needs to know she's not as clever as she thinks she is."

It was surprising that Laura would talk this way to her manager, as if they were peers. But, when had Laura ever been careful with her mouth? She said what came to mind. At least you knew what she was thinking.

"It won't make you look good if you keep gossiping," Janelle said. "It's not going to help you get where you're trying to go."

The two of them were now almost ten minutes late to the staff meeting. They'd walk out of the break room any second. Vanessa stepped around the corner and started down the hall toward the second floor landing. She had no destination, but she could easily loop around and back to her cubicle, then wait a few minutes before she returned. She walked slowly, feeling the sway of her hips, focused on the graceful arc of her legs in her high heels, not thinking about what she'd heard. Not yet. Once she'd secured her donut and espresso, she'd sit at her desk and think about it. Better yet, she'd relax on one of the low navy blue cushioned chairs in the sitting area outside Hank's office, put her coffee on the table, study her cube from a distance and listen to their conversation replay itself in her mind, consider its usefulness.

Fifteen minutes later, she returned to the break room. All that remained was a cake donut, two fluffy glazed donuts, and half of one with chocolate frosting. Glaze had oozed onto the plate, creating a sticky sheen. Luckily, it hadn't made its way to the chocolate covered donut, and that was the one she wanted. She grabbed a paper towel, placed the donut on it, and made a cup of espresso. She carried the donut flat on her palm, and the mug, fingers slippery with steam and perspiration, back to her cubicle. She put the mug and donut on her counter and went to the restroom.

A woman dressed in a polo shirt and jeans, her dark hair pulled into a tight coil on top of her head stood outside the janitorial closet. In front of her was a large plastic garbage can on a cart loaded with a mop, bucket, and cleaning supplies. The woman snapped thin ivory plastic gloves over her hands. She looked down as Vanessa approached and nudged the cart so it wasn't blocking the restroom door. Vanessa smiled. "Are you getting ready to clean? I can use another one."

The woman shook her head. "It's fine." She pulled the cart closer to the open closet.

"Thanks."

The woman smiled carefully. The cleaning crew crept around the building like ghosts. They rarely looked the Avalon employees in the eye, rarely spoke. It seemed to Vanessa they were treated like a nuisance as they wiped down counters in the break rooms, cleaned toilets mid-day, and replenished paper towels. The company saved money by utilizing a cleaning crew during business hours rather than at night, and it made Vanessa's stomach coil in knots when her co-workers walked past as if they didn't exist.

Vanessa pulled open the restroom door and went inside. Her heels echoed violently on the tile. Metal stalls, tiled floors and walls, porcelain, all designed to shout back at her. Even the rush of water became a roar. She washed her hands. The paper towel dispenser whirred as it spit out the amount of towel considered appropriate for a thorough drying of two hands. She waved her hand in front of the electric eye and tore off a second sheet to pat dry her wrists and make sure no moisture lingered between her fingers.

She walked back to her cube, past inspirational posters and photographs artfully framed, their messages ignored. She settled in the chair closest to Hank's office door facing the half wall forming the front of her cubicle. The cubicle was nice enough — an L-shaped desk and work area with a large computer screen. Behind the desk was a credenza that held four snake plants in pink ceramic pots, each well over twelve inches tall. There was plenty of space for the iron coat tree and a six-foot cabinet full of office supplies. Everyone else on Hank's staff had an office. They closed their doors when they didn't want to be disturbed. From eight to six, five days a week, she was constantly available.

She took a careful bite of the donut. The flakey dough and chocolate dissolved on her tongue. She chewed slowly. She would have to tell Hank what she'd heard. It was part of her job to be his eyes and ears, mostly his ears. He'd even said so once, or something like that. It was difficult to imagine what his reaction would be. She closed her eyes and tried to picture his face, impassive, waiting for the full story. He never interrupted, assuming he knew what she was going to say. He was like that with everyone — gathering all the facts before forming an opinion, even before posing a question to gather additional information.

It was exciting to think about how he'd respond, whether she'd see shock or fear on his face. Would he let down his guard when he looked at her? Reveal something? She crossed her legs and studied her ankle. She'd been told her ankles were beautiful. They were slim with bones that made them look as though they'd been carved out of marble. It was shameful to admire yourself, but she wasn't being arrogant, just honest. She ate the donut in small, precise bites. The chocolate and sugar slid around her mouth, drugging her with sweetness.

It was insulting. Laura would never say those things about one of the product managers or an engineering staff member. They were in a different class, too professional and dedicated to their work to let something as ordinary as sex cross their minds. And of course, nothing was Hank's fault. Laura implied it was all on Vanessa — seducing him. A poor, helpless man who had stronger urges, simply doing what a man did. A woman taking advantage of uncontrollable male desire. Dressing provocatively, being too available. And that's not how it was at all. Hank was the one attracted to *her*. She could see it in his eyes, his mouth, his lingering gazes, and his insistence that she sit across from him every day, planning his schedule, but also gossiping, while he looked at her and smiled as the atmosphere of his office filled with warm, liquid desire. Laura hadn't said any of those things, but the echo was there behind her words — *controlling access*. Vanessa didn't control anything. Every single thing she did was directed by Hank. He told her to block out parts of his schedule to make him deliberately unavailable when he needed to catch up on email. He asked her to close the door when they met every day at five.

The truth was, he didn't want to meet with Laura. Especially now, with Laura's ravenous drive to insert herself into that job. She told everyone it was already hers, she was perfect for it, there was no way it would go to anyone else. Hank didn't say anything, but Vanessa could see that Laura terrified him, just a little. He didn't want to lose her, didn't want to incite her wrath, but he wasn't sure about promoting her. He didn't like her sense of entitlement. It wouldn't take much to push him toward hiring someone else.

Laura was right. Vanessa did know things. Hank trusted her. He confided in her. She knew what he thought about every single person on his staff. She knew his plans and she could interpret his concerns. In some ways, she was closer to him than he was to his wife, shut away at their home in Tucson where he lived on the weekends, flying back to the Bay Area every Sunday night.

Vanessa swallowed the last bit of espresso and sat up straighter. She uncrossed her legs. In the crevice where the back and seat cushion joined on the chair to her left was a tiny foil ball. Had someone really eaten a chocolate kiss and shoved the trash into one of his chairs? She stood and plucked it out. She dropped it on the paper towel with the flakes shed by the donut. Being an administrative assistant was like being a slave. The product management staff left their empty cardboard coffee cups on the conference room tables and Vanessa stacked them and dropped them in the trash. They ate the foil-wrapped chocolate kisses out of the glass bowl on the counter in front of her cubicle, never recognizing that she supplied the treats out of her considerably lower salary. They stood in front of her desk and talked about the business as if she wasn't there. When she offered an opinion, they gave her condescending smiles. Their eyes widened as if a stray cat had wandered down the hall and begun speaking. The job was like a form of slavery because there was no hope of advancement unless her boss was promoted. Hank was already a vice president. When, and if, he moved up to senior vice president, Vanessa could expect a promotion. Until then, her salary was essentially frozen, already at the top of the range for her classification.

They thought she was pleasant and friendly, wanting nothing, always available to do as they asked — ship packages, schedule conference rooms, order more soda for the break room, and re-fill the always empty candy dish. They were wrong. Much of the time, she hated them all. Except Hank.

VANESSA WAITED UNTIL the staff meeting had been over for half an hour before she wandered down the hall to the restroom to wash donut residue off her fingers. She walked past the break room, slowing to listen for gossip, wondering where the rumor would travel next. She glanced into the room and checked out the donut plate — empty.

When she emerged into the alcove between the men's and women's restrooms, Laura was standing near the janitorial closet studying her smart phone. She looked up, but nothing from her slightly pointed chin to her narrow forehead registered concern that Vanessa might have learned she was the subject of vicious accusations. "Hi." Laura slid her phone her into the left pocket of her pants. "I'm late to the pricing review."

Vanessa waited.

"But we never start on time."

"Is that right," Vanessa said.

Laura laughed. "Hey, I meant to ask you. When is Hank setting up interviews for the Ops Director position?"

"I don't know."

Laura smiled. She leaned forward and spoke in a low voice. "Yes you do."

"No, I don't."

"When you get around to it, Thursdays are best for me."

"Thanks for the update."

Laura touched Vanessa's shoulder. "Any chance you'll tell me who the other candidates are?"

"I can't."

"I'll find out."

"I'm sure you will, but not from me."

"It's no big deal. It's not like it changes the playing field." Laura stepped out of the alcove. "Now I'm really late. Let me know soon when I'm scheduled. And I know you already have the schedule. He tells you everything." When Laura smiled, the curve of her pale lips looked strangely friendly. It was their fullness — a startling contrast to her thin features.

Vanessa glanced down the hall. It was empty. The conference room door was closed. She could ask Laura about the rumor, watch her struggle to find an answer. She could force Laura to explain why she thought Vanessa was the kind of woman who would seduce her boss. But anything she said would get turned inside out. Laura was smarter in almost every way. She thought more quickly on her feet. It was better to talk to Hank. Or not. She had to think about that for a while. Part of her wanted to rush to his office, shut the door, and pull a chair close to his desk. They would laugh about it together. He'd wink and then he wouldn't speak for a few minutes, and she'd wonder what was circling through his mind. The risk of telling him was that it might put something between them, cause him to pull away from her, worried about his reputation.

She watched Laura walk down the hallway. Her glossy brown hair swung across her neck, her narrow hips, covered by a long jacket, hardly moved. She opened the door to the conference room, stepped inside, and closed it with a decisive click.

Two

THE PREDAWN LIGHT had turned the sky a charcoal color, promising the sun would force its way through the waterlogged clouds later that morning. Laura's weather app said the temperature was fifty-one. She pulled a thin white tank top over her navy blue sports bra, and a white sweatshirt with a gold embossed Avalon logo over that. She wrapped her hair in an elastic band, pulling it back hard so the shorter pieces in front wouldn't work loose and fall across her face. The stubby ponytail bounced as she moved across the room to her dresser. She put on thick ankle-high socks, picked up her Nikes, and walked down the stairs to the living area, stepping carefully so the soft cotton on her feet didn't send her skidding across the wood floor.

Built into the freestanding wall dividing the living and dining areas was a 75-gallon saltwater aquarium, the home of two eight-inch lionfish. She stepped up close to the glass and turned on the light. "Good morning, beautiful creatures."

The Volitan lingered among the plants, watching. Its white spines moved gently. The Radiata swam up toward the surface. Laura hadn't named them. She preferred calling them by their scientific names. It wasn't as if they had the persona of a dog or a horse. Still, that didn't mean her affection and concern was any less. After three days without food, they were hungry. "I'll feed you as soon as I'm back from my run," she said.

The fish glided through their silent world. The grace of their effortless movements soothed her and their utter dependence terrified her. The precision of their designs suggested they'd been created for a purpose she couldn't fathom. Despite their venom, their captivity made them weak. She'd thought about buying more fish tanks, overcome with an irrational desire to protect as many creatures as she could. What would they do, all these privileged fish, without humans to sustain and protect them? She supposed they'd live in the wild, but once they were in her home, they were helpless.

Every so often she wondered how she'd ended up with such fragile pets, a distant cry from her childhood dream of owning a horse, riding for miles on the flat beach in perfect control of the powerful animal while the ocean roared at her side. Its hooves would kick up sand, forcing others out of her way, leaving them behind until they faded into fog-shrouded specks on the shore. All through high school, Saturdays had been the high point of the week. After her riding lessons, she'd hung around the stables for hours, drinking in the animals' energy, feeling their heavy grace in her bones. It wasn't too late. She could certainly afford to own and care for a horse. It wasn't as if riding was something you forgot how to do. She just needed to make it a priority.

When her shoes were tied, her playlist set, and her phone snapped into the case strapped to her arm, she poked her earbuds into place. She went out, locked the door, and dropped the key into the tiny pocket inside the waist of her neon green shorts. The polyurethane soles of her shoes thudded on the Spanish tiles as she jogged down the stairs. Goose bumps flared up along her thighs, but she ignored the chill. By the time she was a half a mile into her run, her arms would be bare, the sweatshirt tied around her waist.

The three other suburban lofts joined to hers were silent, the occupants either busy with coffee and early morning email, or still asleep. She was never sure which. One unit housed a couple who were both attorneys. She rarely saw them, they might as well live at their respective firms. A single mom and her four-year-old son occupied the other downstairs loft-style condo, and an older couple lived next door to Laura. They were retired, always anxious to chat, although there wasn't enough common ground on which to develop a meaningful conversation. Mostly they marveled over the cleverness of their four-year-old neighbor and told Laura stories of their grandsons in Chicago where they visited once a year, while Laura fed and cared for their three cats.

She wove her way through the queen palms and past large bougainvillea, stubbornly blooming in the cold weather. She turned right, moving quickly, pumping her arms, covering the three blocks to the high school in less than five minutes. Often, as she walked along the silent sidewalks, she wished she could run the bay trail near the Avalon campus. Jogging past still water and wild grass on a carefully constructed five-mile route would be so much more satisfying, so much more energizing than running in ovals around a track with rows of empty bleachers reaching up into the sky. Avalon offered locker rooms for employees who used the trail or rode their bikes to work, but the thought of walking into the building sweating, her legs and arms exposed, of dressing and doing her makeup in front of other employees, was unappealing.

When she reached the high school, she entered the sports field through an opening in the chain link fence where the two sections overlapped, allowing nearby residents free access for jogging, Frisbee tosses, or running their dogs. Trees and thick shrubbery that towered over her, always in need of a pruning, ran along that section of the fence. Beneath the trees was hard-packed dirt and large clumps of even more non-descript shrubbery, bunched together, some with spaces hollowed out where they didn't grow in a uniform fashion, or where branches had died out. The area offered the kind of secretive places children reveled in, or at least Laura had when she was a child. She pulled the stiff branches away from her arms. It almost seemed as if they wanted to block people from entering, not really intending to share the facility after all. She crossed the grass to the edge of the track. At this time of year she usually had the track to herself. And although she loved the solitude, thin needles of fear pierced her pleasure. *Girls shouldn't be out alone in the dark.* Girls that were assaulted, murdered even, invited it by going to places they shouldn't, doing things they shouldn't do — seeking power in the business world, for example. Girls shouldn't play sports, shouldn't put so much effort into being fit. Girls were soft and needed protection. Despite years of flouting her parents' archaic view of the world, she couldn't erase a deep, irrational certainty that when she ran at the deserted high school track, something bad would happen to her.

She loved the feeling of strength and power in her body when she ran. She refused to believe she was weak and unable to protect herself. It was embarrassing and stupid, yet the whispers wouldn't go away no matter how much her logical, educated brain told her they were lying. She hated watching other female runners who appeared happy and relaxed. Could they see on her face that she was scared to death? From time to time, she worried about the same things at the office — that they saw fear leaking out of her composed expression. She comforted herself that the fear made her work with greater intensity, drove her to run faster, which was a good thing.

The thoughts dogged her until her heart began pumping harder, the sweat rose to the surface of her skin, and she was finally lost in the pure physical sensation, the demands of her body consuming every unwanted thought.

As she completed the third lap, a man emerged from the shrubs covering the opening in the fence. It was lighter now, although the sky was still plastered with grubby clouds. He was six-two or more, his body lean in what should be the perfect physique for a runner, yet when he moved his limbs jerked as though his joints weren't properly connected. Lank hair was tied at the nape of his neck in a thin ponytail. An equally thin beard sprouted from the knob of his chin. There was no other facial hair, just those long strands, the twin of the ponytail. He wore a tank top with gaping armholes that showed his ribs and when he moved a certain way as he lurched across the grass, revealed his nipples. His sweatpants were torn off mid-calf. His running shoes looked as if they'd been dunked in a barrel of tar.

Nothing about him said he lived in this neighborhood, although for all she knew he was a high tech titan with tens of millions stashed in the bank — a geeky software engineer turned nouveau riche, preferring to remain *down to earth* in his style of dress. He walked to the edge of the track. Without pausing to stretch his muscles, he stepped over the concrete border and began to run. His movements were more erratic than they'd been when he was walking. He jerked forward like a caricature of a robot, holding his neck back, his shoulders stiff and straight, yet he moved quickly.

He was near the curve of the oval, about fifty feet in front of her. She took a gasping breath and slowed to a languorous jog. Almost immediately, he slowed. His head jerked from side to side in small increments, as if it were locked in place. Once again she reduced her speed. Within a few strides, he'd done the same. As the distance between them grew smaller, her heart pounded furiously against her ribs. In a sudden burst of energy that didn't seem to have any source within her laboring cardiovascular system, she broke into a sprint and raced past him. Immediately he increased his speed and closed the gap. Then he dropped off slightly and remained about twenty feet behind her.

Moments later she heard him breathing, nasal, and wet with too much mucous. He passed her and slowed. What was his problem? They could take opposite sides of the oval, keep a similar pace, and not engage in this silent struggle. She kept her rhythm steady, but he was going slower now. After several minutes she passed him again.

She'd lost count of how many laps she'd run. She sped up, sprinting around the curve at the top of the field, then slowed because she was now in danger of overtaking him again. She stumbled to the side of the track and walked across the grass. She ducked under the bar that ran along the concrete platform at the base of the bleachers. She pulled herself up onto the platform and sat down in the front row. She put her elbows on her knees, rested her chin in her hands, and leaned forward slightly. She stared hard, willing him to turn and look, better yet, not look, but feel her watching, lose his focus, trip and fall, or become so upset he left and vowed to never return. The horizon was growing lighter — time to head home.

The man continued circling the track with spastic movements. His beard fluttered to the side of his neck but his ponytail hardly moved. She could hear the scrape of his feet on the gritty surface. She was certain he was going to lose his balance, sprawl across the gravel. She'd have the pleasure of watching it tear off fine pieces of skin, leave delicate lines through which blood would bubble out. But none of that happened. He ran as if he wasn't aware she was watching, ran as if he was headed to a real destination instead of racing in aimless circles, seeking purpose for his effort. Each minute that ticked by interfered with her carefully arranged schedule that got her to work before eighty percent of her peers, demonstrating to Hank that she had leadership potential, that she was dedicated and knew how to get a jump on the day, and the competition. Executives respected employees who came in early. It meant you took your work and your contribution seriously, that you were a go-getter — early birds and all that.

The man showed no sign of being winded or tired in any way, no sign that he might have completed his goal for the day. It seemed as though he might keep circling while the sun rose in the sky, reached its zenith, lowered itself slowly, and sank behind the trees. If she left the track, he would win, although it wasn't clear what the prize was. She had no right to expect the track to herself.

She climbed down from the bleachers. She couldn't waste any more time trying to outlast him. Tonight she'd go to a yoga class and make up for her loss. Yoga would re-align her brain and tomorrow she'd tack on an additional mile. She jogged past the point where he was making his way around the curve of the track and stopped. As he drew closer, she pulled her lips down and furrowed her brow into a deep scowl. He stopped and returned the sneering look with far greater intensity than she'd managed. She shivered and looked away. She turned and ran toward the fence, regretting what she'd done.

LAURA PULLED INTO THE PARKING LOT outside building four. At the Avalon coffee shop in the adjacent building, she purchased a non-fat latte and an apple. She entered her building and climbed the stairs to the second floor. She looked over the rail of the landing to the lobby below. As she watched, the security guard who manned the reception desk pulled out the desk chair and settled in his place.

Laura turned down the hallway leading to her office. Sunlight came through the windows surrounding the lobby and open space up to the second floor, shimmering off the gold-painted walls. The effect was warming and designed to be soothing, but she felt amped up. The latte was probably a mistake since she'd already had a large mug of coffee at home, and was still jittery and more than a little angry. That freakish guy had disrupted everything. She'd forgotten to feed the fish. She squeezed her eyes closed and tried not to picture them making their way to the surface of the water, hunting for food. They'd be fine until evening. Still, she was sick with guilt.

She put the coffee cup and apple on her desk and tilted the blinds to keep the glare off the computer screen. Her first meeting wasn't until ten. As soon as she finished eating, she'd find Brent and talk to him about a strategy for getting around that fucking roadblock sitting outside Hank's office. She blew on her coffee and took a tentative sip. Still too hot. She typed in her password — N0$topping.

For twenty minutes she nibbled on her apple and made her way through the virtual piles of mail from Europe and the East Coast that had arrived since she'd last checked before her run, if you could call it that. By eight-thirty she'd heard the espresso machine fire up twice and the sound of voices traveling down the halls. She picked up her cardboard cup, still half full, and went out and around the corner to Brent's office.

A blue tooth device clung to Brent's right ear. He nodded and gave clipped answers while he nudged charts around the PowerPoint slide open on his screen. He lifted his chin at her in a silent greeting, then tilted his head toward the chair facing his desk. He held up three fingers and mumbled, "Uh huh, sure."

Laura sat down. Sitting there while he talked to someone who was unaware of her presence made her feel like an eavesdropper. She should have turned and walked away, forced him to come looking for her, but that would make her look prickly. He would have tracked her down eventually for their daily chat, but she really wanted to talk now. She couldn't afford to lose another day helplessly waiting for things to happen around her. Getting this promotion wasn't something she could leave to chance. She was absolutely qualified and the position was rightfully hers. Hank knew her skills were outstanding. Janelle had given her a *one* rating on her last two performance reviews and Hank had signed off on those. The only hurdle was the upper layer of execs who sometimes entertained a fanatical devotion to hiring from outside the company. They got all wrapped around over-valuing a fresh perspective and new ideas. Well she had lots of ideas. All she had to do was make sure Hank had a firm grip on how the organization relied on her, and the job was hers. She didn't have to prove she had leadership abilities, could make the tough calls, understood all the financial and technical aspects of the business. He already knew that.

Vanessa's evasiveness was disturbing. Laura worried the interviews had already started. The previous Director of Operations had been gone two weeks. She would have thought Hank would start talking to potential candidates the minute he knew the guy was leaving. And that was the other thing. Hank's organization needed more women in management roles. Diversity requirements had to factor in, even if it would never be spoken about. HR would be tracking it.

"Alright then, thanks." Brent pressed the Bluetooth and pulled it off his ear. "Sorry about that. Thanks for waiting."

Laura smiled and sipped her latte. Why did he have to act so self-important? It was disrespectful, behaving as though her time were less important than his. He should have ended the call more quickly It was bad enough that he'd already acquired a director title of his own, asking him for advice made her feel even more subservient. There had to be a way to make him more eager to help her. The Director of Operations was critical support for his product line. Surely he recognized that. If she had the job, he wouldn't have to fight for executive sign-off on every decision he made.

"You're quiet." He pushed his chair away from the desk and stretched out his legs. His size-twelve feet were clad in those ridiculous shoes, no laces, like some weird hybrid athletic shoes and a pair of boots.

"Not really, just thinking."

"Did you see that email from Janelle?" he said. "*Please make sure to dress properly for the launch event — no jeans, even with suit coats.* What does she think we are, a bunch of high school kids?"

"Evidently. And why is she sending it now? The launch isn't until the end of March." This was why she liked Brent. He could slip off his alpha male attitude and gossip as eagerly as a girlfriend. It was an admirable trait, although he wasn't alone. Plenty of men she worked with had it. Maybe as women had become an integral part of the business world, both genders had adapted, developing more similarities than differences — ambitious women, learning to control their emotions, men wallowing in gossip. The one thing that hadn't changed, despite being well into the twenty-first century, was the dearth of women in upper management. She and Brent had talked about it more than once, but it didn't concern him as much as it should.

"What's new?" he said.

"Nothing's new. I just talked to you fourteen hours ago. But there is the job."

"Did he set up an interview?"

"No. I don't get what the hold-up is."

"Too much going on." He folded his arms across his chest and pushed his chair back further. His office was larger than Laura's, easier to move around in — the physical evidence of being a director instead of a senior manager. There was space for a small table and two chairs, even though you had to shove the desk chair up against the desk to make room for three people. Not that the office was what attracted her. Not at all.

"Maybe I should just ask him. I'm playing by the rules too much. He'd respect some aggressiveness, don't you think?"

"It won't do any good. When he's ready, you'll find out."

"I tried picking Vanessa's brain, but you know how she is."

Brent laughed. "Don't waste your time."

"It pisses me off."

"There's nothing you can do about it."

Easy for him to say. He had more access to Hank. There wasn't another layer of management in between like there was for Laura. Sure she attended Hank's weekly extended staff meetings, but there were twenty people in the room. Those meetings were more like an audience with the pope. In addition to the staff meeting, Brent met one on one with Hank every week. She took a long, slow breath. If she wasn't careful, she'd end up feeling jealous. It wasn't as if her desire for the promotion was all about getting the inside scoop that the rank and file employees weren't privy too. Although that, like the larger office, was a pleasant side effect, satisfying a latent craving to be included in the inner circle, wanting to belong — whatever that meant. This was the next step in her career. She'd been planning the timeline since she walked out of school for the last time with an MBA attached to her name. And she'd be awesome in that role. Brent saw it, didn't he? "Who do you think the other candidates are?" she said.

He shrugged.

"You know, don't you."

"Focus on selling yourself, not on everyone else."

The sun was suddenly higher in the sky. Rays sliced through the blinds that Brent hadn't angled sharply enough. Her eyes watered. The walls, the office furniture, even Brent's long, evenly sculpted features, wavered as if they were under water. She thought of her fish, hungry and confused. She shouldn't have let that creep get under her skin. If she saw him again, things would be different. But she wouldn't see him again. He was an anomaly. She'd had the track virtually to herself for three years. It wouldn't change now. It couldn't.

"Don't get sulky," Brent said.

"I'm not sulky!"

"You stopped talking."

"I'm thinking."

"About what?"

"First, that you know the other candidates and you won't tell me. Ditto for Vanessa. She treats it like an issue of national security. Second, that you don't understand why it's important for me to know who the internal candidates are, and how many are from outside, and third, that there has to be a way to get around Vanessa. She acts as if she owns him. Simple things like asking him a question shouldn't require an appointment."

Laura slipped her arms out of her jacket and let if fall across the back of the chair. The sun was making it too hot but she would not ask him to adjust the blinds. She squinted.

"Want me to fix those? The sun's right in your eyes."

"Brilliant observation."

He smiled. He wheeled his chair around, stood, and walked to the window. He turned the wand, tilting the blinds further toward the ceiling. "Vanessa isn't going to change. And at the end of the day, her gate keeping isn't going to impact whether or not you get the job. Focus."

"I know that."

"Did you want me to look at your resume again?"

"No, I'm good."

He stared at her. His phone buzzed. He glanced at the display but didn't pick it up.

"All I asked her is when will the interviewing start. Why would she refuse to answer that? Fine if she's worried she'll get in trouble for telling me the names of the other candidates and how many there are. But when the interviews start? Why is that a secret?"

"Let it go."

She pressed her fingers against the base of her skull. She was going about this all wrong, looking too needy, handing all her power to Brent, and even Vanessa.

"Maybe I should tell her what I heard about them having a thing. Then she wouldn't act so superior."

"Don't do that. You don't even know if it's true."

"I think it is true."

"You're the only one who gives it any credibility."

"Really? You really think that? Look how he is around her."

"Okay. Maybe. But so what?"

"It's wrong."

"That's between them and their spouses."

"She's not married."

"Whatever. It's no one's business."

"But it is. It impacts the organization."

"How?"

"It makes things that should be simple, complicated."

"Like not getting advance notice on the interview schedule?"

"It seems like you're not even on my side."

"There aren't any sides. I'm not sure what we're talking about any more."

"You said she knows things she shouldn't."

"Did I? Either way, there's nothing you can do about it. And it doesn't matter, it's just politics."

"In this case, the politics are affecting me. I'll do better if I can prepare for the interview. If I have an idea when it's coming. I don't need her calling me and telling me it's in two hours."

"I doubt that will happen."

"It could. I'm right here. She doesn't have to juggle schedules like she does with someone outside the company."

"You need to relax and concentrate on your skills and your background. You're completely qualified, but it's not a slam-dunk. You're obsessing over trivia."

Again, with the condescending attitude. Well that would change when she was his peer. Ninety percent of the time, he treated her like his peer now. The other ten percent, he maintained a barely perceptible wall that said he was a lower level executive and she was a worker bee. Despite being friends, the balance of power was off. He was right about one thing — she was focused on details that didn't matter. And he was her friend, she should stop worrying about who had more power. It wasn't healthy. But what was that comment about it not being a slam-dunk? Was he her friend or not? Surely he wouldn't express doubts about her to Hank. Her head ached, thoughts turning solid as iron, pressing against bone and nerves.

After she left his office, she walked down the corridor to the back of the building. The gold and cream walls, gold on one side, cream on the other, the weave of the carpet tying the colors together stretched before her, empty. At the far end was a window in a small alcove. She walked toward it. The bland emptiness did nothing to calm her, instead it made her feel more crazed, as if the institutional colors and furniture inside the offices she passed were designed to subdue all her ambitions and desires, but the attempt failed. She walked more slowly, taking long, deep breaths.

"Hey, Laura."

She stopped near the doorway of Janelle's office. Janelle curled a coral-tipped finger in her direction. "Come in for a second. My daughter's selling Girl Scout cookies. Want some?"

Laura stepped inside. "Sure." Janelle's perfume, heavy in the air, soaked into the fabric of the chairs was cloying, but for Girl Scout cookies, she'd endure anything. She smiled. "I'll take three thin mints and two peanut butter."

"Are you sure?"

"I love them." She glanced at the photograph of Janelle's

daughter, her hair the same honey blonde as her mother's, the same eager smile. "Besides, how can I pass up helping your cute kid."

Janelle fiddled with the hook of her long earrings — gold hoops larger than her ears. For a woman so full of bravado, she turned into something else entirely when her daughter was mentioned. "Thanks," she said.

"No problem." Laura wrote down her information on the order sheet. "I'll bring a check tomorrow."

"Great. Thanks."

Laura stepped into the hallway and continued toward the window. She looked out across the parking lot. The distraction of Janelle had provided a calming effect. After a few minutes, she walked back toward her office. It wouldn't hurt to review her resume again. Just to be sure. She couldn't take anything for granted.

Three

VANESSA STARED AT HANK'S OFFICE DOOR. Through the glass panel she saw the VP of software marketing. He sat with his legs crossed, hands clasped behind his thin neck, leaning back as far as the chair allowed. It didn't look as though he planned to leave any time soon. It was already five-thirty. Hank should be directing the conversation to a close, urging Sandeep, with his bony neck and sharp elbows and knobby ankles, prominent beneath the cuffs of his jeans, out of his office.

This was protected time, blocked on Hank's calendar. It had been scheduled every single weekday as long as she'd worked for him. It was the one point in the day when she felt like a critical part of Hank's staff. The time when she knew she was more important to his success than five senior product managers. Of course, he needed them or there wouldn't be a business to run, but he needed her in a different way, in a more urgent way, to help him function in every minor detail. And minor details that weren't carefully looked after led to catastrophes. If she scheduled his connecting flights too tightly, he could miss one and end up sitting in the Frankfurt airport for seven hours. If she didn't properly document his expense reports, he'd wind up wasting hours emailing explanations to accounts payable. Most important, if she didn't control his schedule, his calendar filled with appointments that lacked a clear purpose — people fishing for praise, wanting attention, needing him to notice their contributions, wasting his time. During her daily appointment with Hank she enjoyed his focused attention, his implied dedication to her. His well concealed, consuming need for her.

Why did Sandeep have to go on in such precise detail? He uncrossed his legs and leaned forward. His elbows dug into his thighs and he rested his chin on the heel of his hand. She heard the rumble of his voice but couldn't decipher the words. Not that she wanted to. She probably wouldn't understand the conversation, something about software bugs. She opened her purse and pulled out a tube of lip gloss. She turned her back to Hank's door and ran the wand over her lips. She'd already glossed them twenty minutes ago but a few sips of water from her refillable bottle had dulled the shine.

"What are you doing?"

Vanessa spun her chair around.

Laura leaned on the counter. She nudged the candy dish away from her forearm. "Getting ready for a date?"

Vanessa dropped the gloss into her open purse in the drawer. She closed the drawer and turned to her computer. "What do you need?"

Laura laughed. "So you do have a date?"

"My lips were dry."

"Uh huh."

"Do you need something?"

"I need to get a few minutes with Hank." Laura glanced at the closed door. "It looks like he's finishing up with Sandeep."

"He doesn't have any time today."

"It's the end of the day. Does he have a meeting at five-thirty?"

"Yes."

"Really? That's unusual, isn't it?"

"He doesn't have any time, Laura. When he's done going through resumes and doing phone screenings for the external candidates, I'll set up your interview."

"He's interviewing external people first?" Laura plucked a chocolate kiss out of the bowl. She put the round base on her thumb and pressed her index finger gently against the pointed tip. She stared at it as if she were inspecting the quality of a diamond, holding it out in front of her so it would catch the light.

Vanessa clicked to her open Facebook page. The angle of the screen made it impossible for anyone leaning on the counter, even Laura straining forward, to see what was displayed. She scrolled through the latest update. She clicked *like* on a funny quote about women's shoes and a picture of her cousin's Golden Lab puppy. Laura smiled, her eyes wide, waiting expectantly, as if Vanessa were eager to share any bit of information that might help Laura get an inside track on landing the operations job. Laura acted as if she'd never repeated the rumor, as if she wasn't even aware of it. She broadened her smile as though she wasn't hiding judgments about Vanessa dressing to seduce her boss, as if she didn't believe whatever was between Hank and Vanessa was only Vanessa's doing — a helpless man immobilized under a woman's spell.

The rumor was a funny thing. One minute she was furious, her neck growing hot, blood rushing to her face as it did when someone ignored her or treated her as unimportant. Another part of her liked thinking that others were aware that Hank noticed how good she looked, that he might want her, or at least wondered what it would be like to make love with her. Not that she would ever cheat on Matt. Not that she would even want a relationship with her boss. She just liked the thrill of possibility. The occasional dreams that lingered into daylight, and the daily hum in the atmosphere around his office when they talked with the door closed, when he came out and sat on the credenza in her cubicle, so close she could feel the heat of his skin.

"Are you okay?" Laura said.

"I'm fine." It was exciting to think about the jokes between

Hank and her, their easy conversations turning into something more.

"Well I asked you a question," Laura said. Her lips were darkened with chocolate-laced saliva.

"I thought it was rhetorical," Vanessa said.

Laura raised her eyebrows. She swallowed the remains of the candy and smiled. "It wasn't."

"Yes, he's doing phone screens first."

"Does that mean he's leaning in the direction of hiring from outside?"

"I really can't talk to you about it."

Laura peeled the foil off another chocolate kiss, flattened the wrapper and spread it out it like a tiny blanket on the counter. She popped the kiss in her mouth, and as she chewed, plucked another out of the dish. Vanessa grabbed the loose piece of foil and tossed it in the trashcan under her desk.

"I was going to throw it away," Laura said.

Vanessa squinted at the computer screen.

"I don't see why you can't talk about something as unimportant as a group of job applicants. I've done lots of phone screens — usually half of the candidates are completely unqualified. And it's not like it's going to hurt anyone if you tell me what's going on. I'm not asking you to give me their names."

She shook her head, tossing her hair away from her face. She balled up the remaining piece of foil. She pushed the dish away from her. "These are too tempting."

"When he's ready to set up your interview, you'll be the first to know."

Laura snickered. "So does he have five minutes after he's done with Sandeep? I just need to ask him a quick question."

"About what?"

"Nothing you'd understand. It's about the offsite."

"What about it? I might be able to answer it."

"Does he have five minutes or not?"

"No."

"Then I'll just hang around and see what happens when Sandeep stops going on. And on." She winked and glanced at the closed door.

Vanessa pulled a small cherry red spiral notebook off the narrow shelf under the counter. She took a red pen from the holder and held them out to Laura. "Leave him a note and I'll make sure he gets it."

Laura moved away from the counter. She folded her arms, wrapping her fingers around her biceps. The tight folds of her jacket covered the pinky finger of her left hand making it look as thought she was missing a finger. "I'm not going to write him a note." She laughed. "If that's all I needed, I'd send him email. I have to talk to him."

"You can't talk to him today. He doesn't like it when people hang around my desk and try to ambush him."

"How do you know what he likes?"

"I know."

Laura smiled slowly. "I'm sure you do." She turned. The light hit the top of her head. A fine gray hair glittered, stiff, separating itself from the others. "Tell him I stopped by."

"Sure."

Laura disappeared around the corner.

It was dark outside and the security lights in the parking lot glowed bright as if there were holes cut in the sky, letting light shine through from another place. The sitting area near Hank's door was bathed in shadows, the lights having gone out without the motion of people walking by for the past hour. Vanessa took a sip of water and tried to think where she'd made her misstep with Laura. It seemed as if Laura felt she'd scored a point, although it wasn't clear what game they were playing.

On the other side of Hank's door, Sandeep sat up straight. He crossed his arms. She took another sip of water and glanced at her email. Nothing new. It was five-forty. Sandeep stood and continued talking. When he finally opened the door, it was ten to six.

"You're still here?" Sandeep said.

"I have to go over Hank's calendar for tomorrow."

He nodded. "Have a good evening."

Evidently he felt no need to apologize for running well past his scheduled time, for making her stay late. Did he realize she was paid hourly? He must. It was one of a hundred ways they knew she lived in a different world. The extra cash would be nice, although Hank would likely rush their meeting because it was nearly six. She went into his office and closed the door.

Hank was half hidden by his giant computer screen. "Ready?" she said.

"Yes." He moved his chair to the left.

They talked for a few minutes about the offsite, whether she had everything taken care of for the two and a half days in Napa Valley. The event would be expensive, but Hank felt they needed to have some serious focus. When planning meetings were held locally, inevitably people showed up late, ducked out for other meetings, and generally failed to put their entire heart and soul into the company. He wanted their hearts and souls. He would never say that, but it was true. At the resort, they'd be a captive audience. Even their cell coverage would be spotty among dense pine trees and rolling hills blanketed with grape vines.

"Laura wants to know when you're going to start interviewing," she said.

His cell phone buzzed. He glanced at the screen and picked it up. "It's Deb, just give me a minute."

She'd hoped gently introducing Laura's name would be a good way to feel him out about the rumor, give her clues about whether or not to tell him. The phone call would force her to start over, killing the subtlety. Maybe she should wait. Knowledge was power. Once she told him, she'd no longer have the advantage of knowing something he didn't. In some ways, this proved she had no power at all, considering a silly bit of gossip as some sort of collateral. Yet it was important. He would notice her, she'd be on a different level in his eyes, not just a member of his staff in a life full of employees and staff. Nearly everyone in his life existed primarily for him, even his adorable dark-haired, round-eyed son.

She'd never met Kevin, never met Hank's wife. All she knew were the things he told her, and the photographs on his desk. Large, obviously expensive photographs. One eight-by-ten was a studio shot of his wife dressed all in white, holding three-month old Kevin. The background was a clear blue, the color of the sky on a summer morning, filled with a yellowish suggestion of sunlight. Deb was plump with the weight of childbirth, but there was something angelic about her with the ankle-length flowing white dress, not unlike a nightgown. Holding the round soft flesh of her naked son, she didn't look overweight, just pleasantly maternal. A goddess, with her hair long, draped over the baby's legs. More recent photographs told a different story. Deb's hair was cut short, sliced in a sophisticated style with sharp lines that brought out her large eyes. But she'd never lost the baby weight, and it seemed to have packed itself on more solidly over the past few years. She was still a beautiful woman with dark hair and dark eyes, but there was no getting around the fact that she needed serious weight loss. Vanessa couldn't understand why a woman who stayed home with her child and enjoyed the financial success of being married to a vice president didn't put effort into getting in shape. Especially with her husband gone, living in his Bay Area apartment five nights a week. Didn't Deb worry about him looking at other women? She should.

Hank was still listening, interjecting an occasionally muttered, *okay.* Vanessa wondered if Deb knew Hank met with her every evening. When Deb called, did she assume he was already home in his apartment? Did she even ask? And did he ever tell her?

Vanessa shifted in her chair, crossing her legs. She stroked her ankle, feeling the hard line of her bone. She straightened and looked at him. He was watching. She gave him the suggestion of a smile and scooped her fingers through her hair, letting it fall down over the back of the chair.

Deb might be the one person who didn't exist solely for Hank. She existed for her son. He didn't complain, he seemed pleased she was such a devoted mother, but he worried, casually, vaguely that because Kevin was seven now, Deb should be letting go a bit more. Instead, she was tightening her grip, signing up to help the coach with Kevin's soccer team, whatever that meant. She volunteered in his classroom, she chaperoned field trips, she helped out in the school office, and organized the fund-raising carnival. The list of things she did for her son was long. Hank insisted he couldn't blame her. Since she was alone all week, he was glad she kept busy. Yet he worried. Even when he didn't say it, Vanessa could see it in the tightness around his lips, the unfocused look in his eyes. And he did say it often enough. He never asked Vanessa's opinion, never opened the door for her input, just recited his thoughts, almost as if he'd forgotten who she was. She wondered if that meant he was jealous of his son. All Deb's affection was wrapped around the boy.

In fairness, the woman was essentially a single mom, although a single mom with a boatload of money. She probably had to build a protective wall around herself. Maybe that was the reason for her failure to lose the weight. Hank had never mentioned any siblings for Kevin. It was possible there wasn't enough between them to conceive another child. So many things Vanessa wondered about. But he was here, now. And so was she. Like they were every day. Deb was simply a face in a photograph and the indecipherable rattle of words on Hank's cell phone. Hank and his wife lived in two different worlds — different climates, different concerns. Hank said his weekdays belonged to Avalon, the weekends to his family, seeming to suggest that he never spoke about Avalon at home. And except for the hints of worry, and status reports on Kevin's school and sports success, he didn't say much about his home when he was at Avalon. Vanessa had no idea what their house looked like, what they did on the weekends aside from soccer and gymnastics events, and she knew nothing about their friends or extended family.

He ended the call and hooked the phone to his belt. "We were talking about interviews," he said.

"Yes."

"Did you print the resumes and do a first pass to get rid of the wackos?"

"Yes. The rest are in those folders." She pointed to the shelf behind his desk.

"The internal candidates? And Laura."

She nodded. She sucked in her breath and held it for moment, feeling the stillness in the office, the dark sky outside clinging to the windows. If she touched the glass it would be like a sheet of ice.

He stood and walked to the window. She half expected him to touch the glass, feel the chill against his fingertips, as if he'd read her mind and wanted to experience it himself.

"On paper, she's the best candidate," he said.

"You haven't looked at the external resumes."

"I can guess what I'll find." He turned and walked to his chair. He put his hand on the back and grimaced. "I have doubts about her."

"But you have to interview her."

"I can always count on you to bring me back to earth."

She picked up her water bottle and flipped up the top. She put it to her lips and took a small sip, careful not to smear gloss around the opening, making all the subsequent drinks unsatisfying. She could ask him whether she should schedule interviews for Laura and the other internal applicants — only two of them. But why rush things? It was more fun this way. She could watch Laura worry and get increasingly aggressive, which would only make her look weak and desperate. Vanessa took another sip of water. "There's something else about

Laura. Just so you know."

He sat down. "What's that?"

"I heard her talking about me. About us."

The ventilation system came on with a soft ticking sound. Warm air drifted into the room, well controlled, not blasting out in harsh gusts like her furnace at home. "She told Janelle we're having sex." That wasn't quite what Laura had said, it was more complex, more full of suggestion, but that was what she wanted Janelle, and everyone else, to believe.

Hank ran his fingers through the sides of his hair. It was almost as if he hadn't heard what she'd said. She'd hoped for a change in the set of his lips, that his gaze would turn completely to her. She'd thought he'd sit forward, or stand. Something. There was nothing to indicate whether the words excited him, or scared him, or if all his attention was on Laura's flaws and not on the suggestion of he and Vanessa together. It had been her only chance. She shouldn't have spoken so fast, should have made him question her, drag the information out so he was forced to respond.

He lowered his hands. He pulled his phone out of his pocket and glanced at the screen. The clock behind him said ten past six. "What did you say to her?"

"They didn't know I was listening."

He nodded.

She studied his mouth. There might be the suggestion of a smile, but she couldn't be sure.

"And why are you telling me?"

She swallowed. She was still clutching the water bottle in her right hand. A sip would give her time to think, ease the tightness in her throat, but she was afraid she'd dribble water down her chin. She hadn't expected him to ask a question. She wanted to see the muscle move in his jaw, something to acknowledge his desire. No matter how carefully she studied his face, there was nothing.

"I thought you should know what's being said."

"There's nothing I can do about it."

"She made it sound like it was all me, that I was coming on to you."

"Okay."

"It's not okay."

"Don't get upset."

"I am. I don't want to hurt your reputation, but it's not fair. She made me sound like . . ."

"Ignore her."

"She came by while Sandeep was here. And she said things. That she bets I know what you like."

"Don't let her get under your skin. This is one of the reasons I have concerns about her."

So. He was going to make this about Laura and her lack of discretion and her pettiness or whatever he wanted to call it. He wasn't going to let Vanessa see inside of him. She could feel his desire, she knew it was there, but he refused to let a single word slip through his lips. Had he ever said something he regretted? Or only at parties, when he'd had a few too many drinks, and then promptly forgot what he'd said? In the office, every single word was crafted before he spoke. Did that mean all their conversations weren't friendly and confidential after all? He only told her what he thought was safe, just putting on a show of intimacy?

She uncrossed her legs and took her phone off the table. "It's late."

"It is." He stood and put on his jacket. "I'll walk you out."

They didn't speak while she got her coat and purse and locked her desk. They walked down the stairs side by side. They were the same height when she wore her highest heels, and she felt as if the rhythm of their steps was identical. They had an ease around each other, knowing how the other would move, familiar with each other's gestures. Anyone watching would assume they were close. If they weren't in the office building, they'd look like any couple going to dinner. Vanessa with her hair tangled in the collar of her coat because she'd put it on hastily. Hank's hand in one pocket, his thumb on the button of his remote, his other hand free to take her elbow when they stepped onto the wet pavement outside the overhang of the building. Except he wouldn't.

Things between them were unfinished, but it was too late to speak in the cavernous lobby. The silence was companionable but beginning to stretch into something awkward. He walked with her to her car. "Have a good evening. Sorry I kept you so late." He turned and headed to his car, parked far away from the others so he could count on having plenty empty spaces around him to protect the paint job of his black Mercedes. He pulled out of the parking lot before she started her car. She waited a few minutes, fixing her hair and checking her phone to be sure there weren't any text messages from Matt. Why had Hank apologized? He'd never done that before.

Four

THE FISH IGNORED Laura when she approached the tank. It was as if they were saying — *Fine, you didn't feed us, we aren't going to dance and tease you with our exotic markings and our beautiful, dangerous appendages that have the power to bewitch you.*

She went to the kitchen and removed the lance fish from the fridge. She stared at the limp silvery creatures. She impaled the first one on the acrylic feeding stick. She returned to the aquarium and wiggled the first piece through the water, luring her fish with the illusion of life. The Radiata closed its mouth around the flesh and continued its graceful path through the water, pausing to wave its spines, always moving, even when it was still.

After both had eaten what they wanted, she replaced the cover, washed her hands, and sat in the coffee-colored leather armchair to watch them for a few minutes. The room was silent except for the hum of the pump and her own mind, thrumming as the day's events raced through it. The morning seemed so long ago, the intrusive man at the track seemed like a ghost from her past. All of her fear had been written over by the frustrating conversation with Brent, and Vanessa's stonewalling. She never should have let that girl have the upper hand. Laura had gone by Hank's office because she'd foolishly hoped Vanessa was gone for the day. She should have known better, should have checked the parking lot first.

There was no way an admin was going to continue to wield such power. That open position belonged to her and Vanessa was a heartbeat away from actively sabotaging Laura's promotion. She'd hoped the rumor would make its way back to Vanessa, that it would deflate her sense of self-importance. She longed to see a confused, worried look on those pouty, over-glossed lips. But if Vanessa had heard any whispers, she wasn't letting on. It wasn't clear how far the rumor had traveled. Janelle was a big gossip. She liked to pretend otherwise, and she tried to couch her snarky whispers in tones of professional interest — *I'm concerned that something might be going on in Jeff's personal life. He was late on his last three deliverables, and they were riddled with mistakes. That's not like him. Or it didn't used to be.* Then she'd ask, striving to show compassion in the softness and openness of her gaze — *Have you noticed his shoddy work? Do you think he's okay?*

Laura slid off her shoes and tucked her feet close to her thighs. She should think about fixing dinner. In some ways it was her favorite part of the day, now that she lived alone. Even after nine years, she relished the complete antithesis to the life she'd lived when she was married to Tim.

Her adult life had started out well, the poster child for having it all — an MBA from Santa Clara University, a new job in high tech marketing at a growing company, and a fiancé with dark hair, blue eyes, and a lean, muscular body that made him look positively edible in everything he wore. The guy could throw on cargo shorts, a torn t-shirt, and flip-flops, and women would stare at him shamelessly as he passed by.

Tim had doted on her. She was ashamed that it had taken seven years for her to fully recognize that doting was not always a good thing. A real estate agent specializing in historic homes in Palo Alto and Menlo Park should have admired her ambition. He had a constant flow of sterling referrals, which meant he managed to do well whether the housing market was up or down, and when he and Laura got married, it was headed up. Way up.

"You don't need to work twelve-hour days," he'd said.

She laughed. "You're funny. I got an MBA so I could build a career, not stay home and cook for you."

"I love your cooking. And I don't see you enough. Even when you're here, you're not." He stroked her hair, and rested his cheek on the top of her head.

Laura felt a strange mixture of desire and anger. She'd outlined her goals in great detail, many times. Why was he doing this? Still, she'd caved, choosing the desire. She stretched her head back, inviting him to stroke her neck with his lips until the anger washed out of her.

The tug of his demands was gentle at first. He joined her on a business trip to the UK and Germany so they could spend the weekend together in Munich. It hadn't gone well. He'd stayed in the hotel all day and sulked when she got in late at night after dinners with customers and the local sales teams. Every Christmas, he'd bought her a new cookbook. He gave her a set of Demeyere cookware. The kitchen eventually became a showcase of high-end appliances. And she used them all. When she was home.

Slowly, everything between them tarnished. She traveled too much. She should cook dinner five nights a week. "You're my wife. I can't be grabbing fast food all the time because you find Avalon more interesting than me."

"I don't think it's more interesting than you."

He looked at her, his facial muscles slack. He stared until she was forced to look away because his glare was a little bit frightening.

"I thought you liked cooking," he said.

"I don't like cooking when you force me to do it."

"I'm not forcing anything. I'm asking. I need to eat."

"I make sure we have leftovers. And eating out is nice."

"I thought you wanted to be a wife."

"What does that mean?" She backed away from the center island, all the way into the breakfast room. From that distance, he looked like a stranger.

"It means you want to be with me."

"You mean feed you," she said.

"That, and work in the garden, get the laundry done so I don't have to do it myself."

"I'm not a maid. We're supposed to be a team."

"Yes, but I make more than enough. You don't have to work."

"I told you what I wanted before we got married. You knew who I was."

He walked around the island and crossed the kitchen. He put his arms around her shoulders, pinning her elbows to her lower ribs. He put his face in her hair and took a deep breath. "You smell good."

She squirmed.

"Hold still. I need you."

That always got to her. There was something about a man, stoic and tough, unemotional, expressing raw need. Her body softened as if she was sinking into a mound of feather pillows. He ran his tongue down the edge of her ear. She shivered and relaxed her shoulders. When he felt her muscles give way, he released the pressure on her arms. He kissed her throat and unbuttoned the first button on her shirt. She looked down and watched him unbutton the next, exposing the top of her bra, the sheer nylon, her nipples already as solid as the tiny white buttons. He folded his fingers around the edges of the shirt. He took a half step back and yanked his hands away from each other. She heard the sound of threads tearing. Buttons skittered on the tile.

"Stop! What are you doing?"

She tried to pull back, but his grip was so hard his knuckles were white.

"Turning up the heat. We're in the kitchen, aren't we?"

"That's not even remotely amusing. Let go of me. This shirt cost a hundred and fifty dollars! I don't know if it can be fixed."

"Forget about the fucking shirt. You look like a man in it."

"Let go of me."

"I want to see my wife." He unhooked the center of her bra. The cups sprang to the side. He let go of the shirt and placed his palms over her breasts.

She shoved her hands against his chest but he must have been expecting it, he didn't lose his footing. "Let go of me!"

"You want a man to dominate you. That's how it is at work, right? All the men in the power positions? You're a female. Be a female and stop trying to be a guy."

"Get away from me." Her voice was soft. He probably thought she lowered it because desire was overtaking her, but he misread her.

Then things turned a little ugly.

She didn't want to think about it any more. She slid her feet off the chair and went into the kitchen. Cooking was fun when it was on her terms. All the pots and pans and most of the appliances ended up in her column when they split up their possessions. Tim got the home gym, which was fine with her. All she needed were a few dumbbells to keep her muscles strong. She preferred running. It made her feel she had the power to escape. She liked that all she needed was a pair of shorts, a sports bra, and good shoes. There was no need for mats and machines with digital displays and all kinds of settings, surge protectors, and adequate ventilation.

A brown paper-wrapped piece of sole sat on the second shelf of the fridge. She placed it on the counter. She opened the vegetable drawer and took out the bags of baby spinach, a yellow pepper, green onions, and cilantro. In the smaller drawer designated for cheese and lunchmeat was a plastic bag with a single jalapeno pepper, like a worm in a cocoon. She put the bags on the counter and reached down to the open shelf where the colander sat.

After the vegetables were washed, patted dry, and chopped, and the fillet was rinsed, she took a medium-sized frying pan and set it on the stove. She sprinkled in a few tablespoons of vegetable broth, heated the pan, and sautéed the vegetables. When they were ready, she scooped them onto a small plate, covered it with a plastic lid, and quickly cooked the sole. She poured a glass of Viognier from the open bottle in the refrigerator.

It was her habit to eat at the table with a candle in the center, using a placemat and a cloth napkin. It wasn't so difficult to enjoy delicious food served with class. There wasn't a single evening that she missed Tim. It would be nice to have a partner, but it had to be someone who supported her goals. For now, she needed to concentrate on securing her new job. She also needed to figure out how to get Vanessa out of the way and lock down some time alone with Hank. She'd gone about it all wrong. An interview would put her on the same footing as the other candidates. She needed face time, one on one. She needed a way to show him she was indispensable.

Over the years, her interaction with Hank had been one of mutual respect. Recently, he'd started coming directly to her with requests, rather than going through Janelle. When there was a pricing exercise, even if it wasn't for a product she was responsible for, he asked her to review the data. He knew she was brilliant at understanding discounting and lining up products and add-ons so there wasn't any confusing overlap or one product wasn't disadvantaged. Once or twice, he'd looked at her so long, with such interest in what she was saying, she had the feeling he was taken with her. She wasn't unattractive, and that, in combination with her intelligence, had captured his interest. Hank gave the impression he understood women were just as ambitious as men, and he liked that. It was a mental connection beyond words. She wasn't aware of that dynamic with Brent. But Brent didn't have the power, hadn't achieved the status Hank had.

The director position required a much broader view of the business. That was the problem. Hank saw her as a pricing guru, narrow in her scope of knowledge, and maybe a little geeky — a pricing savant. He was less familiar with her leadership skills. He didn't see her as someone with authority. It was funny that you had to be in a position of authority before they saw you that way. If Tim were here, and he was not, she didn't know why she was thinking about him, but the memory of his voice forced its way in. Tim would say it was here fault she wasn't advancing. He'd say she must have screwed up, she needed to stop blaming things she didn't like on other people.

She stabbed her fork into the last strip of pepper and put it in her mouth. She took a sip of wine. She'd poured too much, as usual. Still chewing, she stood and carried her plate and glass to the kitchen. She poured the rest of the wine down the drain, washed and dried the glass, and put the other things in the dishwasher. She returned to the dining room and blew gently on the candle flame. It bent away from her then flickered back. She couldn't blow too hard or she'd spray wax across the table like spittle from someone laughing while they chewed their food. It required a perfect touch.

If it weren't dark, if she hadn't just eaten, she'd go for a run. That always cleared her head, introduced ideas she hadn't considered. Instead, she'd watch a little TV and set her alarm to wake her at four-thirty. Screw the whispered threats about the dangers of going out in the dark. She needed a longer run and a clever idea. Tomorrow, she'd run six miles, and while she did, a new thought would plant itself in her mind. She was sure of it.

WHEN SHE REACHED the Carlton High School track, the curb along the athletic field was empty of cars. Good. She was alone. She went through the opening in the fence and clawed her way past the shrubs and vines, tearing them off her skin like they were long fingers stroking her body, trying to claim it as their own, pulling her down into the earth. The area hadn't been pruned in months. Budget cuts were causing small signs of decay everywhere. The roads were covered in ragged black lines in an effort to patch without resurfacing. Weeds sprouted in the strips of ground between sidewalks and streets, and last fall she'd seen a roach scuttling along in the gutter on her way to the track. The city no longer sprayed for bugs. Independent companies had swooped in to offer bi-annual spraying contracts, stirring up the fear of insects attracting rats now that the city *couldn't afford to do its job*. Laura resented it, but she'd signed up. She hoped her neighbors had as well.

She walked to the edge of the track, stretched her calves and quads, and took off in a burst. Screw warming up with a slow jog. She was still rattled from the previous day. She needed to push herself hard this morning. Besides, getting to a state where her body was working close to maximum capacity was more likely to free her mind to discover a new way for dealing with the situation at work.

It looked as though she couldn't rely on Brent to give her any insights, and she wasn't about to ask Janelle. Both of them had been at her level two years ago, promoted up. She was really the only one left in Hank's organization that had the potential to move higher and hadn't. Sometimes there was

a niggling thought that Tim's imagined voice was right —
there was some flaw in her, an unattractive blind spot that
was keeping her back. But she was rigorous with herself so
that couldn't be the case. And look at Janelle. Her open back
high-heeled sandals slapping down the hall, her oversized ass
that she took no effort to conceal, her precariously low cut
tops that bordered on unprofessional. The cloud of perfume
and long, coral fingernails. There was nothing about Janelle
that inspired respect or indicated she was serious about the
business. Although Laura had to admit Janelle was smart,
despite her bimbo impression. It suggested that all that
dressing for the role you wanted, acting like you had the job, was
pure bullshit.

Four laps around the track equaled a mile, and she'd already
completed the first one. She pushed Janelle and her hip-
jiggling walk out of her head. Obsessing over that, feeling
resentful, wasn't going to help her get where she wanted to
go. Brent was right about one thing — she needed to focus.

The semi-darkness made everything surreal, made her feel
as if the world was deserted. That was exactly what she
wanted and now she was wishing it was something else. It
pissed her off that a thread of fear was beginning to wind its
way through her heart and up her throat, even though she
knew it was nothing but years of paranoid brainwashing. This
was the suburbs. And an upscale suburb at that. There was no
crime to speak of — the occasional car break-in when stupid
people left laptops in plain sight, or an unlocked bicycle

stolen off a front porch. Non-crime, really.

She rounded the end of the track. To her right was the equipment storage shed. Next to that was a closed up stand where they sold hot dogs, chips, and soda at sporting events. The untrimmed shrubs along the fence were crowding up to the snack stand, ready to overtake it. She glanced past the small building toward the opening in the gate. It must have been her gut telling her to look. The skinny creep with the weird hair stood amongst the shrubs, as if he was determined to keep himself hidden. She stumbled. She regained her footing and increased her speed. With her back now turned to him she began sprinting. He had no right to be here. He could hardly run, his movements were ridiculous. He didn't appear to enjoy it so he should find something else to do. This was her time, meant for clearing her head and draining all the tension from muscles and bones that spent too much time immobilized sitting at her desk and in meetings.

Unless he was stalking her. He'd seen her somewhere else when she wasn't aware of him and he'd followed her home, then watched her movements, figured out when and where she ran and was now inserting himself into her life. Her hands trembled and she gasped for breath as she struggled to maintain the full-on sprint. Already she'd looped the track and seen from the corner of her eye that he remained partially hidden, watching. Her lungs burned and her heart pounded like an alarmed neighbor slamming a fist against the door to warn of a fire. It wasn't possible to have a heart attack at her age. Well, maybe it was, but she was in good shape, and she ate well. Her legs were getting rubbery. She slowed but continued running. She could stop and call the police. The very act of taking the phone out and putting it to her ear might frighten him off. But if it didn't succeed in scaring him, she wasn't sure what she'd say to the dispatcher. *A man is staring at me. I think he's following me.* There was no way to communicate the alarm she felt without sounding unbalanced. But the fear was real, and it wasn't just her mother's hysterical caution. This was her gut, screaming that the man was dangerous. As she rounded the top of the oval she glanced at the equipment shed. He wasn't there. Had he left, or moved further into the shrubbery? The sky had lightened, but the thick clouds still kept it darker than normal. She didn't want to slow down or he'd think she was vulnerable, he'd realize his presence had upset her.

Behind her, she heard feet thudding on the track. How had he slipped out and started running without her noticing? She couldn't keep up her pace. She glanced toward the opening in the fence. The best move might be running right across the grass and slipping out to the street. It wasn't impossible to jog around the neighborhood, she just didn't like it because running on concrete would eat away at the integrity of her joints over time. She rounded the curve again and as she did, she saw he was about twenty yards behind her. She ran toward the outer edge of the track and slowed. She was breathing so hard it would be impossible to speak, to tell him he needed to leave her alone or she'd report him. He ran past her, not turning to look, as if to make her more unsettled. She bent over and put her hands on her thighs. She gulped in air, closing her mouth slightly to let it out in a thin stream, trying to get her lungs to calm their frantic search for oxygen.

By the time he'd rounded the track and was coming up on her again, her breathing had slowed enough to allow straightening and taking in air through her nostrils. She folded her arms across her stomach and widened her stance. When he was about fifteen feet away, she took a single step forward. "Stop following me."

He came to a standstill so quickly and smoothly she wondered if he'd been waiting for her to speak. The thin beard trembled like it had a pulse of its own. His skin was pale and his hair almost colorless in the cloudy, pre-dawn light. "What?"

"Leave me alone. I mean it."

"What are you talking about?"

She glared at him. He was not going to get away with an innocent facade. She was not backing down no matter how much he tried to make her appear foolish. "I want you to stop following me."

"I'm not *following* you."

"You're here every day."

"I've never seen you before."

"That's a lie."

He backed away and returned to his slow, stilted jog.

She ran after him and grabbed his upper arm.

His left foot skidded on the track. "Let go of me," he said.

"I'm not afraid of you. But I want you to find another place to run, if that's what you're really doing."

"You're crazy. Let go of my arm."

"You're clearly not a runner. You can barely put one foot in front of the other."

He wrenched away from her. "What's wrong with you?"

She couldn't let him see she was trembling. "If you don't know what you're doing, you're going to hurt yourself. You shouldn't be running if you have a handicap."

"I'm not handicapped, you bitch."

She gasped. Her instinct was correct — there was a layer of rage very close to the surface. He was after something, he just hadn't been prepared to make his move. Yet. She'd thrown him off his plan. Too bad she couldn't leverage that skill at work. Maybe that was the approach to take with Hank, knock him off balance. She smiled.

"What are you laughing at? There's nothing wrong with me."

"Your body jerks when you move. You can't really run."

He turned and started up again, as if to defy her.

She crossed the track and stepped onto the lawn. She made her way through the shrubs and out to the sidewalk. There was something wrong with him. There was a reason he was there, watching her, and she was going to make it stop. But for now, she was pleased that she'd confronted him, and even more pleased that she'd figured out an angle for getting Hank's attention. All that needed to be worked out were the specifics.

Running a few miles on concrete wouldn't damage her body forever. She started a slow jog up to the corner and turned toward downtown. Something would come to her or an opportunity would present itself. All she needed to do was pay attention.

Five

VANESSA'S LEGS WERE like sticks of ice when she woke to the alarm on her phone chiming in her ear. She tapped it into snooze mode. The dream was slipping away. If she opened her eyes, it would evaporate. It was so much easier to retain her dreams on weekends when she woke naturally rather than to an electronic sound, no matter how well it was tuned to be calm and soothing.

She'd been walking down a street in the dark. Hank was at her side and Matt was a few steps behind them. The air was thick with the scent of gardenias. It was warm. She'd been naked. Matt hadn't seemed to notice, although she'd had the impression Hank was very well aware. They'd both been speaking to her, but it was impossible to distinguish their voices. Then, she'd been in a hotel room. It was familiar — the palatial room in New Orleans that she'd stayed in during the electronics trade show last summer. The dream was identical to one she'd had many times since she'd returned from New Orleans. Hank was in her hotel room. It was dark. He was kissing her. She was half enjoying the kiss and half trying to decide what to do, whether she should take charge and stop things from careening down the side of a mountain. Before she had time to make her decision, Hank was removing her clothes. He was very methodical, taking each item and folding it, placing it on the dresser before he proceeded to the next. When he was finished, he carried her to the bed and made love to her, although she couldn't figure out when he'd taken off his own clothes. Then, the hotel room was filled with blinding light and she woke. Every single time.

The alarm chimed again. Sticky thoughts plastered themselves across her mind like spilled food. She turned onto her side. Thursday. She opened her eyes and tried to think what was on Hank's calendar. And his apology — *sorry for keeping you late*. What was that about? She closed her eyes and let her mind skim through her closet, considering the tops that seemed to trigger a second glance from Hank. The comforter and top blanket were piled on Matt's side of the bed. If it had been a Saturday, she would have slid up close, wrapped her right arm around his waist and worked her fingers up to his chest, stroking the soft hair, running her index finger in a circle around his nipple and putting small kisses along his shoulder blade until he woke with a longing groan.

Now that it had gone on for nearly thirty seconds, the

phone's trilling became more annoying, boring into her ear like a mosquito. She kicked the sheet off her legs, sat up, and silenced the phone. The room was dark. Matt was deep in blissful ignorance of possessing all the blankets. She grabbed her robe and walked down the hall while she put it on. The main bathroom more or less belonged to her, the one she used to get ready while Matt slept. It took him all of twenty minutes from climbing out of bed to walking out the front door. She envied him, but she was not going to be one of those women who cut her hair short and avoided the work of a finely made up face. She liked looking good and considered the process fun.

The bathroom had a tub and shower combo. It was a nice shower with solid water pressure and the tub made it easier for shaving her legs without slipping and slicing out a piece of skin that bled faster than the rushing water could wipe it away. There was a long counter around the sink and next to that a closet with towels and four gloriously deep shelves. One shelf held baskets of make-up and face brushes. Another held first aid supplies. The two center shelves were filled with bottles of nail polish, lined up like tiny soldiers in perfect formation. Matt rarely even used the toilet in the hall bathroom. He never opened the closets or drawers, so he was unaware of just how much nail color she owned. Far too much for one person to ever consume. Some of the bottles were probably dried out, the chemicals separating from one another. But she couldn't stop acquiring it. She felt her choices were endless when she opened the door and saw all the glistening bottles.

Every evening she removed her polish and painted on two coats of a new color. Her nails were shaped into short ovals so she could type easily without damaging the polish or having to hold her fingers at awkward angles to perform practical tasks. When she was a teenager her nails had been dagger-like. Once the realities of adulthood settled in, she'd trimmed them back, but she would never give up all the brilliant colors. Even when she was an old lady, she'd have gem-like nails next to her worn skin. Colored nails provided pockets of happiness in her days when she glanced down and saw ten glossy red or pink or taupe fingertips.

She showered and dried herself. She pulled on a black thong and a black bra with lace straps. While she dried her hair, she studied her reflection. Her pale skin looked dramatic next to the black lingerie. It fit well and it made her feel good under her clothes. As her hair dried, it changed color from a dark blood-like red to creamy strawberry blonde, making her face and her gray blue eyes look soft and welcoming. When her hair was falling around her shoulders and arms in long layers, she put on dark brown slacks, high-heeled brown boots, and a light green sweater with a scoop neck that showed the swell of her breasts without being flamboyantly low cut.

First, she smoothed on moisturizer, a bit of concealer, and a transparent layer of lightly tinted cream. Making up her eyes was the most fun. She worked slowly so the various shadows were evenly applied on both sides. For the smudged navy blue liner beneath her lower lashes, she pulled out the magnifying mirror. After she brushed her lashes with mascara, she put everything away, wiped the counter, and washed her hands.

She made coffee and checked email while eating spoonfuls of blueberry yogurt. Matt walked into the kitchen and poured himself a cup of coffee. He carried the pot to the table and refilled her mug. "You look good. Anything exciting going on today?"

He asked her that question a lot, but today it took on a new flavor. Last night, she'd opened her mouth three times to tell him about the rumor. Three times she'd blurted out something nonsensical, not sure how to begin or whether it was the right time.

There'd always been a slender thread of jealousy in Matt's attitude toward Hank. He never complained when she worked late. There wasn't any suspicion over the need to stay past six, sometimes seven o'clock, but there was something — a shadow in his eyes followed by a looking away from her as if he subconsciously wondered whether she was drawn to Hank. Matt sometimes complained that Hank could do as he pleased, speculating about how Hank's power insulated him from consequences, separated him from the world everyone else lived in. Things didn't touch people like Hank, they could buy their way out of trouble, in his view. *Guys like that think they can have whatever they want.*

Matt wasn't an overly ambitious guy. Doing graphic design for a boutique company that serviced high tech corporations satisfied him. He liked working with computer tools and he liked the praise he received for his creative ideas. His salary was good enough and he couldn't see the point of trying to climb up to an account director role or launching his own company. He didn't want to be rich and he didn't want to be in charge. *We have so much more than most people on the planet.* She couldn't argue with that, but there was nothing wrong with wanting more. It was human nature. Occasionally she thought there was something wrong with him. He was barely thirty. Didn't he want to travel more? To retire before he was too old to enjoy it? To have a bigger house with more property in a nicer area? To not have to budget their income so precisely? She wanted more, even if she couldn't define what that was; and she wasn't going to apologize for it.

Matt was happy with his crime shows and sports for entertainment. He seemed to get a thrill out of rooting for the bank robbers, even the murderers, if Bonnie and Clyde were any indication. *Everyone roots for Bonnie and Clyde.* She'd asked him once why he was so addicted to crime shows — it didn't matter if it was true crime — overdramatized — or fiction, he couldn't get enough. Classics like the Elliot Ness series and Sunset Boulevard, and brand new classics like Breaking Bad. It was their cleverness, the way the anti-heroes lived life on the edge, he'd said. She'd wondered why he didn't make any attempt to live life on the *edge*, even a little, but she hadn't asked. Maybe living on the edge was over-rated. Fun to fantasize about, but the reality wasn't all that great. He thought it was obscene to spend hundreds of dollars on a single meal or stay in a hotel room large enough for five people. *I'm a simple guy*, he said. And she loved him for that. But still, there was a craving inside her, a need for something . . .

When she backed her Miata out of the garage, the sky was cloudy, the sun making a half-hearted effort to pierce the blanket of white. Something had kept her from telling Matt about what she'd overheard in the break room, from telling him how Hank reacted, or rather, didn't react. And now it was too late. She couldn't stop the car in the driveway and run back into the house just as he was locking up. Blurting it out would be worse. And tonight, or tomorrow night, or next weekend, would make it appear that she'd withheld it, which would cast it in an entirely different light. Although, he didn't have to know exactly what day it had happened. She accelerated into the street and headed toward Avalon.

It was early. She liked to beat Hank into the office, to be sitting at her desk when he came in rather than having to stop in his doorway to let him know she'd arrived. Maybe it was just that the longer she worked at Avalon, the more at home she felt sitting in her corner of the building. As if her desk and computer and the sofa and chair and the windows surrounding the sitting area were all becoming more familiar than her house. She was necessary and important here.

Everything was clearly defined. With Matt, there were certain areas of the landscape that were soft, as if a garden hose had been left running all night and you never knew where you'd sink into a pocket of muck that had built up beneath the lawn. They'd lived together for nine years now, engaged for six, and the idea of marriage was almost a joke. Matt had made the down payment on the house with cash from his parents' estate. He paid the mortgage and Vanessa paid the utilities, money that trickled away every month and left her with nothing. She wasn't absolutely clear on what her part in the house was, if it was even her home at all. She decorated it, but Matt didn't care much about those things, the color of the drapes or the layout of the furniture, as long as his recliner was at a good angle for watching TV. Of course, her cubicle belonged to her even less than the house did.

The building was cool, the heat lowered overnight and just now starting to fill the empty hallways. She was glad she'd worn boots, keeping her feet comfortable and snug as she climbed the stairs. At the top she lifted her chin and tossed her hair behind her shoulders. She proceeded along the landing.

The minute she rounded the corner, she stopped and took a large step backward, stumbling slightly. The entire counter in front of her cubicle was draped in a swath of ants. The stream undulated, making it appear as if the counter itself were moving. They covered the candy dish and continued down the half wall where they narrowed to a thin stream headed across the carpet, along the bottom of the wall in the sitting area, and disappeared into a space where the window joined the molding on the floor, an opening visible only to the ants.

She felt sick to her stomach. She turned away, not wanting to see how far they traveled on the other side of the counter, whether her desk and chair were also covered with the tiny creatures, insignificant on their own but able to dominate whatever they chose when they joined forces. Her skin tickled and twitched making her feel they'd already found their way up the heel of her left boot and were climbing the back of her leg. She grabbed her pants and rubbed furiously. She moved further away from her cubicle, leaned against the wall, and tugged up the hem of her pants, inspecting her boots for even a single ant.

She wanted to blame someone. It was irrational, but it was her first thought. It wasn't the candy that attracted them. She'd kept the candy out for years without this kind of result. Now it was on her to call someone to spray. Her space would reek of insecticide all day. Stray ants that managed to dodge the deadly fumes would linger. She swallowed and took a step forward. She looped her purse strap over the handle of Hank's office door and walked slowly toward the end of the counter in front of her cube. She peered around the corner. The stream of ants was draped over the side of the trashcan. Of course. Someone had tossed out unwanted food. Maybe it wasn't malevolent, but it was a lack of respect. The admin's cubicle was public property. They left candy wrappers, tossed coffee cups and soda cans in her trash, took pens and sticky pads off her desk, and every so often, when she'd left early for a medical appointment or an errand, they wheeled her chair around the corner and into the conference room to accommodate an overflow crowd.

It took maintenance twenty minutes to show up. She couldn't imagine what they were so busy with at seven-forty in the morning. They were still spraying when Hank arrived. He turned up his nose at the odor, went into his office, and closed the door. Vanessa sat on the chair furthest from the spot where the ants disappeared into the joining of the window and wall. The smell of insecticide was sickening. The guy in a blue jumpsuit wiped away the carcasses with damp towelettes. He carried her trashcan into the hallway and tore out the liner. He tied the top edges in a knot and dropped it into the huge trashcan on wheels.

"That was your problem," he said.

"What?"

"A donut."

"I didn't eat any donuts." Well, she had, but only a half, and there hadn't been anything left.

"There was a jelly donut in the trash."

"It wasn't mine."

He winked and went back to wiping up the remains of the ant army. "Might not want to sit here for a while, until the spray evaporates."

"I need to get to work."

"Your choice."

She grabbed her purse and slung it over her shoulder. It thudded against her hip as she walked down the hall past the empty offices and along the landing to the stairs. She descended slowly. It made no sense for someone to carry a donut from the break room to her cubicle when there was a good-sized trashcan with a protective flap built into the counter. Unless someone planned to eat it while waiting for Hank, and had been invited in sooner than expected. But she was almost certain it hadn't been there when she'd left the night before.

She walked out of the building, shivering as the blast of cold air slapped her cheeks. She hurried across the breezeway and into the adjacent building to the coffee cafe. The line snaked past the glass case with fruit and muffins and croissants, among the small tables and thin chairs meant to look like a commercial coffee shop, and out into the hallway. She got in line. Like the others ahead of her, she pulled her smart phone out of her purse and scrolled through email, looking for messages that might be short and easy to read on the phone, deleted if they didn't require a response, always striving to reduce the gush of electronic messages cluttering her psychic space.

When she had her coffee and a blueberry muffin, she returned to building four and sat in the lobby to eat it.

Upstairs, she turned the corner toward her cubicle and

Hank's office and took a deep breath. No odor of insecticide here. She walked down the hall. Hank's door was open. He was speaking but she couldn't make out the words. They were always dropping in unannounced. It was a game, as if they lurked down the hall waiting for her to leave her desk. Normally he kept his door closed. The poor guy couldn't read email or make phone calls when they dropped in unannounced — there were twelve people on his direct staff alone. Yet he didn't want to be the kind of executive who was unapproachable, so when they showed up in his doorway, he greeted them as if he was glad to see them and gestured them in, although with a clipped, *What can I do for you?* Keeping them away, protecting his time, was the most valuable thing she did for him. She moved closer to his doorway. "Thanks for bringing it to my attention," Hank said. "Tell Janelle and Brent and the others to run through their numbers again."

"The new ops director will make sure that sort of thing doesn't happen." It was Laura speaking, a higher pitch to her voice than usual. There was almost a giggling quality to the tone of her words.

Vanessa's cell phone rang, drowning out Hank's response. While she fumbled in her purse to silence it, Laura spoke again and Vanessa didn't catch that either. She walked around the counter into to her cubicle and hung her purse and jacket on the rack. She pulled out her chair and looked up.

Laura stood just inside of Hank's doorway. She leaned against the doorframe, her arms folded. Her watch face caught the florescent light and shone like a tiny moon on her thin wrist. Her nails — smooth, unpolished ovals — were like smaller moons floating nearby. She wore a skirt that looked shorter than it probably was on her long legs. She told Hank she'd take care of it and stepped across the hallway to Vanessa's counter. "Did you have an ant problem?" she said. "It stinks."

"Yes." Vanessa stood behind her chair. She wasn't going to sit down until Laura left. Apparently Laura wanted to revel in her petty victory.

"It smells awful. I don't know how you can work with that smell."

"I'll manage," Vanessa said.

"It looks like Hank had some time to see me after all, and it's a good thing."

"I'm glad he could squeeze you in."

"His schedule isn't quite as tight as you make it out to be."

"Next time, make an appointment."

"I'll do that."

Laura walked to the counter. "The candy's gone. I guess it had ants?"

Vanessa leaned forward and moved the mouse to wake the computer from sleep.

"Hopefully they're gone for good and you can re fill the dish."

"Let's hope so," Vanessa so.

"You know, you shouldn't act like Hank is over-booked or

people might stop believing you. That wouldn't go well for you, if no one believed what you said." Laura turned and walked around the corner.

The world was so unfair. Vanessa had worked hard to be independent, to support herself from the minute she turned eighteen. Because Laura had a platinum college education handed to her, she thought she was smarter and more deserving. Instead of working, Laura got to play all the way through college and come out with ten times the earning potential, entitled to opportunities and respect. Vanessa supposed it was equally unfair to be born beautiful while some people were born plain or downright ugly.

Six

THE HARSH ODOR of insecticide permeated Vanessa's cube and the sitting area outside Hank's office. It wafted down to the hallway leading to the break room. Laura hurried toward Brent's office as if the cloud of poison was chasing her. She stopped just outside his doorway. "Any time to walk over for a coffee?"

"Sure." He stood and grabbed his coat.

"It's only twenty feet, I don't think you need a coat."

"It's cold."

"Wuss."

He let the coat fall back over the chair.

"I lucked out," Laura said. "They sprayed Vanessa's cube for ants so she had to get out of there for a while. I did an end run around her and got a few minutes with Hank."

"You just dropped in?"

"I did." As they started down the stairs, she grabbed the railing. She hated feeling compelled to hang on, but there was something about walking down a long flight of stairs that shifted her equilibrium, filling her mind with images of her body propelling itself down without her permission.

Brent spoke quietly. "You know she's a hard ass about his schedule because he wants it that way. Dropping by isn't a good idea."

"It wasn't about the job. Well not entirely. I did get a chance to mention the job, and I would have said more, but she showed up. Then her phone started ringing and I lost the moment."

They crossed the lobby and Brent opened the door. He held it for her and she went out. It was cold and breezy. The sky was clearing and a strong wind had kicked up. It rushed through the space between the buildings, gathering force as it was funneled into the narrow channel. Laura shivered.

"If the job is meant to be yours, it'll happen," he said.

"Aren't you the philosopher."

"It's true."

"I didn't go in there just to talk about the job. I told him I'd reviewed all the pricing inputs and not one single person had accounted for the drop in power supply prices."

"Why didn't you talk to me about it?"

"Nobody factored it in, you weren't the only one."

"So you threw us under the bus just so you could have an excuse to get in front of Hank?"

"I didn't throw you under the bus. It's understandable."

"You should have told us directly."

"Sorry. It goes for final approval today, I didn't think I'd have time to run around and tell each one of you."

"That's what email is for."

They stepped up to the counter and placed their coffee orders. While the barista prepared Laura's latte and Brent's cappuccino, he was silent.

"Don't be pissed off," she said.

"You didn't need to tell him."

"Well it was a chance to let him see how good I'd be in that job."

"Things like that can backfire, you know."

"How?"

"He doesn't like to be bothered with every little detail. He just wants it correct and on time."

"And now it will be correct. And still meet the deadline."

"But you created work for him. Now he has to contact each one of us."

"No, he told me to do that."

"Like you should have done in the first place. Don't you see that? He was letting you know you're wasting his time."

She took a sip of the latte. It seared her tongue. Why did she always have to rush into action before the timing was right? She knew the coffee was too hot. She'd watched the girl steam the low fat milk. She'd wrapped an insulated sleeve around it to keep from burning her fingers.

They sat at a small table near the back corner of the cafe. Brent stirred his drink. "I hope it works out for you."

"You hope?"

"Stop trying so hard."

"If you want something, you have to go for it with everything you have."

"By giving a great interview and selling yourself, not by manipulating the hiring manager's admin and irritating him with petty issues."

"She controls him more than she should. I don't think he realizes how that looks."

"I don't think he gives a shit how that looks." Brent leaned back. He stretched his legs out to the side and crossed one ankle over the other. Two guys in suits that were walking toward them turned to the side and went around the table next to Brent's outstretched legs.

"You're blocking the aisle," she said.

"There is no aisle."

"Those guys couldn't get past."

"They managed."

She pried the lid off her cup. After a minute, she took a sip. Much more tolerable without the lid trapping heat inside. "It bothers me that no one can talk to him without going through her. And I don't like the way she dresses — all that hair and makeup. She looks like a girl at a car show."

"Meow."

"Not really."

"I think she looks pretty good."

"Of course you do. That's the point."

"What are you talking about?"

"It's not the right look for the office. It makes men think about women as females instead of colleagues. It brings in this other dynamic."

Brent re-crossed his ankles. He slid his cup toward his left hand, then back again.

"You don't understand. Since you're a guy."

"She's always looked the same. Why is it suddenly a problem?"

"Now it's affecting me."

"Because she won't set up an interview before he's ready? Or because you think you have an inside track and you should get to lock it down before he talks to anyone else? She sees through you and you don't like it? None of which has anything to do with what she's wearing."

"That's not fair."

"If you're the right person for the job, you'll get it. And you have the best shot. Why are you so worried about it?"

"I'm not worried."

"You sure act like you are."

"I'm not. You don't understand how it is to be a woman in the industry. Even now."

"The glass ceiling is a myth." He sipped his cappuccino.

"It is not."

"If women don't get promoted into executive positions nowadays, it's their fault. You have an equal chance. Look at all the women CEOs. Look at Janelle. Look at Claire Wong, look at . . ."

"Okay. But isn't it interesting you can name them? You couldn't begin to name examples of men in high level positions because ninety percent of the executives are men."

Brent was only thirty-three, and for the first time she felt the difference in their ages. Or maybe it was only because she was female. Men didn't have a clue what it was like to contend with half-naked women splashed all over every magazine rack you passed, every Internet page you browsed, every channel you passed on the TV, and every movie theater you walked into. He was right, women weren't prevented from getting into powerful positions, but they still had to be better — smarter, more articulate, better educated. More everything. It required a lot of additional effort. It was work to not seem too female, to ask yourself every god damned day — *Is this blouse too low cut? Is this skirt too short? Are these pants too tight? Are these heels too high? Do I look too prim if I wear flats?* It was exhausting. And that was before she even arrived at the office. Those questions didn't even brush past the minds of her male co-workers. Women like Vanessa made it worse. Everything about her oozed sex and it made men look at all women in that light. Or maybe they already did, but it sure didn't help. Janelle was the same. It hadn't stopped her from getting promoted to Director, but that was because she shouted like a man and was generally obnoxious. Maybe Brent was right — Laura was trying too hard, she was too professional in the cowboy environment of high tech.

"What's your point?" Brent said.

What *was* her point? Why was she letting a clerical worker get under her skin? Vanessa shouldn't even be on her radar. It was because Vanessa acted like she owned Hank, acted like she knew things about the company that Laura wasn't privy to since she didn't report directly to him. It wasn't right. Vanessa acted like she had enormous power over him because, on some level, he wanted her. And Vanessa knew it. He spent more time meeting with his admin than he did with people who actually drove the business. His calendar wasn't that fucking complicated. "My point is, she has too much power and it's because she's sexy and it reflects on other women."

"You're nuts."

"Do you think she's sexy?"

"Come on, Laura."

"Do you?"

"We should get back to work." He pushed his chair away from the table, stood, and picked up his coffee. He turned and dropped the half full cup into the plastic-lined trashcan.

The corners of her mouth twitched. She wanted to laugh, but he wouldn't get it. She pressed her lips together before she took a sip of her drink.

"Let's go," he said.

"Just a minute."

"Did you want me to give your resume a look?"

"I already told you it's fine."

"You still need to market your successes in the right way."

"Whatever." She stood, took another swallow of the latte, and replaced the lid.

They wove through the tables and down the hall to the side doors. She'd won the argument. He refused to answer her question because the answer was *yes*. If he never thought about Vanessa in that way, he would have said so. Of course he noticed, he couldn't help it. Even if Vanessa wasn't sleeping with Hank, she was using her looks and her age, everything she could, to grab power. Or maybe there was something else. Laura wished she could figure out why men were so drawn to the girl. Maybe it was that secretive look in her eyes, maybe they felt she understood them.

At least once a week Laura caught Hank looking at Vanessa a half second longer than he should. She'd seen him help Vanessa with her coat, and she'd seen through the window in his door how Vanessa sat across from him, too close to his desk, and talked to him every fucking day of the week. What she couldn't see through the door was the expression on Hank's face. What did they have to talk about for thirty or forty minutes every day? It couldn't possibly be his calendar. He just liked sitting there looking at her. Maybe it was unconsummated, but it was still some sick relationship that gave him a voyeuristic thrill. Brent would tell her she had a crazy imagination. Maybe she did, but she knew enough about men to know that some of them, maybe more than she realized, had weird desires. Like Tim. She shivered. She felt the coffee tremble inside the cup, sloshing up the sides.

Brent was going on about resumes, or something. She couldn't concentrate. When they reached his office, she murmured, "See you later." She returned to her office and sat staring out the window. Hank traveled nearly fifty percent of the time. And he lived in the Bay Area four days a week, his wife and son sequestered in Tucson, Arizona. Maybe he wasn't doing it with Vanessa, but there was something going on there that wasn't all business. Sex was a powerful thing. It could destroy people. Not having it made people crazy. It made them do terrible things.

IT WAS ALMOST one-thirty by the time Laura felt a stirring of hunger. She'd accomplished next to nothing. She'd sent email to Janelle and the others about their pricing errors. So far, she'd heard nothing back. It was their mistake, yet her breathing grew tighter as the minutes ticked closer to the time Hank needed the updated spreadsheets. Why had she involved herself? Now it was on her. What started out as a brilliant plan to make herself look good could turn into something that left her on Hank's shit list for a week, or at least a few days, until other fuck-ups captured his attention.

She went to the break room and opened the fridge. All four shelves were packed solid with plastic containers, lunch bags, cardboard containers from the cafeteria, Chinese take-out boxes, and bottles of juice. There was no reason to bring half-gallon jugs of orange juice or giant tubs of yogurt to the office to store in a refrigerator shared by twenty people. She removed two plastic containers, a takeout box, and a rubbery lunch bag. When she pulled out her container of soup, it had a spot of someone else's food on the side. She replaced the other lunches and turned at the sound of high-heeled shoes on the linoleum. "Hi, Vanessa."

Vanessa greeted her and pulled the coffee carafe off the burner. She filled her mug with stale-smelling coffee. Only half a cup remained when she was finished. Someone needed to make a fresh pot, but Vanessa made no move to dump the aging coffee.

"Are all the ants gone?" Laura said.

Vanessa put her mug on the counter and pulled her hair over her left shoulder. She twisted it into a coil and laid it alongside her breast. As she bent slightly and ran her fingers along the side of her knee, her hair fell across the side of her face. She straightened and pushed it back.

"Well are they?"

"Yes."

"Good. They always come inside when it rains."

"Do they?"

"You've never noticed?"

"The jelly donut in my trash all night didn't help," Vanessa said.

"I guess not. But still, the rain brought them in."

Again, Vanessa rubbed vigorously at the side of her knee.

"I hope you don't have an ongoing problem with them."

"Why would I?"

"Once they invade, they keep coming back. It's instinct or something. Groupthink. A new contingent might already be scouting it out, now that the spray is evaporated."

"I think they came in because of the donut and if people don't throw their garbage in my trash, there won't be a problem."

"People don't always do what they should," Laura said.

"No, they don't."

"In fact, you could almost say that most of the time they don't do what they should."

Vanessa stared, her eyes dark and smoky with artfully smudged liner. She put her fingertip in the corner of her eye and rubbed it gently. She lowered her hand, opened her mouth as if she were going to speak, then poked the tip of her finger at her lashes. Her red polish shone like M&Ms glued to her short nails.

Laura moved toward the microwave. It sounded as though Vanessa blamed the jelly donut on her. There were many things that could be blamed on her, but not that. "You look upset," she said.

"Did you throw the donut in my trash? To attract the ants? You seem to know a lot about them. It sure gave you a chance to sneak into Hank's office without an appointment."

"That's ridiculous."

Vanessa rubbed her leg again.

Laura smiled, imagining the phantom sensation of the ants'

thread-like feet beneath Vanessa's silky slacks where she couldn't scratch very well. Even tickling the corner of her eye. "It's hard to get rid of *all* of them. Unless you spray every single crevice. It takes a lot of diligence."

Vanessa folded her arms across her ribs, pinning her hair to her side.

"What's that on your wrist?" Laura said.

Vanessa gave a little shriek, stepped back at an awkward angle and flapped her arms away from her body. "Where?"

Hank appeared in the doorway. "What are you doing?"

Vanessa didn't turn. "Where is it? I don't see anything."

"Maybe I saw that little mole," Laura said.

Vanessa folded her arms again. Her eyelids were lowered, darker than ever, hair tumbling around her shoulders and arms from her rapid movements. She turned toward Hank. "I thought I had an ant on me."

Hank lifted a paper cup off the stack. "Would you make me an espresso?"

Vanessa reached for the cup. He didn't immediately release it, hanging on as if he wanted to hold the cup while she operated the machine. After a few seconds, he let go and she nearly dropped it. The moment she had a firm grip on the cup, she poked the fingers of her left hand under the sleeve of her sweater and rubbed in small circular motions. She reached further until the webbing between her middle finger and ring finger was taught.

The silence continued. Speaking now would sound forced,

trying too hard to break the thick mood. Laura didn't want to be the one. Didn't want to have a conversation with Hank on any topic that Vanessa might take and reshape, making it her own. If Laura said something weather-related, food-related, pop culture-related it would leap from her lips like the toads and lizards that fell from the girl's mouth in that fairy tale. She was beginning to feel like an intruder in a private moment. Hank — waiting for his espresso when he could easily prepare it himself. Vanessa . . . who knew what was going through her mind. Perhaps she thought she'd been demoted to kitchen help, or possibly she was thinking about ants, longing to scratch vigorously but not wanting to appear disgusting in Hank's eyes.

Now, Hank was staring at Vanessa's throat, the opening of her sweater, the way it spanned her collarbone, the soft hint of her breasts that might introduce themselves into the workplace when she leaned down to get the coffee grounds out of the bottom drawer.

"Is something wrong?" he said.

"No. I got distracted for a minute." Vanessa stepped closer to the machine and pulled out the receptacle packed with wet grounds left from the last user. She opened the cabinet and dumped them into the trash.

While she prepared a fresh scoop, Hank backed away and leaned against the counter. He glanced at Laura. "Are those updated spreadsheets coming soon?"

"Yes."

"I'll see them in my in-box when I get back to my desk?"

"I don't know about that. But soon." She twisted the silver band on the middle finger of her left hand. It felt solid and cool.

As his gaze moved away from her, Laura studied his profile. It wasn't right that a man could look like that — dark hair, dark brown eyes, and the shadow of a beard that always made a man look dangerous. She couldn't figure out why that was the case, or why it was so appealing. It was biological, most likely. A man that's dangerous is strong by implication. He can provide adequate protection, and a woman was wired, as much as Laura resisted it, to find a man who would keep her offspring safe. Although she had no offspring and didn't require safety, she couldn't ignore Hank's power. It hovered around him, invisible yet pungent. There was no way Vanessa was immune to that. If Laura noticed, then so did Vanessa. The three-quarter carat diamond on her left ring finger didn't erase biology.

"Do you need anything else?" Hank was looking at Laura again.

"Not really." Was he dismissing her?

He continued to hold her gaze. No, he wasn't dismissing her . . . she had it backwards. His look was admiring. He was thinking about how sharp she was, about how she'd caught an oversight made by people that theoretically should have a better grasp on their pricing structure. He seemed unable to look away. They understood each other perfectly. All the irritation she'd felt after talking to Brent dissolved.

The espresso was done. Vanessa poured the thick liquid into the cup and handed it to Hank.

"Thank you." He put it under his nose as if he was inspecting the bouquet in a freshly opened bottle of wine. He turned toward the door. He walked into the hall and quickly turned the corner without looking back.

Laura picked up her soup. "That was odd."

"What?"

"That he came all the way down here just to ask you to make espresso. Why didn't he text you?"

"Maybe he needed to stretch his legs."

Laura laughed. "He was stretching something all right."

"What does that mean?"

She didn't even know. It just shot out of her mouth. There was no doubt in her mind there was some kind of deeper connection between them. She was going to find out what it was. Brent would tell her she was fucking up her goal, but the truth was, she'd grown beyond her current job. It was time for more responsibility. While they dragged their feet about giving that to her, she needed something to entertain herself. Besides, maybe she could use it as leverage. Whatever *it* was. In case Hank had doubts about promoting her to Director of Marketing Operations. She savored the title on the back of her tongue. The job was hers. She could feel it. But a contingency plan was always good.

Seven

AN ARTIFICIAL BLANKET of light spilled across the flower garden that ran the length of the front porch. It looked worse in the harsh, too bright spotlight than it did during the day. Everything brown from frost, but instead of remaining brittle, the rain had turned the stalks and dead blossoms soggy. The stems of the gladioli, which had bloomed late, lingering into the Indian summer days of early October, were split open, revealing black gunk. Vanessa had meant to dig everything out in the fall but the weekends slipped past. Unseasonably warm weather in early December and all the holiday tasks had pushed her into complacency. When the frost hit, followed by heavy rain, the last thing she wanted to do was shiver in the garden.

That small flower garden was the only part of the house that felt like it was truly her own. She supposed it was distrustful to think of it that way. Matt made it clear the house belonged equally to both of them. And it was her tastes that carpeted the floors and ran up the drapes and colored the walls. He made more money, it was only right that he carried more of the financial weight. But in truth, he carried all of it, and it only belonged to her because he loved her. Still, when she felt distant from him, as she did now, it seemed as if she were a guest. Her piece was filled with decay. She wasn't really cut out to be a gardener. She liked flowers, and she loved shopping for new plants, getting them settled in the ground. But the constant plucking of dead leaves, the forgetting to water, the weeding, all of it slipped her mind once the newness wore off. After ten hours in front of a computer five days a week, she wanted to go to dance class or do yoga, not crouch in the dirt until her knees stiffened, making her feel like an old lady at the age of twenty-nine.

She unlocked the deadbolt and went inside. She turned off the porch light throwing the dead flowers into darkness. Matt would use the remote to open the garage and enter the house through the pantry door. She removed the cork from a bottle of Zinfandel and poured a small amount into a glass. She took a sip and opened the refrigerator. She'd planned ravioli for dinner. It was a simple task — breaking apart the frozen raviolis, but it left a fine dusting of flour all over her fingers that congealed to a pasty coating. Washing and cutting vegetables for a salad was equally unappealing. She closed the door. It would be nice to go out. Matt rarely suggested it. If she casually introduced the idea, hoping it would become his, he'd pick Chili's or Black Angus — dull, repetitious, chain food. Tasty enough, but uninteresting.

The garage door rattled open and his sixty-six Mustang rumbled into its spot. She poured a bit of wine into another glass and set it on the counter. The metal door panels clattered back into place and he came into the kitchen. He kissed her, picked up the glass, clicked hers, and took a sip, all in a single, fluid movement. "Let's sit down and relax before you start dinner. I didn't have lunch until almost two." He picked up the bottle and carried it into the other room. She followed and sat next to him on the couch. He poured another splash into both their glasses. She crossed her legs and took a sip. Her high-heeled boots made per position awkward with her knees jutted up. She inched forward. She sipped her wine while he talked on about his day, problems with clients and a complete structural overhaul of a web site he was building for a software startup. By the time his words trailed off, her glass was empty.

Matt picked up the bottle.

"I shouldn't have any more yet, I didn't eat much," she said.

He put the bottle down. "I guess I could eat something now."

She tipped her head back and shook her hair away from her face. She ran her tongue across her upper lip. "It's nice to sit and relax."

"Well which is it? Hungry or more wine?"

She could drop hints and lead him right up to it and by the time he got there, it wouldn't be anywhere close to being his idea. "I feel like going out," she said.

"Okay. Sure." He put the bottle on the table. "Even though I'd rather stay here and get naked with you." He leaned toward her and pressed his face into her hair. He took a slow, deep breath and exhaled. "Black Angus sound good?"

"I guess."

"If that's not where you want to go, tell me. The way you look right now, I'll take you anywhere."

"Anywhere?" What fun was it if she had to suggest eating out and also come up with an interesting restaurant?

He put his glass on the table. "Not anywhere, I guess. If I could, I would, though. You know that. But we're common people with common tastes, right?"

She loved him. A lot. But the last thing she wanted to be was common. The word made her feel there was nothing remarkable about her or him, or their lives. She was nothing special. Hank could afford to take her anywhere, he wouldn't have to qualify it. She stood and stepped around the table, anxious to escape the betrayal seeping into her thoughts. It could never happen. Would never happen. "It's kind of insulting to call me average."

"I said *common*. And there's nothing wrong with that. It's what the world is made of. It's the key to happiness — not wanting things you can't have."

She knew he had these views, but tonight they struck her as defeating. It was important to go for everything you could get in life, not settle for what was easy or what everyone else had.

She wasn't even sure he appreciated what he had. Not really. Men would kill to have a woman who looked like her. Matt accepted it as his due, or somehow failed to recognize how lucky he was. It wasn't that she thought she was better than him. She wanted him to act as if he would die without her. A small, unattractive part of her wanted to feel she had power over him.

He was staring at her. And not in that way. "Are you okay?"

"I'm just hungry. We can talk at dinner."

"Is there something we need to talk about?"

"Don't twist things around. Let's go. We'll probably have to wait for a table. And I'm really hungry." She wasn't that hungry but she couldn't stand here any longer, doing nothing. Minutes dribbling into the past, the evening disappearing, her life slipping out of her grasp while they talked about trivia and she felt nothing but dissatisfaction.

IT WAS NEARLY seven-thirty by the time they were seated. It was another ten minutes before the bottle of Cabernet was open and their glasses filled — too full. Vanessa hated the wine glasses here. They were too small with a narrow opening, and the glass was too thick. They were practical and dull and designed for utility, not the elegance of delicate, beautifully sculpted glass, a work of art in itself, complementing a moist cork and silken liquid. She took a sip. The taste was as sharp as her thoughts, as if the wine hated her as much as she hated it. Or at least hated the glass it was served in. The food here was fine. Good, actually. But there was always too much of it. The plates were so big they made her feel she was in a cafeteria, even though the lighting was dim and the booths were quite private with tall sides so you weren't aware of how vast the restaurant was. It seated hundreds.

Matt unwrapped his utensils and spread butter on a hunk of soft, whole grain bread sitting on the wood cutting board between them. "You haven't told me how your day was." His voice was firm, almost demanding.

"It sucked, actually. There was an ant invasion in my cube. Thousands of them." She scratched the hard bone behind her ear. "It was like a piece of black fabric running across the counter. Some jerk left a jelly donut in my trash."

He chewed and took another bite. "Gross."

"They sprayed and it still smells like chemicals." She thought about telling him how Laura had defied her, snuck into Hank's office. The timing of it made her wonder again about the owner of the donut. But it was just too fantastic. And too much effort to explain.

"Maybe you should lock up your trashcan at night."

She laughed. "Then they'd leave shit on my desk."

"Yeah." He pulled off another piece of bread. "I thought you were hungry."

"Not for bread. I'll wait for my salad."

She took a sip of wine. "Some other stuff is going on."

"What's that?"

"There's this rumor . . ."

"Isn't there always?" He leaned back and pushed his bread plate away as the server set their salads in front of them. Vanessa accepted the offer of fresh ground pepper. Matt declined.

"Do you want to hang out with Chuck and Caroline this weekend?" He stabbed a slice of carrot but his fork wasn't able to penetrate the thick slice. He stabbed again.

"Sure." She waited for him to ask about the rumor. He didn't. He wouldn't. Like he'd said, there were always rumors and his thoughts had moved elsewhere. Sometimes she felt like a pre-school teacher constantly directing a child's attention back to the task at hand. After a few minutes of eating in silence, she took a sip of wine. She put down her fork, then picked it up. "The rumor is about me."

"Yeah?"

"They think Hank and I . . ."

"Are doing it?"

She put down her fork. She reached for the wine bottle. She added a bit to her glass and took several sips. "Why did you say that?"

"It's the most logical rumor about a boss and his secretary."

"Administrative assistant."

"Right. A boss and his admin."

"It doesn't bother you?"

"Not unless it's true."

"Why doesn't it bother you?"

He put a forkful of lettuce with a crouton balanced on top into his mouth and chewed. Would he ask whether it was true? It didn't seem as if that had crossed his mind, except as a factor contributing to his lack of concern. She should have expected it. He was calm, she liked that about him. Nothing rattled him and he didn't draw irrational conclusions. But neither did he seem inclined to worry that there could be a hint of truth, or a possibility, of Hank wanting her.

"I don't like people talking about me behind my back."

"There's nothing you can do about it. That's how people are. *You* do it."

Tears tickled the edges of her eyes. He should defend her honor, he should worry that Hank was nearby every day, aching for her. She wanted Matt to want her so badly that even the suggestion of a threat would enrage him. Not enrage, exactly. But fill him with passion. Instead he was crunching through toasted bread and lettuce like cattle dining on wild grass, oblivious to anything but the food in his mouth and the food still to be consumed. "I'm worried it'll hurt Hank's reputation."

"That's his problem."

"Aren't you . . . don't you feel anything?"

He swallowed and turned toward her. "I trust you." His pupils were large, filling the blue, as if an eclipse of the sun was taking place inside each eye, the universe condensed to a pair of eyeballs.

"It's not about trust." Her voice was slightly louder than it should be. She'd talked to him in a public place to prevent him from over reacting, but what had ever made her think he'd over react? That was a fantasy. A fantasy where he was consumed with desire for her — where he stroked her skin and kissed her slowly all over her body, surprised her with a steaming bathtub sprinkled with rose petals, where they sank into the warm water and drank wine and ate chocolate. Or whatever. Something wild. Where he showed up at work and couldn't keep his hands off her and they did it in Hank's office. On his desk, pushing Hank's outrageously expensive Montblanc pen and leather covered calendar on the floor.

"Then what is it about?" he said. "I know you love me. I don't think you'd cheat on me."

The main course arrived — steaks with foiled-wrapped baked potatoes and a heaping pile of steamed vegetables. The salad plates were cleared and they began slicing into their meat. Matt spread open the potato and slid the butter over the exposed surface. Once it was melting evenly, he smeared sour cream over the flesh, poking it into the crevices. "Should I be worried?" he said.

She shook her head. "They made it sound like I'm . . ."

"I'm sure no one really believes it. You aren't going off in the middle of the day with him or anything like that."

"I think most guys would be jealous if their fiancé told them something like this."

"I'm not most guys."

She smiled so he couldn't see the disappointment leaking

through her chest. At least Hank acted like she was something special, he noticed she was desirable. She'd seen it. He couldn't stop looking at her, and some weird part of her not only liked him looking, she liked that other people noticed. She didn't want them thinking she was sleazy, or not good at her job, but she liked them wondering. She liked them knowing a man as powerful and successful as Hank might potentially risk his career for her. It was intoxicating. Much smoother than this dull, character-less wine.

She dragged the serrated knife across the steak, tearing at the fibers, the knife not quite as sharp as it needed to be. Her ID bracelet clanked on the edge of the plate, the chain too long for her wrist so the extra piece hung loose, tapping against the keyboard when she typed, and ringing on plates if she wasn't paying attention while she ate. It had been a gift from her father on her sixteenth birthday. Her name was engraved in elaborate script almost impossible to read it was so cluttered with curlicues. From the time her father moved out of the house when she was twelve, until now, he'd given her jewelry every year on her birthday. While her mother's gifts were things Vanessa wanted or needed, mostly needed, her father was on a jewelry streak. Most of the other things were in a tarnished, tangled heap in the maple jewelry box he'd given her when she turned eighteen and moved into her own apartment.

The heavy links and the flat plate with her name felt solid on her wrist. She liked seeing her name written so beautifully and she liked knowing that the opposite side was engraved with the words — *my princess*. It was silly. And her father certainly hadn't acted like she was his princess, worthy enough to make him turn away from the woman he chose over her mother. If she were a princess, he would have tolerated her mother. Not just tolerated, he would have loved the mother of his only daughter, his only child. If Vanessa had been more interesting, her father would have stayed. He wouldn't have been able to tear himself away.

Things didn't go wrong with her mother until he left. Before that, before he found someone prettier, her mother had laughed and cooked wonderful meals. She'd been fun. Why wasn't that good enough for him? Why wasn't his daughter good enough for him? Unanswerable questions. She should consider giving up the bracelet, wearing something else, because all it did was clank on things as if it was ringing a chime to remind her of the questions that would never go away, that only he could answer, and maybe even he couldn't. She didn't know, she'd never asked him.

She chewed her steak, letting the taste soak into her tongue, the aroma of cooked beef permeating every pore. After putting another carefully sliced piece in her mouth, chewing it slowly and thoroughly, she said, "I hope the ants aren't back tomorrow."

"Maybe you should bring in your own can of spray."

She put down her fork and scratched the back of her wrist. The bracelet caught on the cuff of her sweater. She freed the hook and scratched harder, the tickle now aggravated by the bracelet chain.

"So do you want to hang out with Chuck and Caroline?" he said.

"I said it was okay."

"Don't bite my head off."

"I already answered you."

He put his hand on her leg. He squeezed gently and moved his hand up her thigh. The lower part of her belly softened. She slid closer to him on the semi-circle bench. He took his hand off her leg and put it on her lower back, then slipped it under her sweater. He stroked her skin, but all she could think of were ants creeping up her spine. With his other hand he poured wine into their glasses.

She moved closer to the table. "Do you want dessert?"

"You're my dessert."

The words sounded false, as if he was trying too hard. Or maybe it was all her. Not trying hard enough. It's just that she didn't want it to be work. Relationships weren't a job, they were beyond thinking, full of things you couldn't spell out and make sense of.

Eight

A MODERATE DRIZZLE promised an empty track. Even the monster wouldn't come out in this mess. The rain stung like shards of glass falling on her face. Whenever the temperature dropped to thirty-eight and it was raining, everyone hoped for snow in the Bay Area. Once every forty years or so, they got their wish, but most years, as it sank below thirty-five the rain evaporated, leaving nothing but a dusting of hard frost followed by dead plants and high heating bills in the inadequately insulated California homes.

Laura swatted her way through the tangle of shrubs. Too bad they hadn't been damaged by the three days of frost before this splatter of rain started. As she emerged from the shrubbery and cluster of small trees, she saw him. She stepped back.

Logic insisted he had every right to use the track. She couldn't understand why he set off this visceral storm of rage, shadowed by fear. She hated herself for that reaction, but it refused to dissipate, no matter how much she chattered to herself about her foolishness. Therefore, her gut must be warning her there was something off about him. Or was her gut nothing more than the deeply embedded voice of her mother hissing that nice girls shouldn't be athletic, didn't beat the boys, didn't go out in the pre-dawn hours trying to hone their figures to look like boys' bodies by running too much and too hard?

She needed to get rid of the irrational expectation that she deserved a public track entirely to herself. If she wanted to run in solitude, she needed to haul her ass up to a secluded trail or run on a treadmill like a gerbil. If she planned to continue running in a convenient location, she needed to get a grip.

She pressed the toe of her left shoe against the metal fence pole to stretch her calves. She switched to her right foot, then balanced on one foot while she grabbed the opposite ankle to stretch out her quads. She did ten jumping jacks, touched her toes, bouncing gently a few times, and sprinted across the grass to the track. He wasn't going to frighten her. She was not giving in to female directives from another era. Her mother had come of age in the late sixties, it made no sense that she lived by rules from the fifties and fed them to Laura along with spoonfuls of pureed carrots and peas.

She ran three laps, remaining exactly half the circumference behind the monster. As she started the fourth lap, the drizzle faded, but the sky grew darker, the clouds gathering more rain, or possibly, the longed-for snow. Her face was slick with moisture. Her lips and the tip of her nose were numb. The backs of her hands were wet and her sweatshirt was damp and leaden. She lifted it up to her armpits. She slowed to pull it over her head, but it was too wet and didn't want to slide off. She wrestled with the fabric, knowing she was stretching it out of shape, but not wanting to come to a complete stop. She'd slowed to a laborious jog now, unable to see where she was going. If she wasn't careful, she was going to trip.

Finally she was forced to stop. As she pushed the sweatshirt up her arms, another's hands grabbed the sleeves and gave them a tug. She screamed. The damp sweatshirt was tight, gripping her skin, pinning her arms above her head so she couldn't move. Although she knew it was the monster, all she could think of was Tim, pulling a sweater slowly over her head, binding her arms as securely as if he'd tied them with plastic cord. He'd hold the sweater tightly in one fist and with the fingers of his other hand trace curves along the tendons at the insides of her arms. He'd stare, his eyes like the flat, dark surface of a lake when a storm was building, revealing nothing, a shimmering expanse of darkness. He'd run his fingertip across her ribcage, up the other side of her body and along the delicate skin in the hollow under her arms until her body convulsed. She writhed and thrashed, trying to move away. The harder she fought, the more he smiled, but his eyes remained blank. After several minutes, she'd be sobbing, unable to breathe.

Now, she could feel her body respond as if the monster were tickling her bare skin even though he hadn't touched her, just keeping her immobilized long enough for her mind to complete the memory loop. After a moment, the sweatshirt came free.

"There you go," he said.

She jerked around to face him. "Don't touch me!" Her vision was blurred, her nose plugged with mucous. Tears ran down the back of her throat.

He smiled. His teeth looked as though they'd been molded by years of braces and retainers. They were such a contrast to the rest of his body, they gave off their own disconcerting threat. "You were caught."

"I didn't need help." Her hands shook. She wrapped them inside the sweatshirt so he wouldn't laugh at her helplessness.

"That's what you think."

"Don't come near me ever again." She turned and started running. Her heart slammed inside her, rattling through her bones.

A moment later he was at her side. "You're nothing special."

"Leave me alone."

"You think you're one of the elite, but you're exactly like me."

"I'm nothing like you. Get away from me."

He laughed. It was a cackling sound like some kind of bird,

or something otherworldly. She increased her speed. He kept pace with her. Anyone who walked onto the track now would think they were running partners. She couldn't go any faster. She'd lost count of the laps. She was caught on a spinning playground toy, whirling faster. Any minute she'd be flung off, skidding along the rough gravel, tearing up her skin, and bruising her knees. He continued laughing. Her breath was quick and tight. He must be in excellent shape, to laugh and keep up this pace. Of course, he was eight or nine inches taller than her, so he didn't need to take as many steps, no need to push himself as hard as she was.

She stopped. As if he'd seen it coming and prepared in advance, he stopped immediately, only a few feet ahead of her. "What is your problem?" she said. She was almost shouting. "If you don't leave me alone, I'm calling the police."

He raised his hands in mock horror. "Calling the police? What will you tell them? That someone else is jogging at the same track you are? They'll arrest me on the spot. What will happen to me? I don't think I can afford an attorney."

"Why are you doing this?"

"Because you think you're all that. And you're not."

"What's it to you?"

"People like you are why there are people like me."

"What the hell does that mean?"

He backed away. He laughed softly. His hair was plastered to his skull. Water dripped from his beard. Talking to him had been a mistake. He was unbalanced, maybe completely mad.

He could be more dangerous than she'd realized. Maybe the police would come, if she told them he was a lunatic. She hadn't seen a car parked anywhere along the side of the high school. Had he escaped from an institution? She looked down. His feet were still bare inside the stained, tattered, oversized shoes. He wore the same torn off sweatpants and his shirt had small holes along the seams.

She started running. If she didn't speak, he'd lose interest. She could tell he'd gotten agitated when he talked. If she didn't engage with him, he'd calm down and go back into the private world inside his head.

He followed her for three more laps. She was exhausted. She wasn't sure if it was because she'd run with so much intensity for a countless number of laps, or it was mental weariness from having to think, glancing to the side, straining her peripheral vision to see where he was, trying not to look over her shoulder when he disappeared from sight. She slowed to a walk. In a moment, he was beside her again, laughing softly. She continued walking calmly, as if he wasn't there, allowing her breathing to return to normal. When she rounded the curve she cut across the track toward the grass. He was right behind her. If he tried to follow her home, she was definitely calling the police. Her hands began shaking again as she pushed away the shrubs to make her way out through the opening in the fence. He was a few steps behind. Wet branches slapped at her arms and face. When she was free of the shrubs and vines, she walked to the corner. As she crossed the street, he turned and crossed in the other direction. She was halfway down the block before the sound of his laugh faded to nothing and all she heard was the whoosh of tires three blocks away on El Camino Real.

She walked past older homes set well back from the street, most of them still dark. She clutched the wadded up sweatshirt, unable to stop her shoulders and legs from shaking, memories of Tim shoving themselves to the front of her mind — his torture that sometimes turned sweet.

She'd been so stupid . . . Tim had been sitting in bed, three pillows supporting him as he stared at the doorway expectantly. She stepped into the bedroom and pulled off her high heels. "You're in bed early."

"I was waiting for my wife."

"Well here I am." She took off her jacket and walked into the closet to hang it up.

"Come back," he said. "I have an idea." She heard the click of his iPod wheel spinning in the bedside docking station and the soft sound of music, a tune she couldn't make out, the closet insulated by slacks and shirts and dresses. She stepped back into the bedroom.

Tim thumbed the iPod, turning up the sound. Now she recognized it — The Stripper.

"No," she turned.

"Please. Come on. Please. We need to crank things up."

"Then you do it."

"You know you want to — all women do. I read an article

about it."

"There's nothing that all women want to do."

"Okay, most. Lots."

"Then don't say *all.*"

He paused the music and crept to the foot of the bed. He reached out his hand. She folded her arms. His hand remained outstretched. He wore nothing but blue jeans. His bare feet were pale, the soles smooth and tender. "You get upset when I'm too dominating. This would put you in charge. Right?" He smiled.

"You're cruel sometimes."

"I know. I'm sorry. Please, please, please?" He batted his eyes.

She laughed. "Okay, whatever. Go pour me a shot of vodka and I'll do it."

He leapt out of bed. His feet thudded down the hallway, almost running. He returned with the bottle and set it on the dresser. He poured a shot, dribbling a bit on the pine surface. She swallowed it and handed the glass to him. He drank a shot and climbed back on the bed. He flicked the music back to the beginning. She poured a second shot and drank it more slowly. The alcohol melted across her brain, warming her neck and face, softening her shoulders.

As the music thumped its way through the trite, but strangely intoxicating tune, she undid her blouse, letting her fingers linger at each button. After she'd slid it off and dropped it on the floor, she slithered out of her skirt. Tim grinned, but his eyes were needy, longing for her. Seeing his desire sent a flame up the center of her body. She danced more slowly turning to show him she was unhooking her bra. Her instinct was to speed up, so she forced herself to slow down even further. When the bra was on the floor she moved toward the bed, pressing one knee into the mattress. She lowered her eyelids and ran her tongue around her lips. She backed away and moved her hips forward as she tucked her fingers inside the elastic of her underpants sliding them down her legs. She looked at Tim, his open mouth, his look of complete absorption. When the lace and nylon was pooled around her ankles, she brought one foot up and grabbed them off her foot. She tossed them at Tim's face. Her aim was perfect, the force accurate. They hung for a moment, then slid down onto his lap.

He laughed. She swayed slightly, glancing at the bottle of vodka, wondering if she should have another shot. He laughed harder. He balled up her underpants and threw them back at her. They landed on the dresser and he fell on his side, laughing so hard his voice began to sound like a dog barking, and then he was gasping for air. His face was red, his eyes wet with tears.

Laura grabbed the bottle of vodka and went into the bathroom. She locked the door, put on her robe, and sat on the edge of the tub and took a sip, marveling at her stupidity. After that, she'd started lifting weights, determined to make herself stronger than him. Even if she didn't need to battle him physically, she had to know in her mind that she was tougher, smarter, more capable. She'd thought he couldn't do anything more to humiliate her.

Nine

HANK WAS IN his office with the door closed when Vanessa arrived on Friday morning. A pressure on both temples felt as if a sheet of metal was folding around her brain. It was the red wine. Not very good red wine, and she'd drunk it too fast.

Even though the wine made the inside of her dull and achy, the outside looked good, better than usual. Her hair was loose and wavy to the small of her back. Her makeup was a soft glow of creams that emphasized her narrow nose, large gray blue eyes, and lips that said *kiss me*, according to Matt when they first got engaged. Lips that were soft and so seductive he couldn't stop looking at them, feeling them on his own, no matter what color she wore. And he said he preferred no color. Nothing but her soft, firm skin. He seemed blissfully unaware of the possibility anyone at work, Hank in particular, might also see that silent demand coming from her mouth. She wondered every time she looked in the mirror to put on gloss whether that message was Matt's teasing or something others noticed. It was so hard to tell when Matt was teasing and when his comments were authentic. He wore the same half smile either way.

She hung her coat on the rack, put her purse in the bottom drawer, and pulled out her chair. It appeared to be free of ants. She sniffed. The air smelled as clean as could be expected inside an office building. Because she was leaving early to pick up a few bags of candy on the way home, she'd inserted an early appointment for her and Hank at eleven-thirty. Whenever she changed their end of day meeting, she tried to squeeze it in near lunch. About twenty percent of the time, he'd glance at the clock and ask if she wanted to grab something to eat. It could mean she'd go to the deli and bring back sandwiches. Other times, grabbing something to eat had a different meaning to him than it did to her. Shunning a deli or sushi bar, he would suggest Chinese or Indian food. And it wasn't a quick kitchen-type atmosphere, but a high end restaurant with tablecloths and linen napkins, water served in tall narrow glasses that weren't scratched by too much time spent under harsh detergent. Once in a while they had a glass of wine.

As she sat at her desk and pulled the computer mouse toward her, a small dark spot caught her eye — an ant making its way along the space bar on her keyboard. She pressed her finger on it and rubbed it off into the trashcan. She got up and went to the restroom, washed her hands, and returned to her desk. It would be a long day if she was forced to kill a lone ant every ten minutes, followed by a trip to the restroom and a thorough scrubbing with anti-bacterial soap.

She worked on the menus for the offsite and spent two hours entering Hank's receipts and currency conversions from his trip to Asia in early December. He hadn't given her the receipts until a few days ago. She marveled that he could pay off thousands of dollars on his corporate card and wait a month or longer for the reimbursement. Yet she was the one supplying candy. If she asked, he would let her expense the candy. But she wanted him to suggest it, wanted him to notice it was coming out of her pocket. She hadn't resented it at first. She'd thought it was a nice touch, something she could do to make her area friendly and welcoming. It was difficult to remember when the pinpricks of irritation began. They turned slowly to anger, and now, she sometimes felt a rage that was beyond any sense of proportion. Occasionally a horrific image flashed through her mind — one of her co-workers choking on a hard candy, gasping for air, lips turning blue, eyes bulging. Maybe that's why she'd switched to the chocolate kisses, she was terrified of her desire to see them suffer. Not a single one recognized that she spent her own money.

At eleven-twenty-five she clicked the save button on the expense report for the tenth time. An ant scurried along the mouse cord. She squashed it and used a hand wipe to clean her fingers. She wanted to be ready the minute Janelle stood and walked out of Hank's office. She clicked to the Facebook tab to see if anything new was going on — new and also interesting. There was nothing. That was the trouble with checking it too frequently. Not that much happened on an hourly or even a daily basis, yet if she didn't check, she felt out of the loop.

Hank's door opened and Janelle stepped into the hallway. She glanced at Vanessa and smiled but her eyes didn't linger on the counter. She was one of the few that were never tempted by the candy. Vanessa liked that about her. In fact, in general, Janelle seemed to recognize her as a human being, worthy of respect simply because she existed rather than dismissing her based on her subordinate position.

Vanessa picked up her phone and a notepad and the printout of Hank's calendar. She went into his office and closed the door. She sat down and put her things on the table.

He glanced up. "Why are we meeting early?"

"I'm leaving at four. I need to re-stock the candy on my desk. And I'll pick up the hats for the offsite."

He nodded. She stood and put the calendar on his desk.

"Any changes since last night?"

"Not really. If you're done looking at the resumes, I should start setting up your phone interviews."

"Right. I'll email you the list of who I want to talk to." He leaned back and looked directly into her eyes. "How are things going with you?"

"I'm okay." She lifted her chin and shook her hair away

from her face. "We haven't talked much."

"What did you want to talk about?"

She smiled. He stared at her, but the usual glint of encouragement was missing from his eyes. She leaned forward slightly. "You apologized for keeping me late the other day. You've never done that before. Is it because of what I told you?"

"I shouldn't be keeping you after hours, that's all."

"Oh." She glanced at the door. He was behaving as if they'd never flirted, never pushed the boundaries of boss and admin propriety. He was acting as if he hardly knew her. Nothing she could think of had changed between them, unless the rumor upset him more than he wanted to admit. "Well it's not a problem, to stay late once in a while."

He nodded.

She straightened her back and re-crossed her legs. She rested her forearm on the table beside her. "Are you worried about what they're saying?"

"We don't need to talk about it. If you ignore what she says, it'll die out."

"I don't like her trashing your reputation."

"And yours?"

She smiled, conscious of the coating of freshly applied gloss, making her lips feel soft, so it felt good forming her mouth around the words. "You have more to lose."

"I suppose." His eyes were dark, made more so by his short, thick, nearly black lashes and the shadow under his brow bone. His mouth seemed more prominent, maybe because she was so conscious of her own. He crossed his arms and leaned back again. His chair was ergonomic perfection. It tilted back with minimal pressure, had scooped arm rests with padding rather than rock-hard plastic like the rest of the office chairs, a neck support, and was constructed of fine mesh that breathed but gave solid support to the spine. She'd sat in it once or twice. It was like sitting on a cloud, no chair at all. He pressed his lips into a hard line. "What exactly did she say?"

Finally. Something inside her burned to see him reveal a hint of emotion, a small suggestion of doubt or uncertainty, mixed with excitement over considering the possibility. The yearning made the temperature of her skin rise slightly, the prelude to blushing. She wanted to talk about this, about what Laura had said, get a deeper glimpse into his desires. Not to act on them, but just the excitement of doing something not quite proper, having a secret between them. A bond that was more than admin and boss, more than what the others had. It might be perverted, but she couldn't stop thinking about it. Those thoughts carried her through her choice of clothes, putting on make-up, fixing her hair, and shaving her legs every single day. Matt would be so hurt if he knew her thoughts. Or maybe not. Who knew what things he kept inside? Everyone did, didn't they? "She said we had a thing."

"How do you know she was talking about sex?"

She laughed. "You're kidding, right?"

He uncrossed his arms and tugged at the skin under his chin. She hated that gesture. Other men did it too. She wasn't sure if it was the itch of shaved off hair growing in or something else. Matt did it. She'd seen her father do it, and on him, it was more disturbing because the skin had minimal elasticity and it seemed to sag lower when he stopped tugging. She turned and looked out the window at the bay. More rain was still needed. During summer and fall the water pulled away from the shore, exposing decayed fish bones and dead sand crabs that stank more as the temperature grew mild. Sometimes in the summer the smell infiltrated the building. Usually by January the water level was more normal, a shimmering expanse of blue, but there hadn't been much rain in November and December. Now the water was grayish green, muddy at the edges. She looked back. He'd stopped tugging on his skin.

"What else did she say?"

Her pulse ticked faster. He did want to talk about it. Wanted to enjoy the rush of pleasure from stepping onto forbidden territory as much as she did. "Janelle made a joke about us doing it on the office floor."

He looked at the window, his expression unchanged.

"Janelle said she didn't believe it."

Immediately she wished she hadn't said that. He wasn't responding at all, and she didn't want to give him a way out, end the enticing conversation before it got started. It wasn't like him to be so reserved with her, giving the impression there were things he wasn't saying.

"Did Laura have any specifics, or just trash talk and speculation?"

Were his thoughts racing around images and teasing words from the past, glasses of wine, and things that should not have been spoken? She licked her lips, leaving a tacky coat of gloss along the edge of her tongue. "No. After that she went on about how I have too much power over you."

He laughed and turned back to face her. "Too much power?"

She nodded. "I think it's about the ops director position. She keeps asking to get on your calendar."

"It would explain a few things. But why does she think you have power?" He laughed again.

Did the laugh imply he thought she had no power, or that he recognized that she did? It didn't sound mocking. He sounded surprised, almost pleased, or perhaps she was reading that in. "Because I control your schedule. Because . . ." There was more to it than that. She'd lost her nerve. Looking him in the eye and saying, *it's obvious you like looking at me*, was a risk. He might deny it. Even if his denial was a lie, she couldn't bear it.

"That's your job."

"I know. She wants to meet with you more, have a more personal connection. I think she wants to get a leg up on her competition."

"Why do you think that?"

Vanessa didn't know. And she didn't know why she'd said it. Although it felt true, so maybe it was instinct, an ability she had to read below the surface. "Just a feeling."

He tugged at the skin under his chin. She didn't look away, but shifted her gaze to the top of his head. His hair was so dark and soft, neatly trimmed every four weeks. "Anyway, I guess if you're not worried about it . . . about how it could affect your career."

"It's just gossip. People will get bored with it."

Vanessa didn't think they would. Laura wanted to create something bigger. She was not the type to let a subject die out, and she wanted to use it to keep Vanessa in her place, to worm her way in front of Hank. Although what she hoped to accomplish by doing that was unclear.

"She didn't mention any details?"

"No."

"Then Janelle won't get caught up in it. She's too smart for that kind of bullshit."

Vanessa nodded. She re-crossed her legs. She felt him watching her, no longer tugging at his skin. "Do you still want to interview her?"

"I should."

"I guess so."

"But schedule her after the external candidates. And that guy from sales."

"Okay."

"Don't tell her that. I want her to sweat a little. And I need some time."

"Absolutely."

"Are you okay? You're not upset?"

She smiled. "Not really. It's kind of . . ."

"It is."

She uncrossed her legs and scooted her phone to the edge of the table. She pressed the display button. Eleven-fifty-two.

He glanced at his computer. "Will you run to the deli and pick us up some sandwiches? I need to get through the last of the resumes so I can send you the list today. I've taken too long on this. Too much going on."

"I know. It's been crazy. Do you want pastrami?"

"Yes. And chips."

"Sour cream and onion?"

He nodded.

She stood and walked out, closing the door behind her. It wasn't what she'd hoped. Still, she liked getting his lunch. Her role was crucial to his job and no matter what anyone else thought, she was valuable to the company. Besides, she liked doing anything she could for him.

AT THE DISCOUNT STORE, she yanked the cart away from the others. The force was too much and she stumbled backwards. Maybe she would purchase all *Sweet Tarts* this time. That should stop the greed, but instead, they'd stand there and complain and then she'd have to listen to their whining for something sweeter, tastier, smoother — for chocolate.

Besides, part of this was to please Hank, and he liked chocolate. She walked down the far aisle to the back of the store where there were six or seven racks of cards. First she'd get a supply of greeting cards for her mother's birthday and two friends' anniversaries coming up next month.

She stood for a long time, smiling at jokes, and stuffing the cards back into their slots in disgust over the empty words – cards designed for people who didn't know what they wanted to say, so they said nothing of substance. Usually she purchased cards at specialty shops. That was the only way to find a decent selection of unique, clever cards, cards that were lower on the crude jokes and higher on the ironically amusing end of the scale. She felt that in those stores she could find cards that made her look clever, intelligent, a woman with something witty to say. Finally she selected two cards bearing photographs, one with a simple *Happy Anniversary* written in script and the other with a quote from a Zen master about the meaning of time and aging, and the fluid nature of the passing days. Not what she really wanted, but something crossed off her list.

She rolled the cart along the back of the store, three aisles over to a row of eight-foot high shelves filled with candy. No matter how many times she walked down this aisle, she was overwhelmed by the quantity and variety. There were boxes of classic sweets — cans of Almond Roca and Whitman's chocolate samplers, stiff packages of licorice drops. One entire side was filled with enormous plastic bags of miniature candy bars. The candy was never more than a few dollars a bag, but it added up. Hank's staff scooped it out by the handful as if it were a fountain with a bottomless supply of water. Day after day, they grabbed and chewed and swallowed. The most thoughtless of them, like the skinny guy in accounting who always seemed to have a red pimple in front of his left ear, balled up the wrappers to the chocolate kisses and left them like tiny snowballs on her counter. It gave her the shivers to clean up his trash after his oily fingers had touched the wrapper. During Halloween season she'd felt ill watching his longish fingernails pick at the seam to open the tightly wrapped waxed paper covering a Tootsie Roll. He'd left the wrapper behind for her to throw away.

She paused halfway down the aisle, reached to the shelf at waist level, grabbed two sacks of chocolate bars and five bags of chocolate kisses, and dropped them into the cart. That should last for a few weeks. If it didn't, then she'd consider again whether she should take the dish home. She yanked the cart around and headed toward the side of the store. Her copper colored high heels with the delicate ankle strap made a smart snapping sound on the linoleum floor.

A few aisles over, she turned left to cosmetics and personal care. She slowed her pace past the nail polish, sorted into sections according to the manufacturer. Hundreds of shiny bottles full of a thousand shades of color, from the palest pearlized pink to a brown-red that looked like dried blood, to neon greens and blues, and purples mixed with glitter. Her purse bumped her right hip. She lengthened her stride ever so slightly so that she appeared to be just glancing at the bottles. She took a breath and another step forward and on the exhale, gracefully moved her hand to the side, grabbed a bottle of antique rose, her fingers stretching in curled arcs to also lift a bottle of cornflower blue off the shelf and in one smooth movement, tucked her hand inside her open purse and dropped the bottles to the bottom. She lifted her shoulder so the contents of her purse shifted and felt the gentle movement of her wallet and a small notepad close over the bottles.

She didn't glance back or look above her head, nothing to change her demeanor — no worry, no startled gestures. There could be no indication that she'd done anything more than let her fingers linger for a fraction of a second on the polish labels before moving on toward the manicure tools. Her heart beat thickly, filling her throat. It was difficult to swallow. The surge of blood into every organ of her body was almost as good as an orgasm. Every part of her felt warm and full, with a thrumming tension that made her want to flick out her hands for more goodies. But the two bottles of polish were enough for this aisle. Perhaps for this trip.

Her friends from high school had failed to learn some of these subtleties. When they first started out, eager fifteen-year-olds, they entered stores and took what they wanted without purchasing a thing. Such a foolish move was like holding a pennant over one shoulder, announcing there was no real purpose for the visit, alerting security personnel to a possible theft. Her friends also erred in taking too much. It wasn't good to focus on the value of the take over the rush of adrenaline. The thrill was the important part, the financial reward was secondary. It had to be that way, or you'd be caught. And two of her friends had been caught during their last year of high school, both, luckily, before they were eighteen. The only punishment was probation, but still, it increased the threat ten-fold if they ever wanted to return. They'd given up their free passes by getting greedy and careless.

Vanessa had been successful. Since that first day, she'd never so much as been halted by a clerk, or received a cold stare from a security guard. The discount stores she favored saw her frequently enough that they knew her as a loyal customer. They thought she was typical, average. She was nothing of the sort.

The defining moment of her life was the first time she'd stolen something. She'd been too young to recognize it as a defining moment, but it really was. It made her feel the whole world, the universe, had crystallized into a single spot of glittering light. Someday, she would steal a ruby ring to reflect that perfect moment. A surge of energy had coursed through her, the knowledge of victory. A burning inside wiped out all other thoughts, replaced by a magnificent, silently shouting voice — *I DID IT! I won! I beat them! I pulled it off. I can do anything.* It made her feel she was different from other people.

What percentage of the population had taken so much risk, had stolen even a single item? Simply walked down an aisle and slipped things into a purse or pocket? It was exhilarating and terrifying. It was something that belonged only to her. No one could touch it.

Only a single checkout station was open. Three people stood in line ahead of her. She didn't like that. She preferred a fast checkout. Already the warm rush and the luxuriously slowed pumping of her blood had dissolved. She was anxious, aching for further release. But it was too late. Leaving the line now would draw unnecessary attention. Once you lost a secure grip on your behavior, there was no telling what could happen. And you didn't want to damage the fragile balance between the thrill of doing something unobserved, while knowing you'd proven you were more clever than anyone you knew. None of her co-workers had the calm, deliberate strength to plan and execute something like this. Even though most of her thefts were small items, the consequences were just as devastating. The thought of Laura or Janelle or any of them being able to compete with her in this arena was enough to make her lips tremble so violently, she had to bite hard on her lower lip to keep from busting out laughing.

Sometimes she fantasized about making a career out of this. She was that good. All it required was more planning, more high-ticket items, and some sort of process for turning the items she took into cash. That last part was the biggest hurdle. It meant involving others, and part of her success came from being a loner. No one knew what she was doing, not even Matt. Certainly not her old girlfriends who rarely talked about their high school years. In their eyes, it had all been one huge mistake. In Vanessa's mind, it was the turning point of her life. It not only proved she was smart, it proved she had power — over undercover security, clerks, and sophisticated cameras. She was someone the storeowners feared. She could do whatever she pleased. No one could touch her.

She paid for the candy and cards, finally rid of the tight knot of rage over the unspoken pressure that she must keep her department supplied with sweets. It was part of the job. All jobs had disagreeable aspects. You just had to accept that, and not allow it to eat away at you the way sugar silently ate away at tooth enamel, until one day you woke up in unbearable pain.

Outside the air was cold, the world frozen as the sun quickly descended. Not unlike her life, which, the minute the thrill faded, had its own frozen quality. Nothing changed, despite her frantic search for excitement. She continued on the same rigid track — working for Hank, dismissed by her co-workers, a stagnant engagement to Matt, and petty theft. How much nail polish and cosmetics and lingerie did she really need?

Ten

RAIN WAS THUNDERING on the skylight when Laura woke. It pelted the windows and sliding glass doors and washed across her balcony like waves on the shore. Going for a run was out of the question. Not that she got pleasure out of her runs any more, pursued by the monster every fucking day. She'd tried shifting her schedule fifteen or twenty minutes in either direction, but it seemed he'd found a place to lie in wait for her, stumbling onto the track within minutes of her arrival all week. Nothing prevented him from grabbing her as she fought her way through the tangle of shrubs and trees in pre-dawn darkness every day. Nothing prevented him from deciding to follow her home. She hadn't spoken to him again, and he'd never made a move to follow her. Yet. She felt him watching her. When she inadvertently glanced at his face, she saw pleasure, an almost gleeful expression as if her fear hydrated his body and gave him energy to push harder, running more miles every day.

She sat at the kitchen bar, looking across the living area. The water in the aquarium was nearly black at the edges and despite the artificial light spreading through the center of the tank, she couldn't make out either of the fish. She took a bite of banana and chewed slowly. The banana had started to turn and she didn't know why she was eating it. If she were a more domestic person, Tim always said, she'd make bread instead of wasting so many bananas, tossing the spotted ones in the trash. She got up, pulled open the cabinet door under the sink, and dropped the fruit in the plastic lined bin. She returned to the bar and pried the lid off a container of yogurt. She ate it slowly. When she couldn't go running, her muscles twitched, not caring that the weather was awful, accustomed to their infusion of oxygen. They turned on her, demanding she tax them into a state of weariness. Her blood felt like partially churned butter inside her veins. Every winter she considered purchasing a treadmill. Running on a rubber platform was better than nothing on days like this.

Neither was it the type of weather she wanted on the day of her interview. After another four days of waiting, observing Vanessa's taunting smile, unable to elicit a straight answer about the timeline, she finally had an appointment with Hank at three this afternoon. She was as prepared as she was ever going to get. And in truth, she didn't need any preparation, she'd been preparing for years, maybe her entire adult life. Her only mistake through the years had been thinking good work alone would get her systematically promoted up the chain. If she worked hard, delivered quality results, the recognition would come. At the beginning, she'd tried to avoid politics. She realized now she shouldn't have done that. She should have played the game when she was younger, made strategic friendships with people, just as Janelle and Brent did. They seemed to have a built-in savvy for managing up, putting more effort into getting executive attention rather than buying into the BS that teamwork was important. All teamwork did was get you lost in a sea of other players, all suited up in the same color, indistinguishable from one another. Executives set themselves apart from the outset and she'd failed to do that. It wasn't too late, it just meant she had to be more fierce and aggressive to make up for lost time.

Life seemed poised to pass her by in the marriage and family department. Children were out of the question with her fortieth birthday rocketing toward her. And that was fine. No loss there. Children were a lot of work and a lot of expense for minimal return. If you were lucky, they were there to care for you in your old age, but from what she'd observed, they could just as easily grow up selfish or put so much terrain between you and them, devoted care became a physical impossibility. With enough money, that kind of care could be purchased. Sure, there were moments of joy with children, but she seriously doubted it was all worth it. As far as a mate, that could still happen, but she'd learned her lesson there. A mate that tried to reshape you into his view of a female was no mate at all. Either she found someone who accepted her on her terms, or she was on her own. And for now, for the foreseeable future, for planning purposes, she *was* on her own. Financial security was hers to earn and enjoy. A partner wasn't required and, from what she'd experienced with Tim, could just as easily pull her back from reaching her potential. She'd thought he was in awe of her, but he hadn't listened to a word she'd said, intent on modeling his life after Pygmalion. He had nearly destroyed her career, undermining everything she did, filling her with self doubt rather than cheering her on when she tried to talk to him about work. Living with Tim had been like the proverbial frog in a pot of water, the heat getting turned up slowly until she'd nearly boiled to death.

Interviewing candidates outside of Avalon was a formality required of Hank to demonstrate the company was following fair employment practices. There was no way any of those applicants had the expertise she brought to the table, and if they did, they were probably too old. Still, it was bitchy of Vanessa to wait until late yesterday to schedule Laura's interview. As far as Laura knew, there were no other candidates inside the company, but Vanessa said nothing, so she couldn't be one hundred percent certain.

She smiled at her watery reflection on the sliding glass door. She would try to be kinder, the poor girl had to have some sense of power or importance. Except for hiding the details of Hank's schedule, there was nothing else to give

Vanessa's job meaning.

BY LUNCH TIME she'd memorized, word for word, every success point on her resume — from the three million dollar budget she'd managed when she ran the marketing focus groups, to the four product launches she'd orchestrated before she moved into Hank's organization, as well as all the associated metrics for positive press, analyst quotes, and viewers at the online events. She had the highlights of how her pricing insights had driven increased sales, in case Hank's past kudos to her had slipped his mind. She walked to the cafeteria alone. Rain sprayed under the covered walkway, forcing her to remain near the center. She wasn't in the mood to talk to Brent. Discussing the interview would make her jumpy. She didn't want to be nervous, she shouldn't be nervous, but she was. Supposedly a little tension was good — it would keep her alert, make her brain cells fire more rapidly.

She arrived outside Hank's office door at two minutes before three. The door was closed. Vanessa stood inside. Her hair was pulled over her left shoulder the way she liked to arrange it when she was talking to men, draped alongside her breast. She wore high-heeled boots — treacherous in the heavy rain. Her skirt was knee-length with a slit up the side to mid-thigh. It wasn't particularly revealing, but still, who wore a slitted skirt to work? Unless you worked in the fashion industry. No one in high tech dressed like that. The sound of Vanessa's voice was clear but Laura couldn't make out the words. There was an intimate quality to it, a soft purring sound. Of course, Vanessa's voice was always soft. She spoke in a low tone, yet managed to make herself heard. It was remarkable, actually. When she first opened her mouth, there was a sense the listener would be required to strain to hear her, but that wasn't the case.

Laura refused to knock. She had an appointment. Both of them should know what time it was. This was another attempt to exert meaningless power. There was absolutely nothing Vanessa had to talk about with Hank right this minute. He should be reviewing Laura's resume. She'd only worked in his organization for three years, and he knew very little about her career successes before that. Yet Vanessa had to insert herself, had to bring up some bit of trivia about an expense report or a meeting or whatever else it was that she spent her time doing for him. The lack of respect was shocking. The admin should be deferring to candidates for this position. In addition to working for Hank, it was the job of all VP admins to provide a minimum level of clerical support for the directors on his staff. In a few weeks, Vanessa would essentially be working for Laura.

It was three minutes after the hour before Vanessa stopped talking and glanced at the glass panel in the door. She lifted her hand and looked at her phone. She looked back across the office. Her mouth moved rapidly, her voice burbling like a small fountain. As she spoke to Hank, she raised her arm toward Laura and held up her index finger.

Laura turned and walked down the hall. The break room smelled of fresh coffee and the metal sink was stained with water spots. The counter between the espresso machine and the pots for regular and decaf coffee was crowded with a stand holding packets of powder for hot chocolate, stir sticks, and tea bags. Since most people drank coffee, it was possible some of those tea bags had been sitting there for years. Right in front was a stain where someone had spilled coffee and not bothered to wipe it up. The liquid had dried, leaving a dark ring and the shadow of a puddle. She took a bottle of sparkling water out of the company-stocked cooler. The cap was so tight she had to strain for a few seconds before it broke loose from the plastic threads holding it in place. She took a sip. It bubbled up too fast and fizz landed on her upper lip. She yanked a paper towel out of the dispenser. It tore, leaving her with a fragment of rough paper. She dotted it against her mouth.

"There you are." Vanessa stood in the doorway, hands on her hips. "It's time for your interview."

"It was time for my interview six minutes ago."

Vanessa disappeared around the corner. Laura ripped another paper towel out of the dispenser, put it under the faucet for a moment, and wiped up the coffee stain. She dropped the towel in the trash and used another to clean her fingers.

As she approached Hank's door, she heard Vanessa, out of sight but just inside his open door. "I told her you were ready.

I don't know what happened to her. I thought she was right behind me."

Laura stepped into the doorway. The focal point of Hank's desk was a state of the art 24-inch computer display. Sitting nearby were all his other electronic gadgets — an iPad, an iPhone, a laptop. How many ways did one man need to access email that he then chose to ignore more often than not? At the end of the desk were a leather datebook and a dark red Montblanc pen. Artfully displayed on the shelves behind his desk were industry magazines with cover stories about Avalon, a diamond-shaped chunk of glass engraved with Hank's name, and other awards for sales excellence and the successful introduction of new products. The whole team worked to design, develop, and bring products to market. They debugged software, they wrote white papers and thousands of PowerPoint slides, they priced and positioned the products in the marketplace, and met with customers. The team was often given cash or stock recognition, but the awards sat in Hank's office. Alone on the bottom shelf was an enormous silver Japanese sword with a jewel-encrusted handle. Two of the office walls were floor-to-ceiling windows that looked out over the bay. Even though the sky was cloudy and the bay water a murky gray, it was a calming view. In front of the south-facing window was a conference table with four chairs. More magazines were spread on the table. For the digital age, there were a lot of print magazines. Did anyone ever read them?

Vanessa left without speaking, hopefully embarrassed that she'd been caught sniping at Laura when the reason they were starting late was entirely her fault. Laura smiled. Once she had the job, she'd never have to fight for respect again. From anyone. It came with the territory. And this interview was only a formality. She pulled out one of the chairs and sat down.

"I know I don't need to describe the position for you," Hank said.

"Why don't you anyway, so I can hear what your expectations are."

He stood and went to the window near his desk. He looked out at the bay as he explained the role, the number of direct reports, how success would be measured, and the overall areas of responsibility. It was nothing she didn't know, but she'd wanted to hear him say it. She needed to force him to take this seriously. His shoulders appeared stiff under the white shirt. He was one of a few VPs who wore white shirts and slacks every day. Especially in engineering, most of upper management dressed in jeans and sport shirts unless they were meeting customers. They usually threw on a suit jacket to give a nod to the power positions they had. But really, they were in love with their work, in love with electronics and design and making cool stuff. Sometimes she wondered if her biggest mistake had been focusing on business and not getting a technical degree before her MBA. It seemed easier to move up the ranks if you were an engineer. She supposed the thousands of mid-level engineers didn't see it that way. But most of those guys didn't want power positions. They were happy with their cool stuff. The ones who did rise to the top appeared to do it almost effortlessly.

The cloudy sky made his shirt look whiter and his hair darker, the shadow of his beard more prominent. There was something about his always visible growth of hair, never satisfied to be shaved off, always pushing through the skin again, demanding to make itself seen, insisting everyone notice this was a man, not just an institutional figure defined by white shirts and education and experience. Underneath all those things was muscle and bone, skin that was tender in parts, desires that were never evident but must be simmering there like they did with every human being on the planet. He'd learned to keep all that hidden. She wondered when it emerged. Only on the weekends when he was with his wife and son? In the evenings? When he traveled and spent long nights alone in expensive hotel rooms?

She was alarmed at the direction her thoughts were taking. She didn't need this kind of distraction. On the other hand, he was a man and maybe she hadn't used that fact to her advantage. It worked for Vanessa. Maybe Laura needed to connect with him on a more personal level. He really was good looking and . . . okay, sexy. She'd be lying to herself if she believed she'd never noticed. His power was like a distinct aroma inside the office.

She realized she hadn't heard what he was saying. She

shifted in the chair, pressing her spine against the back.

Without facing her, he said, "Tell me why you're the best candidate for this job."

It was not the question she'd expected. There should be others first. This was a concluding, bonus points, summarize-your-strengths question. He hadn't asked about the highlights of her career, the challenges, the accomplishments. He hadn't asked about her management style. He hadn't asked the tricky questions about how she handled conflict or failure or pressure. Maybe he was going to proceed backwards?

He turned. He folded his arms across his chest, and as the shirt pulled at his shoulders, she thought again about his raw maleness. If she didn't get a grip, she was on the precipice of fucking this up. She crossed her legs so she looked less prim. "I think we both know why."

His expression didn't change. As if he'd expected this answer, unless he was just a master of the poker face, which he was. The silence continued. She uncrossed her legs and crossed the left over the right. Her answer was too flip. She should be treating him like a stranger, it was beginning to seem that's how he wanted to approach this. But if that was the case, he should have started with her resume. It was completely unfair, as if he wanted to sabotage her. Maybe this was a test. She needed to re-adjust. She wouldn't acknowledge the awkward pause. "I have an MBA from Santa Clara University. I've worked at Avalon for eleven years doing product marketing, product management, and business analysis. I have experience managing people and I know the product line better than any other candidate."

"How do you know that's true?"

"Are there other internal candidates?"

"That's not important. I'm curious how you can make an assertion like that without having all the facts."

So he was testing her. He didn't want her prepared, he wanted to make her squirm so he could see how she responded in the face of conflict instead of listening to her rattle off a planned spiel that made her look good. Fair enough. She smiled. "You're correct. I don't know all the facts. It was an educated guess. I've been in this department for the introduction of every product we have in the portfolio right now except for the AX series. I know the specs, I know the positioning in the marketplace, I understand the high level competitive landscape, and I know the price structure and the revenue run rate. I know the value proposition and why our products are chosen over the competition."

He nodded.

"I . . ."

"Why did you stop managing the product marketing team for the AL series?"

He'd read her resume after all. He went on without letting her answer. "Whoever is hired as the Ops Director will have eight direct reports, and for the past four years, you haven't been a manager."

She'd been prepared for this question, although it, too, was out of order. She'd known it didn't look good to be a manager and then return to individual contributor status. It implied failure. It hinted at incompetence. Hank had been running the Western Region sales at the time. He'd come on board shortly after she left the management job and she'd thought someone might have told him what happened. Maybe they had and this was another test.

Pressure was building in her temples, the hint of a headache accompanied by a distant tone that she couldn't quite hear but thought was there — a high-pitched, piercing sound. All she had to do was act the part, be confident. It was all in your confidence and then they couldn't see the gray and black growth of fuzz, the soft, pulpy decay inside, ready to collapse in on itself once it was fully rotted.

"I received positive reviews from my team. Three of them left the company, and before I could hire replacements, we had a freeze." She shivered as if the euphemism for a hiring pause were real. "Right after, there was a small reduction and the rest of my team was impacted by that."

"Did you fight the decision to eliminate your team?"

Why did she sense that he already knew the answer? It could be his flat tone, as if he wasn't really asking a question, but leading her into a trap of some kind.

"At the senior manager level, you don't get to fight, you execute."

He laughed. "No pun."

"No."

His demeanor and the course of the conversation was different from anything she'd experienced in the past. This might be what he was really like, and when you were a director, there was no more hiding the rough sides of business, no more pulled punches. She could handle it, she just wasn't prepared because she hadn't seen it from him before. All the things that went on in conference rooms with his direct staff. Meetings that Vanessa was sometimes privy to. Did he treat Vanessa with the same harshness? It would be interesting to know. Until now, that hadn't been Laura's impression.

"Why did the first three leave? And why did they target the rest of your team? You must have been given an explanation. There must have been a lack of results at some point."

"My team did great work. I got a lot of kudos for it. I was rated a one, two years in a row."

"What ratings did your team members receive?"

"Aren't we getting a little of course into details that aren't relevant any more?"

Hank sat down. "Management is a big part of this role, driving a team to deliver. When three staff members leave at once, it could indicate a problem."

"There were rumors of a RIF. I think they saw a chance to jump and they did. It had nothing to do with the success of our group."

"I see."

She sensed he didn't believe a word she was saying. The tone resumed its shrieking in her left ear, louder this time. There was no reason to doubt her word, to imply she'd failed or done something wrong to make more than half her team scurry out the door. "Unfortunately my manager from that time isn't here, so you can't check. I could give you his number. He's at Google now."

"No, that's fine. Just getting a sense of your perspective."

The rest of his questions were a mixture of topics that she'd never considered, mingled with the interview standards. He informed her she'd have to interview with Sandeep and two others on his staff. He informed her there was a large pool of highly qualified candidates. He didn't wait for her to assure him she was more so. He told her Vanessa would set up her next interviews and once he had feedback from the others, he'd narrow his list, and then he'd meet with her again. She couldn't imagine what else he might ask. She was exhausted.

She stood. The back of her shirt was damp. She'd wished she hadn't worn her jacket. On the other hand, if she hadn't, and she'd still perspired, the moisture would show when she walked to the door. She tugged the hem of her jacket to make it hang more symmetrically and extended her hand. "Thanks for your time. I know you'll be thrilled with my performance."

He took her hand. His fingers were firm and dry. His grip wasn't as tight as she remembered although it certainly wasn't of the dead fish variety. As quickly as he'd taken her hand, he dropped it and stepped back. "I need the forecast by four."

She felt as if she'd been slapped. He put her through all that, treating her like a stranger, and now, in the breath of a phony handshake, he reverted to being her manager's boss? For half a second, when their hands were touching, she'd felt genuine warmth, as if he recognized her as a person, as if he felt she had qualities beyond what would come out in any interview, that he knew she'd be an asset to his direct staff. She'd felt a warmth beyond just hiring manager and candidate. She'd felt noticed and, if it wasn't taking things to an extreme, like the two of them were simply a man and woman who appreciated each other on many levels.

"No problem." Her voice was hoarse. It sounded weak and had a slight quaver that she hoped he didn't notice.

Eleven

MATT WAS SITTING in the living room drinking a whiskey and coke. The TV screen was off, a solid sheet of black that revealed flecks of dust. He put his drink on the table. "Are you okay?"

She took off her coat. "I'm a little hungry. I was thinking mac and cheese and Italian sausage. Sound good?"

He picked up his drink and worked an ice cube into his mouth. It rattled against his teeth and made his lips wet. Matt loved mac and cheese. Usually his face erupted into a huge grin when she suggested it, but he continued sucking on the ice cube, staring at the blank TV screen.

"Don't you want mac and cheese?"

"I wasn't talking about dinner."

She combed her fingers through her hair, bringing it over her shoulder, inspecting the strands as they threaded around her knuckles.

"What did you mean?" She leaned one hip on the back of

the couch. "I'd rather have wine, did you open any?"

"I needed a drink after what I saw."

"What?" She pulled her hair up and held it in a pile on top of her head. "It's warm in here."

"I was in the hall bathroom looking for a band-aid." He held up his finger to show a piece of damp toilet paper stuck to the cuticle. A small spot of blood had soaked through.

"The band-aids are in the other bathroom."

"We're out. I thought there might be some in the hall bath."

"I don't think there are."

"That's why I had to resort to toilet paper." He squeezed his tissue-covered finger with the index finger and thumb of his other hand.

"What did you do?"

"Just a hangnail. I bit it off and it bled like hell."

"I don't see much blood."

"I used half a roll of toilet paper."

"Half a roll?"

"There's a lot of nail polish in that closet."

"So?"

"It's breeding like rabbits in there. The pink mates with the blue and you have twenty mauve babies or something? It's crazy. I've never seen so many bottles in my life. Why do you need all that?"

"I like variety." She let her hair fall to the side. She bent her fingers admiring the cotton candy color she'd painted them the night before. Tonight she was thinking of changing to purple.

"Well it's not variety. There must be thirty bottles of cherry red alone."

"They aren't all cherry. There are differences."

"It's a little scary."

"I like to do my nails every day. You know that."

"This is beyond every day. You have enough polish in there to open your own Walmart. It's kind of sick. How much did all that cost?"

"It's not sick. You spend money on baseball tickets and other stuff. I like nail polish."

Ice rattled against the glass as he lifted the drink to his lips. "Why so much?"

"I told you." There was no way he could manage to guess she'd stolen it. His mind would never go there. Every single bottle was a badge of honor, telling her how good she was at taking things. She'd collected them for years. She supposed she was lucky he'd never noticed, that he never looked in the bathroom cabinets and drawers. The back of her neck was damp. She put her hand under her hair and lifted it again. He thought she'd spent too much money, that was all. Despite his crime-oriented entertainment tastes, Matt was the most honest guy she'd ever encountered. If a clerk left a pack of gum or a box of dried soup off his receipt, he'd return to the store and wait in line to get the error corrected. "I'll try to stop buying so much." It was a lie. She couldn't stop, didn't want to stop.

"Too late. You never need to buy another bottle."

She laughed. "It dries out."

"It's not only the nail polish."

She went toward the kitchen.

"Where are you going?"

"To open a bottle of wine."

The leather creaked as he got out of the chair. A moment later he stood in the doorway. Metal squeaked against cork as she twisted the corkscrew into place. The lever to extract it clinked on the glass. The cork slid out with a satisfying pop.

"Do you have some kind of hoarding addiction?"

"I don't think so."

"The bathroom drawers are full of unopened stuff. And the back of your closet. A lot of tops and stuff I don't remember seeing."

"You're familiar with every piece of clothing I own?" He shouldn't have gone in there. She liked looking at the things she'd taken, liked knowing she owned lots of delicate tops, lacy bras, and thongs in every color of the rainbow. Not expensive things from Victoria's Secret or department stores. The things she collected were from discount stores, but no matter where you bought lingerie or cosmetics, the cost added up — fast.

"I have a pretty good idea. There's stuff in there that still has the tags. Summer shirts. And it's the same as stuff you already have. What's going on?"

"All men say that. Women just like more variety. Choices."

"It doesn't seem right."

"Don't worry, it's no big deal."

"How did I not know about this?" he said.

She drank her wine. She flicked the cork with her index finger. It rolled across the counter and bumped against the bowl holding an apple that had been sitting there so long she wondered if it was still edible. "I should start dinner."

"What is it with you and your nails anyway? Does Hank have some kind of nail fetish that you have to change them every night?"

"No. He has nothing to do with it."

"Well it sure isn't for me. I don't care what color your nails are."

"It's for me." Her nails glowed under the kitchen light, shimmering like stones plastered to the outside of the wine glass. Part of her wanted to put her hands in her pockets, but she liked looking at them. She took a sip of wine. It calmed her, blotting out the fear that Matt was about to figure out her secret. What if he went through her receipts? They took care of their own credit card bills. Maybe when they were married they'd put all their cash together, but for now, it seemed easier this way. He'd never looked at hers, never asked what she spent on anything unless it was for the house. If he'd gone through her closet, he might go through the box where she filed her statements. He might start looking at everything in a different light, wondering why their grocery bills were lower than those of other couples, asking about how she managed so many clothes on her income. It was easy when you never had to pay for cosmetics. Lingerie . . . men had no idea how much it cost, that you couldn't keep bras for years like you could with . . . well, he didn't even wear undershirts. "Aren't you hungry?" she said.

He finished his drink and poured a glass of wine for himself. "No woman I know changes her nail polish every night."

"Well I do. What's the big deal? You never said anything about it before."

"I always thought it was a little crazy. And now that I saw all those bottles, it got me thinking. And what you said — the gossip about you and Hank."

She put her glass on the counter. She picked up the cork and tossed it into the trash. She pulled out a pot to boil the macaroni. The pot clanked against the sink and the rush of water spraying against the bottom drowned out anything else he might have planned to say. She liked her job and she liked Hank. He was a good-looking man, and yes, she liked being around him, liked flirting a little, liked looking good and knowing he noticed. It was fun. She liked that her co-workers wondered about them, but she didn't want to upset Matt, start him worrying. Although maybe a little competition was good.

Matt stepped out of the doorway and returned to the living room. Over the sound of rushing water, she heard the TV, too loud. He wasn't going to let this go now that the idea was in his head. He'd be relentless, asking questions, trying to understand. Wanting a detailed explanation that made sense, something that erased the idea of her and Hank from his head. It was her fault that the idea, the image he'd formed, now sat inside the soft tissue of his brain like a piece of rusting metal that it would take monumental effort to remove. She couldn't remember why it had seemed so important to tell him about the rumor. Possibly she just wanted him to be more taken with her. He underestimated the impact she had on people, on men. She didn't want him worried, suspicious, just . . . something . . . aware of his good fortune. Thrilled that she was with him.

It wasn't as if their relationship was one of complete transparency. At least it wasn't on her side. Matt certainly didn't know every single thing about her, despite the fact they'd moved in together when she was twenty. He didn't seem to have any secrets, but how did she know that for sure? And he didn't know everything about her and Hank, what Hank had done. It was nothing really. Not an affair. Just this . . . this thing. A desire to linger in his office for as long as possible at the end of the day. The warmth of his eyes on her, even if his expression remained bland. She knew. She'd known for a long time, and she enjoyed it. Was there something wrong with her? Was it a sickness, like the shoplifting? It was certainly something normal people didn't do. Maybe she was an exhibitionist without the nudity part.

Wanting Hank to look at her with longing but not actually wanting to have sex with him. And that's what it would be, because she certainly didn't love him. She wanted his attention. That was it. Being around him felt good. He made her feel important, made her feel she was better than the others. More valuable.

Five months. It was hard to believe it had been that long. They'd been at a trade show in New Orleans. No one could imagine a worse place to host thousands of people at the start of hurricane season, the air so full of water, it dripped. Air that kept you from ever being dry — giving up trying to keep your skin smooth and your hair silky. Except when you went inside, and then it was so cold from the air conditioning your skin turned hard and flakey.

The employee event was held at a quaint hotel. Prior to the party, she'd ushered Hank around at a customer reception, making sure no one sucked him into a discussion of product quality issues, a smiling, small-talk event designed to make the customers who were chosen to attend feel like the elite. After ninety minutes they were done.

Hank was different before they even arrived at the party and started drinking. More relaxed, having shed his corporate skin. The humidity certainly contributed. It was impossible to remain pressed and polished and aloof when your face was smeared with oily perspiration and your clothes stuck to your body like gummy wet suits. They walked down Bourbon Street in the dark, laughing at the people tripping on their own feet, women with the straps of their dresses falling off their shoulders, revealing the paler flesh at the top of their breasts, their damp feet sliding off high-heeled sandals, clutching shocking orange and gold hurricane drinks and other cocktails in large plastic cups. The men were equally foolish, leering at women they didn't know, splashing beer on their clothes.

Hank took her elbow and steered her into the hotel lobby. He picked up a glass of white wine for her and a whiskey and soda for himself and they walked to the room where the others were already dancing. The noise was as heavy as the humid air outside — people shouting with laugher over the predictions of a fortuneteller, or simply trying to make their voices heard above the music.

For a while, they separated. Vanessa sipped her wine and let the laughing, drinking, employees spill around her. She leaned against an adobe column, the surface cool on the skin of her upper back. It felt good to have something solid and hard holding her up after an entire day on her feet, and then, smiling at customers, repeating the same simple, empty phrases over and over — *So glad you could join us. Our pleasure. Thank you for coming. That's great to hear. Thanks. Thank you.*

Cheryl Adler came up to her. She grinned and sipped her slushy drink. "Can I share that post with you? I could use someone to hold me up right about now."

Vanessa wriggled to her left to make room for Cheryl.

"Nothing like free booze," Cheryl said. She giggled. She

stirred her drink and worked some of the thick icy stuff into her mouth. "Mmm. So nice to have something cold after all that sweat!"

"I know." Vanessa sipped her wine. It was no longer chilled, she needed a refill.

"Did you see Hank? He is wasted!" Cheryl giggled. "I've never seen him like that."

"He's not wasted."

"Have you seen him? He can hardly talk."

"You shouldn't say that. Even if it's a party, he's still the boss."

"A boss who's drunk off his ass!" Cheryl raised her glass as if she were making a toast. Cheryl tripped away, wobbling on her three-inch heels.

Vanessa wanted to grab the strap of Cheryl's dress and reprimand her. Even if it were true, it was so disrespectful. Hank worked hard, and he struggled at home, she was sure of it. He deserved to party a little. Everyone did. Cheryl acted as if he had no right because he was an exec, but he was human. And it's not like he compromised the company. There weren't any customers or industry press at the party.

When she saw Hank again, he'd clearly had a few more glasses of whiskey. "Ever' one wants a piece of me." He swallowed his drink. "Roll out a new product line on time and you're the star." He laughed. They talked about the customer reception. His gaze drifted toward the group of people dancing to classic rock. A Stones song came on. Hank took the cup of wine out of her hand and set their drinks on a chair. "Dance with me."

He could have said *Let's dance*, or *do you want to dance?* The phrase he'd chosen surprised and thrilled her. It was commanding and seemed to come from a need that went beyond the music and the drinks and the atmosphere. It came from something that had been dormant between them for a long time. She slipped off her shoes and kicked them under the chair where he'd left their drinks. She picked up her cup of wine, took a quick sip, and hurried after him. The music vibrated in her bones and her body felt loose and comfortable in the coolish air. Her dress was short and the hem swirled like a silky ballet skirt when she moved her hips. It felt good to let go, good to be in a place where everything wasn't oozing with heat. His slim hips shifted slightly from side to side. He kept his eyes fixed on hers, the pupils so large in the darkened room they were almost solid black.

They danced until her heart rate was thumping as rapidly as it did during ninety minutes of jazz class. Despite the blasting air conditioning, she was sweaty again. They each ordered another drink. Hank picked up a small plate of egg rolls from the buffet table. They chose two chairs in the corner farthest from the DJ and watched the dancers. The group was larger now, pressed more tightly together, intensifying the energy radiating from their bodies.

Hank sat with his legs spread. He balanced the plate on the leg closest to Vanessa. He swallowed half of his drink, picked up an egg roll, and bit off the end. She would have liked dipping sauce but they'd forgotten to fill a cup with some of the sweet, golden sauce. She reached over and picked up the second egg roll. The empty plate wavered slightly but remained in place. She took a small bite. It was warm, but not too hot. She took a second bite. It was tasty, perfectly moist with vegetables and thin wrapping so that she didn't miss the dipping sauce. They munched their egg rolls, sipped their drinks, and watched the dancers.

After two more glasses of wine, Vanessa could hear the words coming out of her mouth slow, and lazy, her tongue thick so that nothing sounded precise. Hank's eyelids looked heavy, and the darkness of his pupils seemed to have seeped into the whites of his eyes. They were dark, unfocused holes. He looked as if he'd forgotten where he was.

When she told him she was heading up to her room, he insisted on escorting her. At the door, she inserted the card and pulled it out too quickly. The light remained red. It took three more tries before she managed to open it. He stepped into the room behind her. She had a flashing doubt that she'd left yesterday's bra and thong on the dresser. Then he moved closer, his breath warm on her forehead. He was so close she couldn't see his face. He put his hand on her shoulder and slid his finger under the strap of her dress, moving it along her collarbone. The effects of the wine surged through her veins.

"I feel like you belong to me," he said. He put his mouth

close to her ear. "Mine." He held onto the word and released it with an extended breath, letting it turn into a soft moan in the back of his throat.

"Hank, I . . ."

He put his other hand on her opposite shoulder and turned her toward him. Their mouths came together and the taste of whisky soaked through her lips and tongue. His hand moved along the top of her breast. His fingertips danced across her skin until she shuddered.

After a moment, he pulled back. "Do you have any idea what you do to me?"

Her voice was rough, barely a whisper. "No."

He lifted the strap of her dress and slid it off her shoulder. It tickled the side of her arm and the smallest slip of the fabric covered the tip of her breast. He kissed her neck and folded his hand over her breast. She moaned. "I don't know. I don't think . . ."

"Shhh." He dragged his palm across her nipple.

She wanted to cry, the ache was so deep. Her body was melting. But he was drunk. Drunk off his ass, according to Cheryl. The words raced around inside her mind. Was this him? Or was he even certain where he was, what woman's body he was stroking?

"I don't know," she whispered. She moved back toward the wall.

He let his hands fall away from her. "You always keep me on track. You're right. Not now."

She didn't hear him move in the darkness. The door closed behind him and for a long time she'd stood there, trying to think.

When she'd woken the next morning, she wondered how it would be from there on out. But it turned out to be the same. A small part of her wished she'd let it go on longer, waited to see what happened. She might be in a stronger position if she had. Instead, things were uncertain. His memory of the evening was unclear to her. If a memory existed at all.

Thinking about it now made her want more wine. She added some to her glass even though it wasn't empty. She should offer a refill to Matt, but he wasn't complaining, mesmerized by the football moving up and down the field. Besides, he'd already had a whiskey. Mac and cheese no longer sounded like a satisfying meal. She dumped the water down the drain. She pulled a steak out of the freezer, unwrapped the paper, and placed the open package in the microwave. She hit defrost and returned to the fridge. There was enough romaine and half a bottle of Caesar dressing, all she needed were some croutons. The box in the cabinet above the oven had been up there a while but Matt had carefully folded the interior plastic and clipped it shut. She popped one in her mouth. Nice and crunchy. The salty, cheesy flavor made her want more wine. She took a sip and checked on the steak. She mixed dry mustard and a few small pinches of cayenne pepper.

When the steak was done defrosting, the paper was filled

with a puddle of blood. She lifted out the meat and patted it clean. She rubbed the cayenne and mustard mix into both sides, sprinkled it with a bit of Worcestershire sauce, and put it on the grill portion of the stove. She turned on the gas. Within a few minutes, the aroma of beef brought Matt to the doorway. She handed him the bowl of salad.

"No mac and cheese?" he said.

"I changed my mind."

"Good idea," he said. "I'm starving."

She put the steak on plates and carried the salad bowl to the dining room table. She lit the candles in the center. In silence, they sliced the serrated knives through the meat, red and tender. She was impressed with how it had turned out. Cooking up frozen meat didn't always work well.

Matt put down his fork and picked up the last crouton soaked in dressing. He put it in his mouth. "You aren't cheating on me, are you?"

"Is that what you think?"

"I don't know. Something doesn't feel right."

She pushed her plate to the side. She got up and went to his chair. She swung her leg over his and straddled his lap. "You're all I want."

"Even in your head? You wouldn't cheat in your head?"

"How does that work?"

"Thinking about him. Flirting with him. I don't know, stuff like that."

"What brought this up?"

"That nail polish freaked me out."

"It's just nail polish."

"It's not normal."

"What's normal?" She leaned into him. She put her lips on the side of his face and rubbed them gently across his stubble. The soft blonde hairs didn't scratch. She imagined the sharp, dark hairs on Hank's face would be like razor blades on her lips. She gently bit Matt's ear. He let out his breath slowly. Why couldn't anyone ever feel exactly as you wanted them to?

Twelve

LAURA WANTED TO cry the moment she became
conscious. The streets outside were so deserted she heard the
sound of the pump in the fish tank on the floor below her
bedroom. The red lines of the numbers displayed on her
clock stood like bloody gashes in the darkness — 1:11. She
dreaded the seconds advancing, racing toward morning. She
forced her mind to change direction. Running was as essential
as food and water. If she refused to let the monster rattle her,
he'd give up. He had to. She rolled onto her back. A few
minutes later she thrust herself onto her side again. The
numbers were less like cuts across a woman's wrist now that
they read 1:20. She closed her eyes and turned her back to the
clock.

It was four-fifty when she woke again. She dressed and did
four sets of bicep curls, increasing the weight to twenty
pounds for her last set. She was only able to perform two
reps at that weight, but completing even one was exhilarating.

She did twenty-five pushups and fifty-five crunches and went downstairs. While she drank a glass of water, she watched the fish. She took slow breaths, getting the rhythm of her breath in tune with theirs, and then went out into the damp air. The jog to the high school was slower than usual. A slick tarp of wet leaves covered the sidewalk, dotted with worms glistening under the streetlights. She kept her hands in the pockets of her hoodie, curled into fists to warm her fingertips.

Once she was circling the track, her shoulders relaxed and a smile tugged softly at her lips. She ran fast, her feet pounding the ground. After two laps, she pulled her hands out of her pockets and pushed off the hood. As she rounded the curve near the snack stand, she saw him. Even in the darkness, there was no mistaking him. His erratic movements were like a man flinging himself up and down the halls of a mental hospital, no awareness of where his body was going, trapped by whatever story was playing out inside his skull, certain there were insects swarming beneath his skin, voices shouting, torment that existed only in brain waves, distorted images and sounds, acting themselves out in his muscles and bones. Those people frightened her. Their lips and tongues were too red, their faces too pasty. Everything about them was slightly in-human. They did things in public that no one else would, uncaring and unaware of the effect they had on others. There was a look in their eyes, the surface of the eyeballs glassy and too bright, as if nothing from the brain penetrated the eyeballs and they existed simply to reflect sunlight, glass balls, not living organs receiving and giving intelligent thought. They didn't even give off the kind, knowing look of mammals. More like guppies or other species that existed only as food, made of nothing but breath, pulsing blood, and blind instinct.

Seeing them brought you face to face with all the things that could go wrong in the human mind. Your sanity and intelligence were all you had. If that disappeared, all connection with other human beings was torn away, leaving you trapped forever, not by barred windows and locked doors, thick canvas jackets with leather straps and buckles, you were trapped inside that small bony ball, isolated and crazed with trying to make others understand, but maybe not really caring whether they understood because what you really thought was that everyone around you was mad. Reality clouded by madness that prevented them from seeing that you were the sane one — with the voices telling you to pluck out your eyebrows, and slash your wrists with steak knives, and carve messages into your flesh. The sane one who clearly saw the enormous spiders advancing across the floor, the snakes and other deadly reptiles lurking beneath furniture, ready to strike. The world was nothing but threats. Everything from a sliver of sunlight that caused cancer to grow or enabled invisible flesh-eating bacteria to develop in the water, to the glowing moon, staring through the darkness at you — watching, judging.

A sob formed inside her chest, throbbing against her

throat, demanding to be let out. She stopped and bent over. She pressed her hands on her thighs and took in huge gulps of air. She forced her lips closed to push the air through her nose, trying to slow it down so she didn't burst wide open with the pain in all the dark corners of the human mind. So many people weren't safely locked up these days. There wasn't enough money to house them all. Those without a history of violence — yet — were left free to wander. Free to invent their own bizarre world in tiny, filthy apartments. When she walked past houses, she wondered at the occupants. Was that one with the neatly trimmed lawn housing a madman? Or did that one, with the half dead lawn, no shrubs, just bare, exposed plaster meeting up with the ground around it indicate mental decay? Did the closed drapes mean something dangerous lurked inside, or did drapes that were never drawn closed mean that? Which behavior was deviant?

This guy could have a wall filled with photographs of her. A collection of pictures that included images of death. Any gruesome photograph in the world was available to someone with an Internet connection and a desktop printer. With Photoshop, a normal woman's face and body could be hideously altered. Technology was glamorous and exciting, opening up new possibilities, while simultaneously giving voice and fuel to the deranged. It cracked open the skulls of people who had managed to stay on the right side of the line before, now able to pursue fantasies, give free reign to their quirks until they grew, in the dark dampness of lonely rooms, into something horrifying. He might be planning to kill her. If she didn't kill him first.

She gritted her teeth until her jaw ached. Her thoughts replicated themselves like a hydra, growing into something more terrifying each time she lopped one off. There was too much pressure — the possibly botched interview, this creature following her — half man, half monster. The only solution was to stop running at the high school. But she dismissed that thought. This was her place, this time of day was her tranquility. She'd found it and claimed it as her own and he had no right to invade it. Running was supposed to keep her mind awash in soothing chemicals, not push it to fold in on itself, dwelling on dark topics. Soon she'd be the Director of Marketing Operations. The echo of the words in her mind calmed her breathing. She had not blown the interview. That was nothing but ungrounded fear. She'd countered every move Hank made with a perfect parry. He was probably sitting there right now, smiling at how she'd managed to adapt to an unconventional set of questions.

Behind her, the pounding of the man's feet grew louder, his breath was damp and sloppy with mucous. She straightened and started running faster. It was too late. He was only a few paces back. The heat of his body moved closer. She ran faster. Now he was beside her. She kept her gaze focused on a middle distance, the light graying around her so that smaller objects were now visible, the goal posts at the opposite end of the field, the metal pole at the far corner of the grass, marking the edge of the circuit training equipment.

"I know you." His voice was murky, as if he spoke from under water.

"No you don't." She knew immediately that responding was a mistake, but he'd reached inside to a primitive place where she couldn't control her reactions.

"I know exactly who you are."

Surely he hadn't tracked her to her loft, to the Avalon campus, a disgruntled co-worker or employee from the past who'd located her? She tried to run faster but it wasn't possible. His ability to keep up was stunning. The stiff, bony legs and his ill-fitting shoes, bare feet rubbing on the edges, should have slowed him down.

He snickered. "You know I know you."

"Get away from me. I've never met you."

She couldn't return to this track. She'd have to find a new place. She'd be forced to start the morning in her car instead of warming her muscles, loosening her joints, and clearing the dazed residue of dreams with a quick walk. He'd won. Keeping up this battle, trying to ignore him, accomplished nothing. His uncoordinated limbs, that beard, and those eyes, staring at her as if he did know her, when he did not, were terrifying. She couldn't say precisely what she was afraid of. Rape? Not really, but maybe. Murder. Yes. There was the look of a man who might kill just to prove he was right, to realize victory inside his confused head. Did he think she was a woman from his past? A woman who'd dumped him, or treated him badly in his mind, a woman who'd never actually had a relationship with him? He remained beside her, breathing through that wet goop that reminded her of walking barefoot through thick mud. How could he run with all that gunk inside his throat?

"You can't outrun me," he said.

"Like hell I can't." She forced herself to go faster, breathing so hard the ragged, wheezing sound seared her brain. She pushed harder still. Her pulse pounded in her throat and her heart beat so rapidly she was afraid it might give out. She couldn't keep this up. What was she trying to prove? He laughed. His beard blew against his neck, pulsing with life. As she rounded the curve toward the snack shed, another man emerged from the shrubs. He walked to the edge of the track and grabbed his left foot, bending his knee and pulling back his leg. A normal runner. A guy she'd never seen before. There was a slight pudginess around his middle. He had short light hair and wore a crisp white t-shirt. His shoes looked new, white as his shirt. He glanced at the monster.

Did they know each other? She felt herself slowing, the distraction preventing her from maintaining the pace. It was just as well. She couldn't sprint forever. Yet the monster was right at her elbow, almost touching her. She really should call the police. But what would she say? She wanted the track to herself? He ran too close? He talked to her when she didn't want to talk? They'd laugh and hang up on her. But her dinosaur brain insisted something was wrong. The echoes began — *What's wrong with a nice walk? Why do you have to prove you're better than your brother in everything? It's not nice. You need to be careful of the male ego.*

The other man was jogging now. Lumbering, his first time out on the track in years, maybe ever. A man whose doctor told him to get some exercise. A youngish man, thirty-five at most, already carrying the weight of someone twenty years older. Every few steps, he glanced at the monster. His presence changed everything. The monster dropped back a few yards. He continued mirroring her pace, but she could no longer hear that wet, sickly breathing. She couldn't smell his damp skin. She had no idea how long she'd been out here. She reached into her pouch and pulled her phone halfway out. Six-forty and she hadn't made more than six loops — a mile and a half. Or maybe it was more. She'd been running so fast, she must have covered more ground. She slowed to a walk.

A seagull swooped down and landed in the grassy area at the center of the track. There was no discarded food that might have lured it, which meant another storm was coming, creeping along the coast and sending the birds inland. The gull watched her, its white feathers with touches of charcoal gray like carved marble. Its bony legs and large floppy feet marring its beauty. They were designed to look gorgeous in flight, not walking around on the earth, demonstrating how helpless they were without a second set of appendages to help them maneuver food to their beaks. The gull took a few steps and launched into flight. She was sorry to see it go. There was a sense of defeat, as if the bird had abandoned her to these strange men. How foolish the human race was, running in ovals, going nowhere. Life was so sedentary, so distorted from what the human body had been designed to do, what it needed to do — keep moving. They ran in loops and climbed on machines plugged into electrical outlets. They couldn't even use their own force to propel a machine built to keep them moving.

What thoughts were traveling through their minds? A whole universe existed inside each human skull. Maybe the universe inside her own head was false. It could be they hardly noticed her. The creep had only spoken to her because he sensed her fear. She needed to take back her power. Ignore him. She was about to become a fucking Director! Crossing the threshold into lower executive management. Some wouldn't call it that, reserving that word for vice presidents. But it wasn't true. The director level was a whole new realm and it was so close she could feel it as if it were already printed on her business cards in fine, delicate letters. A year from now, she'd laugh at herself, thinking how accustomed she was to being at that level, privy to more company secrets, more financial insight, invited to discuss strategy in a meaningful way. It was the next step before she set her sights on becoming a Vice President. Then she might finally be able to rest, ease her foot off the gas.

Tim had said she'd never get to the top, that she didn't have it in her, whatever that meant. After all the things wrong between them, those words broke it apart for good. She couldn't stay with a guy who wanted to drag her down, even if he didn't come right out and say so.

Slogging around a track and worrying that two losers were getting in her way would be a long-forgotten joke just a few months from now. She laughed. She glanced over her shoulder and suddenly they both looked very different. *They* were trying to keep up with *her*. She ran faster. They couldn't hurt her. They'd never catch her.

Thirteen

BILL'S DELI WAS in a strip mall two blocks from the Avalon campus. The strip mall was also home to a sushi place, a pizzeria, and a chain sandwich shop, along with a Baskin Robbins and a Starbucks. Most Avalon employees seemed to prefer sushi or pizza. Vanessa rarely saw anyone in the deli. In fact, she wondered sometimes how they stayed in business. In the spring and summer, she walked over to pick up sandwiches, unless the temperature was in the nineties, in which case she drove, feeling lazy and wasteful of the earth's resources, but unwilling to sweat all over clothing chosen for an air conditioned office. She didn't feel quite so top-of-the-food-chain wasteful in the winter, but still. Two blocks, three if you added the width of the parking lot. The car didn't even warm up by the time she pulled into a parking spot facing the deli.

Inside, she ordered ham and cheddar cheese for both of them, Hank's on rye bread, hers on sliced sourdough. In front of the register was a rack of candy. The first shelf held Hershey's chocolate bars. Suddenly, she wanted one. It was possible she missed the chocolate kisses as much as the others did, although she didn't miss the mindless unwrapping and eating before she caught herself, a tiny pile of foil balls on her desk. Hank might like a chocolate bar too. He hadn't said anything about the missing candy dish, but he was in the habit of eating one almost every day. Sometimes he grabbed several pieces of chocolate and took them back to his office. He hadn't asked for a chocolate bar. And the twenty was probably going to be consumed by the sandwiches, an extra charge for cheese, two sodas, and chips. She reached into her purse for her wallet. The zipper was rough on her fingers. She pulled her hand out of her purse. It would be fun to take the candy bar. A thrill she'd never enjoyed — taking something this close to work, and with the sandwich maker only a few feet away. The girl's back was turned. Her head was bent over the wood plank, the white of her neck bright as her blue dyed hair fell away on either side. She was still placing cheese on top of the meat. There was plenty of time.

Vanessa glanced over her left shoulder. The deli was still empty. Mini blinds covered the windows, so it wasn't as if someone passing by would notice. She put her hand on the shelf, touched the smooth brown wrapper. Just one, for her. Hank would have asked for candy if he'd wanted it.

The sandwich maker turned. "Pickles?"

Vanessa took her hand away from the candy. "Yes. I said,

everything but onions."

The girl turned back. The phone rang. It was clamorous, too loud for the small space. The sound made Vanessa's ears ache. The girl wiped her hands on a towel and grabbed the handset off the base. "Hello? I mean, Bill's Deli." It was annoying that the girl ignored the task in front of her for someone who had no previous claim on her attention. Hank requested the deli run because he was short on time. The girl should have finished what she was doing, first. Instead, she was now repeating an order, her voice gravelly and low for a girl that small.

Vanessa touched the candy bars. Plain or almond? She took a plain one and dropped it into the waiting mouth of her purse. The girl was still talking. She could take another, just for spite, but the theft had gone well. It was better not to push her luck.

The girl finished the phone order. She wiped her hands on the towel again and returned to arranging sliced tomatoes on the pile in front of her. She cut the sandwiches, wrapped them in paper, and shoved them into the waiting bag containing the Pepsi cans. She placed the Fritos on top. She handed the bag to Vanessa, took the cash, and returned the change.

Vanessa turned. Laura stood just inside the door.

"Oh, hi." Vanessa walked to the door. "Excuse me."

"Sure, no problem." Laura moved to the side.

"I didn't hear you come in."

Laura smiled.

Vanessa pushed her hip against the panic bar and went out.

Driving back to the office, she felt sick to her stomach. By the time she'd climbed the stairs to the second floor, she was nearly hyperventilating. She walked down the hallway, trying to steady her breathing. If Laura had seen, she would have said something right on the spot, wouldn't she?

Fourteen

LAURA WOKE AT three-thirty. It had been several days since her grilling by Hank and she'd heard nothing about scheduling additional interviews. The waiting was exhausting. During the day, she sat at her desk, clicking the *get mail* button every three or four minutes. It was impossible to work on the slides for the spring product launch because she couldn't help wondering . . . hoping . . . *knowing*, they wouldn't be her responsibility. She would not be carrying them through all the review cycles, handing them off to a successor when she started the new job.

The incident outside Hank's office last Friday was a minor rough spot. By now, he would have forgotten all about overhearing her gossip. If anything did come of it, she could leverage what she'd seen at the deli. Part of her wanted to use what she'd witnessed to get another meeting with Hank, but that would be a waste of good information. For now, it was nice that Vanessa knew Laura knew, or at least worried about how much Laura had seen. It was a good feeling, imagining Vanessa waiting for Laura to expose what she'd done, not so damn self-satisfied. Of course, it was her word against Vanessa's and a minor infraction. But it was more about the psychological control. If Vanessa was scared of the consequences, that was enough.

She tossed off the blankets. Getting up this early was insane, but there was no other way to avoid meeting the creep. She would take another stab at the launch slides after her run. It might become a new habit. She could go to bed earlier and work before the world woke up. Once she had coffee, ran, and showered, she'd be as alert as she ever was at eleven at night.

None of her neighbors' lights were on when she stepped outside. Of course not. It was three-fifty-five. She walked softly down the stairs and along the path to the sidewalk. The ground and trees smelled wet. It hadn't rained for several hours, but thick, low clouds blotted out the stars. It was supposed to clear this morning. The flashlight app on her phone lit the sidewalk, splashing onto the toes of her running shoes. No squirrels raced along the strip alongside the sidewalk, no crows hopped down the center of the street, grabbing bits of food that had been dropped out of car windows during the night. Of the houses she passed on her way to the high school, only a single one had lights glowing behind closed drapes. Her shoes tapped the concrete. The cold wrapped around her bare legs, making them both numb and somewhat sticky.

The bushes just inside the fence were sopping wet. Her face was damp and her hair and the cuffs of her sweatshirt were wet when she emerged on the opposite side. Why didn't the groundskeepers prune them? Someone could slip fighting the tangle of branches, skidding on the muck underneath. She walked across the grass, stretched her calves and quadriceps, and started a slow jog. The only sounds were her breath and thudding feet. She couldn't hold the phone to light the space in front of her, but she was confident the track stretched before her flat and empty.

She ran six laps. As she neared the top of the oval to begin her seventh, she heard his wet, thick breath. A second pair of shoes hit the ground with an uneven tempo, a discordant beat to her own rhythm. God damn it! She wanted to stop, turn quickly, and punch him in the mouth before he saw what was coming. How had he known? He *was* following her! He must live across from the high school, a manic person who never slept, watching out his window, waiting for her to pass by, tugging on that ridiculous beard, pulling down his lower lip with the force of it.

"Out early today," he said.

"Get the fuck away from me."

"Such nasty language for a sophisticated girl like you."

"I'm calling the police if you don't quit stalking me."

"Go ahead."

"I will." She slowed and pulled out her phone.

"I know exactly who you are."

"I've never met you."

"Are you sure?"

"Yes. Fuck off."

"You tell me to go away but you keep talking."

With her other hand, she yanked her hood more tightly around her face. She tugged the cord to tie it, but one end slipped out of her fingers and the entire thing slithered out of the casing. She shoved it in her pocket.

"You have to have the last word. You think you're so smart, so much better than everyone else."

Laura smirked. She didn't think it, she knew it. "What are you even doing here?"

"Running."

"We support this school and the track with our property taxes. It doesn't belong to anyone who happens to wander by."

"See. That's the problem. Why do you assume I don't live around here?"

"Whatever. I told you to get away from me."

"Yet you didn't call the police. Because you know it's a public place and you don't get to decide who uses it."

"What do you want from me?"

"You're going down."

"What does that mean?"

"You think you're on top of the world. Well so was I. Four short years ago. I had a nice house, a family. A *career*. A career with *momentum*. And then. Poof. Laid off. Too old to be hirable."

"If you're any good at your job, there's no such thing as *too old*." It was partially true. To a point, to the age of sixty, maybe. If you were an engineer. Maybe. Unless they found someone less expensive with more modern credentials. And if you weren't an engineer . . . MBA grads were a dime a dozen.

"It can all disappear like that." He snapped his fingers, but his thumb slid soundlessly across the others as if he was feeling a piece of fabric.

"I know that," she said. Her voice trembled as tears worked their way down her throat.

"I frighten you because you know you could become me."

She laughed, hating herself for the spontaneous response. She was encouraging him, allowing him to keep talking by not doing something more aggressive to be rid of him. Her anxiety enticed him, making him think he was in control. He was right — she shouldn't be talking at all. He'd tapped into something desperate inside of her, something that compelled her to prove they were nothing alike, that whatever he thought about her was wrong. It shouldn't matter what he thought. It didn't matter. He was disturbed. But she couldn't stop. "I'm not scared of you."

"Another lie."

"Fuck off."

"Listen to that language. I really am upsetting you."

He'd moved closer, the sleeve of his sweatshirt brushed against hers. She poked her elbow out. It stabbed his forearm, but didn't succeed in pushing him away.

"I think you want to know what I have to say. You think you're hot shit. You think you have it all under control, but you're so wrong. The tide turns and suddenly you're a candidate for a layoff. There's nothing remarkable about what you do. It becomes apparent you don't have the right connections. You thought the VP had your back, but he's putting all his focus on saving that other guy. No one is watching out for you. All those years of work, all those high ratings, all those weekends and nights when you thought they couldn't live without you because they were frantically emailing you and texting you and making you feel important, and so you gave up your whole life for them. It all evaporates like someone flushed a high efficiency toilet. Whoosh."

"People who get laid off find other jobs."

"Wrong again. In the past. Now, less is more. They find they don't need as many people as they thought they did. And they sure as hell don't need people over forty."

"I'm not forty."

He laughed. "Not today." He laughed harder. His laughter turned to shrieks and he stopped jogging. He bent over, gasping.

Not only was he charting her running habits, somehow, he was watching her thoughts. It was like a Sci Fi film — he had a futuristic smart camera in her bedroom and it recorded her last thought before sleep, stayed on all night, capturing her dreams. And her nightmares. Now he owned her because he knew everything about her. He'd described her life perfectly. Her stomach swam. Her skin prickled with sweat. Her nerves trembled so that she wanted to slap at her legs and arms to quiet them. She thought of Vanessa slapping at phantom ants and broke into a sprint. She didn't look forty. Not at all. How could he know? Was he one of those people who was good at guessing, who fed you lines and read your responses? Her words had been too defensive, bitter-sounding when she spat out, *I'm not forty*. He picked up on it. That was all. He didn't know a damn thing.

His feet pounded the ground behind her. The sky remained starless and moonless. She guessed it was four-twenty or so. The realization spun her thoughts back in the opposite direction. He'd known she would be out here because he *was* following her. He lived close enough to observe her movements. Had he watched her for weeks, months? Sitting by his living room window, staring, with binoculars trained on her loft, waiting for her to emerge. Suited up and ready to run the minute her front door opened. She'd never seen him follow her as she walked to the track. He never showed up until she'd started. He watched, then gave her time to get going. He allowed her to think she was safe, to let her body exert herself, her defenses lowered.

He was close to her elbow again. She twisted to the side, swinging her arm at him. She missed and lost her balance.

He giggled. "Three and a half *years*. That's how long it's been. Wife — gone. Kids — turned against me. If I want to see them now, I need supervision. My own sons. I did consulting for a while, and now they won't even hire me for that. I'm too out of touch or too needy and slow and not delivering at the caliber that's required. I have a freakin' Masters of Business Administration. Fat lot of good that did."

"I'm sorry for your misfortune. But your life is nothing like mine and I want you to stop bothering me. I'm serious."

"Ohhhh. You're *serious*. Well that changes everything." He giggled again. "Avalon doesn't give a shit about you and your career. Everything will slip through your fingers and you'll be one step from sleeping on the sidewalk, your beautiful hair snarled until you look like a freak, your skin . . ."

She stopped. "How do you know where I work?" She heard his breath, calm compared to hers, even after jogging several laps together. She couldn't decipher his expression. "How do you know?" She swallowed. She shouldn't have confirmed it, should have misdirected him. Although if he knew, he'd also know she was lying. Something touched her cheek. She swatted at it. His fingers, stroking her skin. She flailed, trying to grab his forearm, groping at nothing. She stumbled back and he moved closer, his form ghostly thin and shrouded in darkness. The smell of wet earth wafted off his skin. He bent toward her and the surprisingly silky strands of his beard brushed across her face. She screamed and flung her arms out, trying to get him away as if she were caught in an enormous cobweb, sticky stuff to clinging to her sweatshirt and hair.

They tussled. Their feet skidded on the track. Gravel crunched beneath their shoes like the delicate bones of songbirds. After a moment, she was able to separate from him, gasping for fresh air. She turned and ran across the track, onto the lawn. Her heel skidded on wet grass but she maintained her balance and jogged to the tangle of shrubs. It took only a few seconds for him to catch up. He grabbed the hood of her sweatshirt.

"What do you want?!" She tried to pull away but his grip was too strong.

"I'm you. You're me. You aren't going to get where you think you're going. It's too late. If there was something remarkable, if your destiny was at the top of the food chain, you'd already be there. You wouldn't be living in a pretentious *loft* in a middle-class suburb. If you were going to arrive, you already would have. You'd have a house in Atherton and you'd be running at a private track."

"Get away from me." Her voice had an uncontrolled, atonal sound that filled her with self-loathing. "Why are you following me?" The sobbing stopped suddenly as if a fist had been shoved down her throat. She turned and grabbed his beard. He screamed, his voice like a young girl's, so sharp and piercing that surely people in the surrounding homes would come out to see what was happening. But everything remained dark. If they heard, no one wanted to know. They wanted to capture their last few minutes of sleep, start their days with a normal routine, safe in the sameness of it, assured the future would also be the same.

He pinched her wrist until she released her grip on his beard. She whimpered.

"The reason talented, educated men like me see their careers go up in flames is because women are taking over. There haven't been enough new jobs to double the workforce over the past fifty years. But you'll be punished too. Just wait. No woman really succeeds. You're too weak."

Something popped inside her brain. A tiny fissure in a cranial blood vessel, exploding with microscopic sparks, spreading across the entire organ with white, burning light. The heat raced through her veins, transforming them into thin wires shooting electricity to every nerve, tightening her muscles. She grabbed his beard again and pulled. The sound of hair tearing out of the skin, his shriek, were immensely satisfying. Inflicting pain increased the heat shooting through her body. She yanked harder. His head was close to hers now, his wet, clogged breath the only sound. She kicked his ankle. He yelped and bounced on one foot, trying to regain his equilibrium. Turning slightly she slammed the heel of her shoe against his good ankle. As he stumbled and fell to his knees, more hair ripped out of his chin. The long strands tore at her palms and the rest of the beard slid out of her grip. He fell forward, weeping.

She pushed him flat and slammed her foot onto the small of his back. His cries were bleeding into one another. The sound fueled her rage. The disaster of his life was not a harbinger of hers. She was nothing like him. Women had the same right as men to gain power and influence. Male and female brains were equally capable. He'd sunk into the dregs because he was a loser. Workplace reductions ferreted them out, it was only a matter of time. There were no similarities between her career and his. He knew nothing about her. If he'd been watching, stalking, he still knew nothing and she wasn't going to allow him to behave as if he had some kind of supernatural insight into her future. It was nothing but the mad ramblings of a man who fucked up his life.

She squashed him into the mud under the shrubs like the cockroach he was. You couldn't let up on those things for even a second. If you pulled your foot away too soon to determine whether it was dead, the thing sped along the pavement, sometimes dragging pulverized limbs, never giving up. Hard and so nasty looking it made her skin crawl. She put her foot on his neck. She lifted her other foot off the ground, driving her full body weight through her right leg. He thrashed, flinging specks of mud into the air. They landed on her face and the backs of her hands, like thick, solid raindrops. The cartilage in his neck snapped as if she was stepping on dried tree branches. Another, louder cracking sound followed.

Immediately his thrashing stopped. At the same moment,

the searing that had consumed her blood vessels dissolved. Her arms and back were limp. She wasn't sure what she'd done. Certainly not why. Except that his presumptions reached into some place in the farthest spot of her dinosaur brain and turned her into something else for a moment.

The sky was a deep charcoal gray with the barest hint of light seeping behind the clouds. The scratching of a squirrel or other rodent came from the thicker part of the shrubs but the birds were silent despite the lightening sky. The strength and ferocity that had overtaken her was like something out of a disjointed dream, fading as quickly as the light spread, parts appearing senseless, the imagined scene of a mind that had slipped loose from its moorings. Either he was dead, or in very bad condition. She knelt on the muddy ground and turned his head toward her. A shudder raced down her spine and she yanked her hand away. He was dead.

How many people had seen her running here? A handful, maybe more, at one time or another. Although never this early. This would destroy her career. His prophecy would come true, just not for the reasons he'd said. She stood and lifted her right foot and studied the bottom of her shoe. She needed to get rid of these and purchase a new pair. Just in case. With cash. At a store out of the area.

She was stunned by her analytical focus. She'd killed a man. Stomped him to death in a brutal rage. Yet she was calm. The extraordinary strength and the white blinding surge of desire to shut him up, to be rid of him, had come out of nowhere and returned to the same place. Now she ticked through a list of things to cover her mistake. The first being, she needed to get the hell out of here. In the dull light, there was no way to look for hairs that might have fallen out. Her hair was tied up and she'd had her hood draped over her head, but not secured, since she'd yanked out the string. She felt in her pocket. The cord was still coiled safely at the bottom. What else? She studied her hands. Except for specks of mud on the backs, they looked normal. Her footprints would be the main thing. So getting rid of the shoes. She'd call, tell Brent and Vanessa to tell them she had a doctor's appointment. But if anything came of this, they'd check. She'd tell them she had a headache. She'd take a drive to the east bay, or maybe San Francisco.

She clawed her way through the shrubs. The opening in the fence was suddenly elusive. She might be experiencing shock at a deeper level, below conscious thought, clouding key parts of her brain. She tripped over a root. She landed on one knee, planting her palm to her right to keep from falling flat. Pain shot through her knee and her hand skidded across something thick and soft. She crept forward and recognized that she'd landed on the edge of a sleeping bag. It must belong to the monster. She could drag him over and stuff his body inside, delay the discovery of what she'd done. But then she risked other joggers arriving at the track. She crept forward a few more feet, curious about his belongings — a large backpack to one side, and some clothing protruding from beneath a thin pillow.

The backpack was the type used by campers who spent weeks in the wilderness, carrying all their supplies. The flap lay open on one compartment. She stuck her hand inside, hoping she wasn't greeted with insects or a rat, but anxious to know what objects he'd wanted close at hand. Her fingers closed around cold metal. She knew immediately what it was and pulled it out. A handgun. Also in the pouch was a cardboard box of ammunition, a hand towel, and a knife with a leather case over the blade. She spread the towel on the ground, piled the gun and other things in the center, folded it over and shoved it up inside her sweatshirt. She pushed herself to her feet and turned. The opening of the fence was directly in front of her. She bent her head to keep the branches from scratching her face and pushed her way through. The only thing she would think about right now was walking with solid, casual determination.

The coldness of her thoughts continued to shock her, yet they shouldn't have. She was used to taking care of things, cleaning up messes. The world was better off without that guy. He was definitely unbalanced — his desire to torment her, his laugh. And now this. If she hadn't killed him, he would have killed her.

Fifteen

NOT A SINGLE person had stopped by Vanessa's cube all morning. An unusual situation, but she wasn't going to complain. Hank was at a sales meeting in San Francisco. His empty office was dark one minute, flooded with light the next as clouds, still gray with rain, moved across the sky. They gave an eerie darkness to the inside of the building as they passed in front of the sun, followed by light so bright it sparkled. The heavy silence was broken by the sound of footsteps moving toward the end of the hallway. She looked up. Laura stood in front of the counter. "I'm better."

Vanessa nodded.

"My headache is gone."

"Thanks for letting me know." Vanessa studied the expense reporting tool displayed on her screen. She clicked in the button to enter a line for a new receipt. Only twenty-seven more receipts and Hank's report would be complete. Entering the data wasn't overly tedious, but the tool could be slow.

Waiting for each successive window to appear made her want to smack the glassy screen in front of her.

She was afraid to let her eyes meet Laura's. The vague smirk on Laura's face when she'd stood near the entrance to the deli floated ghost-like across the computer screen. Laura wore that expression a lot — her lips partially curved, her eyes unblinking, not afraid to stare directly into the eyes of others, waiting for them to look away first. There was a steadiness that said, *you can't hide from me. I'll find out your secrets.* There was nothing to indicate whether or not Laura had seen Vanessa slip the chocolate bar into her purse, but something said she knew.

Vanessa glanced up. Laura's hair, normally silky, wafted out from the sides of her face, each strand permeated with static that made it want to stand up on its own. "What happened to your hair?"

Laura shook her head. Rather than falling back from her face, her hair flew up even more. "I forgot to put in conditioner."

"How'd you forget?"

Laura leaned on the counter. "There's a lot going on. Where's Hank?"

"All day meeting."

"For what?"

"Sales review."

Laura nodded. Her hair rose up like it was applauding her efforts, crazed strands dancing alongside each other. She didn't seem to be aware of the unruly cloud surrounding her scalp. She looked as though she'd just pulled her head out from beneath layers of blankets.

"I expect I'll have my other interviews soon."

"I don't know the status," Vanessa said.

"That's bullshit and you know it."

Vanessa wheeled her chair closer to the desk. She cupped her hand over the mouse and moved it gently to the side. The disk at the side of her mail icon told her seven new emails waited in her in-box. If she started reading them, Laura would walk away. Or not.

"Remind me who else is interviewing me."

"I need to double-check with Hank before I work on that."

"Why do you stonewall me like this? I understand you're careful to do what Hank wants, but we're friends. Women should stick together."

"I don't think we're friends."

"Work friends."

"Not really."

"Well we should be. Women need to have each other's backs." Laura's eyes were glassy. The tip of her nose was a bright red bloom. It didn't look as if she'd been crying, but there was an aura of panic coming off her. If she didn't calm down, if she allowed Hank to see how desperate she was becoming, she'd sabotage her chances without any assistance from Vanessa. The stolen candy bar niggled at the back of her mind. Was that what Laura was referring to? Some kind of implied blackmail before she put forth her own demand?

Laura leaned her forearms on the counter. She glanced to her left. "Where's the candy?"

"I told you I'm not doing the candy any more."

"Why not? I thought that was temporary until the ants were under control."

"This isn't a hostess stand."

"It was a nice touch."

"No one needs candy."

"It was friendly."

Vanessa shrugged. She licked the corner of her mouth. Every one of Laura's words seemed to drip with underlying meaning — candy, women sticking together. It was a huge mistake to take something at a place so close to the Avalon campus. It was one of the rules that proved she was smarter than everyone else. She hadn't even eaten the chocolate. It was still in her purse, probably pulverized by wallet and keys and all kinds of other paraphernalia by now.

"We really should go to lunch sometime," Laura said.

"What do you want, Laura? I have things to do."

"I just think I've misjudged you. Knowing you were sleeping with Hank made me . . ."

"I'm not sleeping with Hank."

"Anymore?"

"Ever." She felt like a child, called into the school office for lying. Laura's height, accentuated with heels, forced Vanessa to tilt her head up. Despite Laura's flyaway hair and the manic glaze in her eyes, she still looked aware of her higher rank. "And if women are going to stand up for each other, they shouldn't be spreading lies."

"There's a connection between you and Hank. Everyone feels it."

"I have work to do."

"So you don't deny it."

"I'm starting to think you're attracted to Hank," Vanessa said.

Laura tossed her head back and laughed. The tendons in her neck quivered as she giggled.

"Why else would you come over here all the time? Waiting to trap him when he doesn't want to meet with you? Speculating about his sex life. You're projecting."

Laura snapped her head forward. "That's ridiculous. He wants to meet with me. I'm the best candidate for that position and he knows it."

"You're different around him. More flirty, eager."

"That's ridiculous."

"Look how upset you're getting. You like that rumor about him and me because you like thinking about him having sex."

"You're crazy," Laura said.

"Am I?" The thought had arisen out of nowhere, but maybe there was truth to it. Either way, it diverted Laura from talking about candy and hinting that Vanessa needed her back protected. In all likelihood, Laura was referring to her own back. "The more I think about it, the more true it seems. You don't even like me, but you hang out here all the time for no reason."

"The job I'm interviewing for is a director position. It's a promotion. Do you not even know that?"

"Of course I do."

"I'm not *hanging around* because I want to do the nasty with him."

Vanessa smiled. Laura's voice was tighter. She scooped her hair back, trying to tuck the floating strands behind her ears, but was unsuccessful.

A small thrill surged through Vanessa. This was almost as good as lifting something off a store shelf and dropping it into her bag. She was winning. Laura was getting more upset. "Then why do you come by and talk to me all the time?"

"This interview process isn't being managed correctly."

"Want to tell Hank about that?"

"No." Laura twisted her fingers together.

"It's handled the way he wants it handled. Let me give you some career advice."

"I don't need career advice." Laura laughed. "I've had far too much of that today. And you don't exactly have the credentials to provide it."

"Then why are you here? I can only think you have a thing for Hank. Or you're desperate, which is how you look right now."

"I had a bad morning okay? And I'm getting annoyed that this is dragging on so long. Once I'm working for him, at least you won't be in the way."

Vanessa picked up the giant paperclip she kept on her desk for the rare occasions she had papers to secure. She pressed the inner curve of the metal, sliding her finger around the outside. Touching it helped her think. It was such a clever device — entertaining in its extreme size, but useful. She had four of them — black, white, silver, and a coppery color. An insignificant office supply turned into a small work of art.

"You're very confident."

"Everyone knows the job is mine."

"Do they?"

"Of course."

"Does Hank know you think that?"

"I know he tells you things. You two have lots of secrets, don't you."

Vanessa smiled. She put the paperclip on the desk and lined it up along the side of her mouse pad.

"What did he tell you? Did he say anything about me?"

"I just don't think it's good to be over-confident."

"I'm not over confident."

"I have work to get done. Is there something I can do for you?"

"You can stop being so smug and using sex to cloud his thinking."

"I'll let him know."

"Look, I had a bad morning. Something really shook me up and I just came by to check the status. You don't need to start gossiping to him about me and putting me in a bad light. I mean it — women need to stick together."

"Thanks for the input."

Laura stepped away from the counter. She ran her palms over the sides of her hair again, but the result was more static, and the cloud of hair seemed to grow larger, straining up toward the glow of the lights. She walked around the corner. The sound of her heels thudding and scratching at the carpet faded after a few seconds.

AT A FEW MINUTES past twelve, Vanessa put on her coat, looped her purse over her shoulder, and walked out of her cubicle. She took the back stairs to the first floor and went outside. It was sunny and breezy, not too cold, but she shivered as the fresh air swept up beneath her skirt. She had no idea why she'd worn a short skirt today, she wouldn't be seeing Hank. It was a total waste. Yellow leaves clinging stubbornly to the branches of liquid amber trees planted across the parking lot were shiny and clean from the rain. They fluttered on the branches, tiny spots of color, waving at her as she walked to her car. She unlocked the door and climbed in. Hard, cold leather greeted the backs of her legs. She bent her knees and inched the seat forward to minimize contact.

Finding a space this close to the building when she returned would be impossible, but she needed to get away. It had been fun watching Laura pretend she wasn't worried whether she appeared to be attracted to Hank. Despite Laura's height, her good posture, her elegant walk, and her expensive clothes and haircut, she looked a bit stale and anxious. Desperate was right, and Laura was oblivious to the impression she made. Was everyone that blind to how others saw them? Was she?

She drove out of the parking lot and turned north along the frontage road circling the edge of the bay. Gulls drifted across the low water, still mucky around the edges. She turned left, wound past other high tech companies and then cut through neighborhoods where she could never hope to live. Homes built before the middle of the twentieth century, some hidden behind adobe walls and mature trees, others exposed with the grandeur of pillared porches that reached two stories, enormous heavily curtained windows, and perfectly maintained lawns and gardens.

She drove to the Whole Foods grocery store. It was a strange choice for shoplifting, but they carried a lot of nice lotions and candles. They expected people to sample their fruits, and actually invited sampling with stands of cheese and crackers placed throughout the store. It was an easy target because they were so concerned with being welcoming, trusting the goodness of the human race. It was crowded at lunchtime with people clamoring for healthy deli, salad bar offerings, whole grain pizza, and wraps. She found a parking spot at the far end of the aisle near the doors into the produce section. She grabbed her reusable bag from the trunk and went inside. She already knew what she wanted. Three six-inch beeswax candles, a few bead bracelets, and a jar of vitamin C tablets. Oddly enough, the vitamin C would be the most challenging. That section was littered with wannabe nutritionists hoping to impart their knowledge of natural remedies and homeopathy.

Beeswax candles were expensive. For most people, candles fell into the nice-to-have category, but she considered them a necessity. She had a cluster of them on the dining room table and she loved when they were lit, filling the room with warm light, the glow softening every flaw. There were candles on the kitchen windowsill, a fat candle in the center of the dining room table, and a few candles in their bedroom. She liked having frivolous things, new things that had never been used, in her home, and on her body. She'd put too much emphasis on being discreet. If she would start scoping out more expensive stores for shoplifting, she'd get double the reward with pricier products and a greatly expanded sense of satisfaction. It was a balancing act, enjoying the thrill but not risking too much, not putting herself in danger of being caught, but it was time to take more risks.

She grabbed a basket, tore off three plastic bags, and filled them quickly with tangerines, an avocado, and loose baby spinach. Once the spinach bag was secured with a small knot, she proceeded quickly to the bulk foods where she filled two more bags — jasmine rice and raw peanuts for Matt's favorite Szechwan stir fry. It was good there was a package of frozen chicken breasts at home because she couldn't very well purchase meat mid-day. In this weather, the produce would be fine in her trunk for a few hours.

The psychological victory over Laura felt good, but she wanted the feeling to continue. The need had grown in the minutes after Laura left, until Vanessa had known she had to indulge herself with some freebies. Lunchtime was perfect. The store was mobbed with seniors and stay-at-home moms, along with the lunch crowd. The staff was busy.

In the Whole Body section, she started with the easy items so there was plenty of time to get a sense of the traffic flow and number of clerks manning the area. As she lingered in front of the lotions, she was aware of two employees — one remained inside the confines of the circular counter, answering questions and offering verbal directions. The other was more trouble. He snuck up on shoppers from behind, asking whether they needed help. It was overkill. If they had questions, they could check with the woman at the counter. The only good thing about him was he seemed to stay far away from the adjacent section formed by rows of shelves filled with vitamins, herbs, food supplements, and healing teas. She walked slowly to a rack of handmade bracelets in front of the bookshelves. She slipped several cards off the rack and held them up, comparing styles and colors. The one with tiny chocolate brown wood cylinders interspersed with turquoise beads was most appealing, but why not take them both? The other had yellow and white beads strung along a strip of leather, perfect with jeans and a white tank top. She took a few steps to the side, reached for a book, and let the two cards fall into her waiting purse. She thumbed through the book on gluten-free cooking and put it back on the shelf. She turned and saw the man looking at her. She walked to him quickly.

"Hi, I have a quick question." She lowered her chin slightly, as if afraid to look him directly in the eye.

"I'm happy to help."

"Do the yellow and white beeswax candles both have the same natural effect, or is there dye in the white ones?"

"Let's go look," he said.

She nodded. Half the time they had to read the labels to answer any questions. She could read the labels herself, but she allowed him to assist her. He picked up a white candle and studied the paper wrapper, word for word, it seemed. He picked up a yellow one in his other hand and studied that label. He proclaimed the products identical and equally beneficial to her health. "Which do you prefer?" he said.

"I'll take two of the white."

He placed them in her basket. "Anything else I can help with?"

She glanced to the left. A woman with two toddler girls standing in the oversized basket was waiting, a question making her lips twitch, eager to break in the moment she had a chance.

"Just one more thing." If Vanessa could stall him long

enough to get a line going, it would provide an excellent window of opportunity. "Are all your gluten-free books on display?"

"Yes. Is there something you can't find that you're looking for?"

"I wanted a book with information, not just recipes."

"I'm sure we have a few of those."

"Oh, you do. I just wanted to be sure they were all out. I want to compare everything you have."

"Okay then. Anything else?" He looked anxiously at the toddlers, gripping the edges of the cart, bouncing in their eagerness for action.

"No. Thanks." She smiled. He grinned back then turned to the mother.

Vanessa strolled toward the bookshelves. While she flipped through another gluten-free cookbook, she put the candles into her purse, one after the other. She moved the food around in the basket, returned to the candle display, and dropped a third into the basket in case he saw her at the checkout. She walked quickly to the vitamin section. She avoided the oversized bottles and chose a glass one that was less likely to rattle loudly enough to be detected by the clerk at the checkout. She had the entire row to herself. She bent over as if to consider the supplements on a lower shelf and slid the bottle into her purse. When she straightened, she rearranged the items in her basket and moved her purse to the other shoulder. She pulled out her wallet and zipped the purse closed.

Checkout went smoothly and in a few minutes she was walking to her car, smiling at nothing in particular. She lifted her face toward the sky. The winter sun brushed her skin and the breeze tickled her hairline. She put the shopping bag in the trunk and settled herself in the car.

This was better than sex. After making love, she was sometimes melancholy. The physical pleasure was fine, but the moment it was over she felt a little lost, as if Matt didn't quite notice her, his thoughts already turning to other things. And so the sense of satisfaction faded quickly. Now, her whole body pulsed with victory. The feeling would remain throughout the afternoon. If she was lucky, it would linger into the evening.

Sixteen

LAURA HAD TO get her hands on a copy of the local weekly paper to find out what was being said about the death of a man at the high school track. Last week, the free papers failed to appear on her front path. Checking the scaled down online version of the local weekly news yielded nothing. It might have been too soon — the police weren't ready to speak publicly. But in the following days, she'd searched for every possible term she could think of and nothing had come up. Was the guy deemed not worthy of news coverage because he was homeless?

Yesterday, her mind had drifted several times to thoughts of the paper lying on wet grass or in the shrubs, hoping it was still readable when she retrieved it that evening. When she'd arrived home there was no paper. The weekly wasn't delivered consistently, but she couldn't believe the unreliable, minimum wage carriers had missed two weeks in a row. Seeing the news coverage would reassure her the case was already slipping to *unsolved-murder-with-no-leads* status. She was confident she hadn't left any evidence. No one had seen her or there would have been a visit from a detective by now. She could relax and breathe easily. Except she couldn't.

It was still dark outside. The only light inside her loft came from the fish tank, reflected through the water, giving off a glow that shimmered as the lionfish moved languidly around their rectangular box. The pump gurgled and rumbled, occasionally drowned out by the Cal Train horn half a mile away. She peered out the narrow window at the side of the front door, trying to see if there was a thin folded paper on the front path. Maybe one of her neighbors had taken it in for her, but it was too early to ring the Grayson's bell, even though their lights were on.

She moved away from the window. Every morning since that day, an irrational fear seized her, whispering that returning to the track would draw attention to herself. She'd briefly considered choosing another high school, driving a few miles for her run. But a different, softer voice, murmured — *They'll think of that, they'll notice a new runner.* She had no idea who *they* were, but it was enough to keep her inside, listening to the fish tank, cowering in its glow, waiting for something to happen, hoping nothing would happen.

How could she have been so stupid? She'd let emotion consume her. The one thing she'd spent fifteen years eradicating from her life. She was known for being calm, in control, measured in her words. Maybe the start of her downfall had been fabricating the rumor. She'd deluded herself that her peers had the same suspicions and she was simply voicing their thoughts, bringing shameful behavior into the open. But as she talked to others, she'd realized no one else was fixated on the tension between those two. Could Vanessa be right with her wild accusation that Laura was projecting her own desires? Was there a latent attraction to Hank burning so deep inside, she hadn't recognized it? There was certainly something alluring about him. Something that made her enjoy being in his presence, made her want to impress him, not just with her business skills, but her appearance, her wit. What the fuck was wrong with her? Was she everything she despised after all? A woman attracted to a powerful man, always measuring herself in relationship to men? What a cliché. Her face burned just thinking about it.

She'd hoped to break Vanessa's control over everything, and instead, she'd ripped her own life to shreds. She'd exposed an attraction she hadn't even known was there to the woman who was in a position to stall her career. She'd been reckless, coming across like an unstable neurotic to Vanessa, and worse, to Hank. She could track everything back to that day she mentioned her suspicions to Janelle. And they were genuine suspicions. Despite everything, the conviction that Hank and Vanessa had something going hovered at the edge of her mind. She needed to make good on her suggestion of having lunch with Vanessa. Then, she'd let drop about that minor criminal activity at the deli a few weeks back. The dead man and the delay in her promotion had knocked her off balance. She'd allowed Vanessa the upper hand. Vanessa did not have the upper hand. Not at all. Laura was nothing like that monster, running to nowhere. She would never be caught up in a workforce reduction. She was too valuable, too talented. Why hadn't she laughed it off?

There had to be a way out of this pit. Not peering out at the empty landing in front of her loft had been a good start. She turned and went upstairs. She opened her Avalon email and sent a message to Brent, asking him to meet for lunch — off campus. A real lunch. Not a salad in the cafeteria. Time to start shoring up her network. The offsite was only a few weeks away. She needed to be a star at that event. Fixating on the interview process was messing with her head.

The next thing she had to do was get back to working out. She would look into joining a gym. Running on a treadmill was boring and demoralizing, but at least she'd stay in shape. Already, she could feel her waist thickening. Even running in place would restore her to her previous state of lean and mean. She smiled. Lean and mean. Ready to fight for what was hers.

She brewed coffee, showered, and dried her hair. By the time she'd finished her coffee and a container of yogurt with sliced chunks of apple, it was growing light. She rinsed her mug and went outside. The smell of bacon was thick in the damp air. She walked to the Grayson's door and knocked. Jenny opened the door immediately.

"Laura! What's up with you so early?"

"Sorry if I disturbed you."

"Not at all." Jenny stepped away from the doorway and turned toward the kitchen area. "Come in. I'll make more coffee." Her blonde hair was cut so short the back of her neck had to be shaved. On top, it was thick and floppy. The style made her look younger than her seventy-one years. She and Charlie were slim and fit, although Laura never saw them doing anything active so she wasn't sure how they maintained their youthful appearances. Maybe they were just lucky. Or maybe she was at the office during daylight hours and had no idea what their lives were like.

"No, that's okay."

Jenny turned back.

"I need to get to work. I just was wondering if you saw any copies of the weekly lying around. I didn't see it last week and can't believe they skipped us twice."

"Haven't seen it. Who needs a throwaway paper with the Internet?"

"True. But the Internet doesn't get all the local stories. Or at least they're hard to find."

"What're you looking for?"

"I just like to know what's going on."

"And you have to know what's happening in city politics at six-thirty in the morning?" Jenny laughed. "You're too much. Isn't this when you're usually out running, burning off some of that ambition?"

"I haven't been running." The words came out too fast. Laura smiled carefully.

Jenny's expression didn't change, accepting the abrupt change in Laura's routine without needing to know the reason. But it was a mistake. If . . . when . . . if the police came asking questions about people who used the track . . . Sometimes Jenny seemed to float outside any real awareness of what was happening around her, but she could surprise you too. Clearly she knew Laura ran early every morning.

"I thought you loved running as much as your job."

"I do, it's just . . . the weather."

Jenny laughed. "When did that ever stop you? I hope you're okay."

"I'm fine. So I guess there's no paper again this week. Or at least no delivery."

"If one miraculously appears later today, I'll drop it on your doormat."

"Thanks." Laura shoved her hands in her pockets.

"If you're that interested, you could go by the publishing office."

"I didn't think of that. Maybe I will."

"What's got you so curious?"

"Nothing. I guess I like things to be dependable."

Jenny giggled. "You're going to have a disappointing life, if that's what you expect."

Charlie appeared behind his wife, his tanned, shaved scalp and navy blue sweatshirt and blue jeans stark against the white on white decorating scheme of their loft. Even in January, he looked as if he'd just returned from a trip to Hawaii. Laura wondered if he worried about skin cancer. She could never look at that glossy scalp without picturing it speckled with tiny moles and scabs.

"What's so funny?" He took off his glasses and began to polish the lenses with the bottom edge of his sweatshirt.

"Life." Jenny leaned into him without turning to check his exact position. Charlie wrapped one arm around her and pressed his face into her soft, floppy hair.

They looked genuinely happy. When Laura thought about her own failed marriage, and observed other people who appeared to live completely separate lives despite their couple status, it was easy to think marriage wasn't worth the trouble. A life more lonely than being single. At least that's how it had been for her, and she had the impression it was that way for Hank, and some of her other colleagues. Two lives with no points of intersection beyond a dwelling place, possibly some children, which, in many cases, simply provided more opportunity for divergent views, another topic to argue about. Jenny and Charlie had been married forty-seven years, they'd told her repeatedly. One daughter, two grandsons in Chicago, three cats who remained hidden right now, not displaying their usual eagerness to sniff out someone at the door, and take a peek at the world. Jenny and Charlie gave off the impression of friendship. Not that she knew them all that well, it was just a feeling, one that she had nearly every time she saw them, even if it was just passing them in the front garden. It gave her a twinge of uncertainty about her own life.

She took another step back. "Thanks anyway."

"So nothing you're expecting in the paper that we need to know about?" Jenny rubbed her head across Charlie' chin.

"No."

"I hope there's not some development or issue we missed. It's awfully early to be out hunting for local news," Jenny said.

"Really, it's nothing. I don't know why I came by so early. I was just thinking about it." The longer she stayed, the more she was going to cement the encounter in their memories. But she couldn't seem to extract herself without being blunt and raising more tiny red flags that would flutter if a detective came asking about people who used the high school track for recreation, letting everyone know a man had been murdered before dawn. Jenny and Charlie would think immediately of Laura. There had to be a way to undo this, but her mind was empty, and so she continued to stare at them, disgusted with herself for not using her supposedly sharp and clever mind. She couldn't even lie effectively, or divert their attention. "It's nothing important. I just thought it would have the date for the next curbside pick-up day. I have a bunch of stuff I need to get rid of."

"The Hope Rehabilitation group left flyers last week. Didn't you get one?" Jenny said.

"This is junk, nothing they'd want."

Jenny nodded. Charlie stared at Laura as if she'd asked him for his social security number. "Is something wrong?" he said.

She gave him what she thought was a casual smile, but it felt weak, guilty-looking. "No. Sorry to bother you."

"It's never a bother," Jenny said. "We love chatting with our neighbors."

"Just not usually before the cock crows," Charlie said.

She needed to make her exit, but it had reached the point where no matter what she did it was going to appear awkward. She had to find a way to have the correct details adhere to the surface of their memories and not bring to mind other odd bits of behavior if they were ever questioned about a murder five blocks away. The chances of detectives canvassing the neighborhood were remote. There'd been other crimes in the area — even the occasional murder. No one had ever come to the door to ask Laura if she'd seen anything. Of course, the rare violent crime was most often gang-related. Could the creepy runner's death be written off as a gang incident? Probably not. Unless by some bizarre stroke of luck he belonged to a gang. "Well I'm really sorry to interrupt your breakfast. I've been meaning to get rid of this clutter since the new year, and work has been so crazy . . . And I never see you in the winter. I woke up this morning and decided I needed to stop putting it off. I get up so early, sometimes I forget that it might seem strange to go knocking on someone's door as if it's mid-day." She laughed. "But thanks. Have a good one." She took a few small steps away from their intense cheerfulness.

"If we see the paper, we'll leave it by your door," Jenny said. "And it's never a problem to stop by. We're up early."

"Thanks."

"As long as it's after six," Charlie said. He stroked Jenny's hair. "Although Jenny shouldn't be so quick to open the door at odd hours. Did you hear about that man who was beaten to death?"

Laura stopped. She needed to take a deep breath, but before her body could respond to her brain, it acted of its own accord.

"What man?" Her tone was sharp.

"They found some guy's body in the bushes at the high school. It had been there for more than a day, it was covered with dead branches and weeds," Charlie said.

"That's awful," Laura said. "How did you hear about it?"

Charlie moved away from Jenny. He stared at Laura, not immediately answering. She felt that something was off about her response, about his hesitation to speak, but she was being overly anxious. He would never in a hundred years make a connection between a dead man and her. Never. It didn't matter that he knew she ran there.

"We were out for a walk and saw two cop cars and a taped off area. We asked what was going on."

"Oh. That's so terrible. And he was beaten to death?"

"Something like that. I don't know the details. It's a good thing you weren't running there when it happened. Maybe you should think twice about that — going out in the dark. Alone."

Charlie sounded like her mother. Like everyone. It was unacceptable, in the twenty-first century, to keep treating women like a special class, as if they needed protection and had to adjust their lives, do less than men to be *safe*. "I don't let fear run my life."

"Fear is there to protect you," Charlie said.

"Most of the time fear is irrational."

"And sometimes murder is random. You need to take care of yourself." His mouth remained open, as if he planned to say something else. She saw it coming, saw his expression change to something patriarchal, the assumed voice of male authority, patronizing. "Women are at greater risk for violent crime. Don't be naive."

"You said a *man* was killed."

"Yes, but don't let feminist nonsense force you to take risks you shouldn't."

"I've been running there for years, I can take care of myself."

"I'm sure you can," Jenny said quietly.

"Yet you stopped. So maybe your gut is telling you to be more careful. That's why God invented gyms with beefy guys at the check-in desk and machines to simulate running," Charlie said.

"It's not the same."

Charlie glared at her.

"Anyway, I'm really sorry I bothered you. And if you hear anything else about the murder, let me know. You don't think of that kind of thing happening around here."

"No, you don't," Charlie's voice was louder than it had been a moment earlier.

"We'll drop off the paper, if we see one," Jenny said.

"Thanks." Laura walked back to her loft. She had the feeling she'd made a terrible mistake, but wasn't sure if it was simple, irrational fear, or her mind whispering that she'd said something she shouldn't have.

Seventeen

WHEN HANK TRAVELED, Vanessa was bored. She also became uncertain about what her job entailed. After all, she was there for him, guarding his door, and serving his needs. Her support for his staff was less well defined and made for an inconsistent workload. Very few people came to the end of the hallway without the main attraction encased between his two walls of glass. Missing her daily meetings with Hank left a void that wasn't satisfied by going home early and cooking a more elaborate dinner, or getting her blood pumping at a dance class.

At four o'clock, the sky was already turning gray, preparing for sunset, if you could call it that, since all it meant was a slow fading of light, then a sudden shift to darkness as if a cosmic hand had flipped the switch. She locked her computer screen and stood. She put on her coat and wrapped her cashmere scarf around her neck. The beige scarf was getting a bit limp, showing its age. She definitely needed a new one. A pale green or even a yellow would look good, and brighten her mood. She slung her purse over her shoulder and dug out her keys as she walked out of the cubicle.

When she reached the parking lot, it was full. It was entirely possible that every person with a window office was watching her leave, *sneak out early*, not giving one hundred and ten percent while the boss wasn't there to enforce her punching a virtual time clock. It would cross the minds of some that she was cheating on her time card. But think of all the times she'd marked her departure at six when it actually had been ten or fifteen minutes past. They didn't calculate all of that. Those minutes added up over the weeks and years. Besides, if they had nothing better to do than track the comings and goings of Hank's admin, then they had sad little lives. She lowered herself into the car. Still, she was compelled to glance up at the second floor, wondering if Laura, in particular, was watching.

She pulled into a parking slot at the pharmacy, turned off the engine, and looked at the facade of the building. The thin, plastic sign, the windows plastered with advertisements for things no one really needed — soda pop on sale and store-brand cough syrup, canned soup at four for a dollar — made her feel needy and sad. She was stealing from a store that probably had narrow profit margins, delivering mass-produced supplies to people living paycheck to paycheck. In some ways, she was one of them. It wasn't as if she had a well-planned stock portfolio or more than a few thousand dollars in savings. She had no stake in her house — nothing but her *understanding* with Matt. The disgust traveled from her financial state to her pathetic need to take things, getting a thrill from stockpiling cosmetics and other small items she didn't need. And they were cheap, it wasn't as though she acquired salon-quality nail polish. What was wrong with her? Why did it feel so damn good, and why, now, was she suddenly ashamed? She'd been doing this for almost fifteen years. It didn't mean anything. It made her feel smart and clever for a few hours, or a few minutes. A silly exercise to prop up a questionable existence, a life with no real purpose except fixing herself up every day, trying to keep Hank happy, cooking mostly ho hum dinners, and living in a suspended state with Matt. No wonder he didn't take her anywhere nice, what did she offer him? She drifted from one month to the next, her life melting away while she hardly paid attention.

As if a force outside of her had animated her body, she climbed out of the car, grabbed her purse, and walked toward the store. She never locked the car when her intention was shoplifting. It was one less rough spot in a casual but rapid exit from the scene of the crime, so to speak.

The store was too hot. The dry air forced shoppers to think they needed that cheap cough syrup after all, as their throats and nasal passages seized, resulting in coughing fits. She picked up a plastic basket and walked to the food section. She grabbed four cans of soup. Once the cans were in the basket, the weight made the handles dig into the bone of her forearm. She put the soup back on the shelf.

A clerk materialized to her left. "That's a good deal. You should grab them while you can."

"It is a good deal, but then I remembered I don't really like chicken noodle that much."

"The vegetable is on sale too."

Vanessa nodded. She waited for the clerk to go away, but the girl, blonde hair plastered to her scalp and thick black eyeliner, continued to hover. Vanessa sighed and put two cans of soup in her basket.

"You don't get the maximum savings if you don't get four."

Vanessa added two more cans. She turned and headed toward the end of the aisle.

The girl followed. "Anything I can help you find?"

Vanessa didn't look back. "No thanks. I come in here all the time."

"I think I've seen you before."

A clammy chill seeped between Vanessa's shoulder blades and down her spine. The girl was too young. It wasn't possible she was part of store security. She was just annoying. Trying too hard to do her job.

"I really don't need any help," Vanessa said. "But thanks." She walked quickly to the cold and flu medicine aisle. Thankfully the girl dropped away, but she'd shaken Vanessa's routine. It was best to leave now. She grabbed a bottle of cough syrup and glanced back toward the food section. The girl stood there as if she didn't have any specific tasks assigned, wandering around the ends of the aisles.

In the cosmetics section, Vanessa found herself looking at every item with an extraordinary lack of interest. The nail colors were all the same. Matt was right about that. And she'd known it all along, but now her awareness was sharp and painful. She not only owned every shade of red displayed in front of her, she had three or four bottles of some of them. She inched her way down the aisle. She picked up a package with a pale brown eyeliner pencil. There was no need for it. She returned it to its place on the rack.

To her right, a woman who looked to be in her mid thirties studied the Revlon eye shadows. With long, artificial fingernails done in a French manicure, she plucked a box of shadow out of the rack. She studied the color and placed it on the narrow ledge. She pulled out two more colors and set them beside the first. She moved a few steps away from Vanessa and worked a tube of lipstick out of its slot. She was planning to take the eye shadow. Vanessa could feel it. She hadn't honed her observation skills, her own studied nonchalance over the years without being able to pick up, almost immediately, when someone else was up to the same thing. She smiled and took a few steps back. It was unlikely the woman would make her move while Vanessa was in the same aisle. She should leave and let the woman complete her task. But part of her wanted to see what came of this, wanted to see how urgent the desire and whether that made the other shoplifter dangerously bold. The woman put the lipstick back and walked to the hypoallergenic display.

After a few minutes, Vanessa was tired of watching. She didn't need to duck around the end of the aisle and spy until she confirmed what she already knew. She turned and started walking. She wouldn't look back. It was sad to contemplate and made her feel not so smart after all — just a common petty thief. A gnawing sensation in her stomach, like hunger, but without the accompanying sounds of churning acid, told her she should set the basket down, soup and cough syrup still in place, and walk out. It was impossible to recover her rhythm. Every item appeared useless or unnecessary, a store filled with things she didn't want, encased in excess packaging, more and more plastic and cardboard and flexible ties to be stuffed into garbage bags and thrown in landfills. She put the basket on the floor in front of a rack of lipstick. She walked to the door and went outside where she took her first deep breath in several minutes.

The interior of the car was still warm. She closed her eyes and wrapped her fingers around the steering wheel, sliding them across the hard, smooth leather. It felt solid, crafted to fit her hands. Again, the need to take something bloomed inside her belly. The problem was, she needed to move on. And up. Cosmetics and personal care items, candy and cheap pens, and inexpensive lingerie were beneath her. There was no pride anymore in her success. She needed to explore a higher end store. But that meant stores with more security measures, including RFID tags that weren't immediately obvious. It was a huge risk. Terrifying. She wasn't sure she was up to it. And if she wasn't, then maybe she wasn't all that clever after all. She opened her eyes and started the engine. As she exited the parking lot, she turned right because it was easier, but she had no idea what her destination was.

Traffic on Steven's Creek Boulevard was thickening as if the descending darkness pushed the cars closer together, restricting the flow, like sluggish blood slowing its passage through veins as the beast settled into winter hibernation. She turned onto the street leading to the mall. It was a vast structure with hundreds of stores, re-shaped every five or six years as outlying buildings were connected with more parking garage extensions, more tightly configured outdoor lots, covered walkways to make the lesser buildings feel that an effort was being made to direct pedestrians in their direction. She parked near Old Navy. Was she really going to do this? Without making a plan, she could see that beneath her conscious thought, her desire had selected a target and moved her in that direction. A target that was likely to have fewer security personnel, a smaller staff than a department store, a staff that couldn't possibly watch every shopper, and moderately priced merchandise that wasn't secured inside locked cabinets or connected by locked cables.

It was completely dark now. The lights cast isolated bright spots that didn't fan out as far as they should, leaving dark pockets between them where the cars lost all color distinction. She walked quickly to the entrance and pulled open the door with force — a woman on a mission, a mental list of what she needed, and the determination to find it quickly.

The store was emptier than she'd expected based on the number of cars parked nearby. Two clerks stood behind the large, empty checkout stand chatting with each other. There was a woman with three small children, a couple with an infant and a toddler in a doublewide stroller, and several high school girls. It was likely there were others who weren't immediately visible. She walked toward the center of the store and turned down an aisle filled with outdoor jackets. She needed to browse, take time to make a plan. There were scarves and woolen gloves on the opposite side of the aisle. A scarf would be easy to slip inside her purse, and then she'd purchase matching gloves.

A pair of leggings wouldn't fit under her skinny jeans, but the idea of wearing something out of the store accelerated her heart rate. She'd never done anything like this. When she'd taken lingerie at discount stores, she'd grabbed the delicate things off overstuffed racks and dropped them in her purse, never daring to wear something out of the store. She'd always imagined if she was stopped, she could more easily explain it away as something she'd put in her purse absent-mindedly, tired of carrying it, then forgotten. The challenge excited her. She'd wasted years, too frightened to reach for anything that increased the level of skill required. And it wasn't just skill in being surreptitious, it required her to be more astute. A finesse she could leverage in her job.

A set of sage green gloves and a matching scarf were particularly appealing. She pulled out her wallet and sunglass case and tucked them between her elbow and ribs. She lifted the gloves off the hook and wiggled one onto her left hand. It caught on her diamond ring. She pulled it off and slid her right hand into the other glove. It was impossible to get a true sense of how they fit with the short plastic strap connecting them. She continued studying her outstretched hand as she reached for a scarf with her left hand. She glanced toward the center aisle. No one was there. She stuffed the scarf in her purse and dropped the wallet and glass case on top. Her purse looked quite puffy now, but it was a large bag, meant to hold a lot of things, so there was nothing terribly out of the ordinary about its shape. It was best not to push her luck too hard, but she was having fun. This felt more like the real deal, whatever that was.

Still carrying the gloves, she walked to the center aisle and headed toward the sweaters and shirts. Although it was winter, there was a rack of tank tops meant for layering under other shirts. One of those would be easy to slip under her sweater. As the thought took root, her heart maintained its accelerated pace, but now it beat with a heavier pounding. She walked down the aisle grabbing sweaters and tank tops until she had a fist of about seven or eight hangers. She went to the fitting room. No clerk was around to check what went in and out. Only two of the eight doors were closed. She chose a room and looped the hangers over the hook. She sat on the bench, pulled out her phone, and scrolled through her email and text messages. She wasn't planning to try on all those tops. She needed to spend an adequate amount of time in the room, in case someone had seen her go in, and then at the last moment, slip on the tank top.

After tapping through a few Facebook updates, she put her phone away and pulled her sweater over her head. She looked in the mirror. Even against her sun-deprived winter skin, her sheer white bra was stark. Her breasts swelled over the top edges looking foreign, as if they belonged to a stranger. She studied her face. Her makeup still looked fresh, even after the ordeal at the pharmacy. She ran her fingers through her hair, lifting it away from her face. Her eyes were clear and direct, her lips parted slightly, giving a non-threatening appearance, someone you'd like to know as a friend, someone you wanted to think the best of. The image she portrayed was not that of a thief, which was the secret to why she'd gotten away with her thefts all these years. She sometimes worried that her co-workers looked at her and saw a woman who wasn't very bright because all she had was a high school diploma. Or maybe she was the one who felt that, and they were simply reflecting her own beliefs. But studying her face now, she saw confidence and intelligence.

She chose a pink tank top. The fabric was thin, the type that wouldn't look very good after three or four washings. It was only fifteen dollars, which was another hint of how long

it would survive. But sometimes clothing surprised you.
Expensive, well-made things unraveled quickly and a shirt
that cost ten bucks lasted for years. She pulled it over her
head. It fit nicely. She slithered back into her sweater, fluffed
her hair back into place, and grabbed the hangers. She took
the empty hanger and tucked it under the bench.

When she stepped out of the fitting room, the area was
deserted. The same two doors were closed and no sound
came from behind them. She walked to the checkout stand
and placed the gloves on the counter.

The clerk scanned the price tag. "You get a discount on
these if you buy a matching scarf and hat."

"No thanks."

"They're fourteen on their own. With the hat and scarf,
they'd be less."

"No thanks.

"Are you sure?"

"I'm sure," she said.

"Don't you want to know what it would be with the scarf
and hat? It would be thirty-one-ninety-five."

"I only want the gloves."

The clerk shrugged and ran the total. Vanessa slid her
credit card through the reader.

"Did you bring a bag?"

That was a mistake. If she opened her purse, would the
scarf be visible? She'd have to carry the gloves. "No. Actually,
if you can cut the strap, I'll wear them."

The clerk fumbled under the counter. After a moment of rattling plastic containers and metal tapping against the Formica, she straightened. "I guess I don't have scissors. You could bite the strip, it's not that hard."

"No thanks," Vanessa said. She passed them to her other hand and turned. As she walked to the door, another clerk fell in step behind her. The girl was right on her heels, stilettos that she'd paired with shiny black leggings clicked on the floor, the sound of someone trying to drive a nail into concrete. Vanessa lengthened her stride. The clicking heels accelerated as well.

"Excuse me," the clerk said.

Vanessa paused. She turned. Her breath tightened. Her lips were so dry it was hard to smile without fearing her expression would appear stiff and cracked. She turned the corners of her lips up slightly.

"I need to ask you something," the clerk said.

"What's that?" A small twitch developed in Vanessa's eyelid. Did the clerk see her parched lips, the smile she was afraid to adjust, giving her a phony appearance? A twitching eye, the bulge in her purse? Was an outline of the edging around the neck of the tank top visible through her tight sweater? She should have checked. Too late now.

"I saw you carrying those gloves. And I wondered why you didn't buy the scarf and hat that matches them. It's a much better deal."

"Yes, I know." Vanessa passed the gloves back to her right

hand. "But I only wanted gloves."

"Most people want all three." The girl squinted at Vanessa. Either she needed glasses, or something Vanessa was doing had aroused her curiosity.

"I'm not most people," Vanessa said. She pulled her purse closer to her hip. "Thanks for the suggestion, though." She turned and started toward the door. The girl's shoes began their clicking again, but after a few steps, Vanessa realized they were clicking in the opposite direction. She dared not turn to confirm it. She pushed open the door and stepped outside, letting if fall closed behind her. The air did nothing to help moisten her lips, but the coolness was a relief. As she walked to the car, her heart continued to beat hard against her ribs, as if it had taken over her entire body. She opened the passenger door and dropped her purse and the gloves on the seat.

Driving home, her heart continued its heavy thudding, but her body temperature was stabilized, her lips no longer felt as if they were about to split open and start bleeding. Instead, she felt warm and energized. There was a rush of pleasure that made her want to spend the evening doing something more exciting than usual.

Waiting, as the clerk stood there, staring, not speaking, had been one of the most terrifying moments she could recall. But now, *now!* She reveled in the thrills pulsing through her. This was the best ever.

AT HOME, MATT was in the kitchen, a bottle of wine opened, the cork still impaled by the corkscrew lying on the counter. "I started dinner." His voice was proud, as if he'd harpooned a swordfish, strapped it to the roof of his car, carried it home, and cleaned it himself. The smell of fish was strong, the cutting board littered with red pepper flakes and bits of garlic he hadn't managed to scoop into the pan.

"What are you making?" Vanessa said.

"I stopped for wine and they had trout on sale."

"Nice." She smiled and kissed his cheek. Beneath the rough stubble, his skin smelled comforting, with a warm hint of woodsy-ness from the wine. "I'll put my purse away and be right back." She went into the bedroom, yanked the scarf out of her purse, and stuffed the scarf and gloves into her bottom drawer. She peeled off her sweater, pulled the tank top over her head, and folded it awkwardly. She shoved that in the second drawer. Her sweater was woven with the smell of her sweat. She tossed it in the dry cleaning bag, flung open the closet door, and pulled out a silky navy blue top with a neckline that dropped low and showed lots of cleavage but draped over the arms so she wouldn't end up with skin stippled by goose bumps.

After she peed, smoothed on a layer of lip gloss, brushed her hair, and tousled it across her shoulders, she returned to the kitchen. Matt handed her a glass of wine. He tapped the edge of his glass to hers and held it there. "You look good."

"Thanks."

"Why are you so amped up?"

"What do you mean?" She took a sip of wine.

"Your cheeks are all red."

"I don't know. Maybe the cold."

"I've never seen them like that before."

She smiled. "Well I don't really know."

"You're kinda late." He turned toward the stove and put his glass on the counter. "I guess you had a long meeting with Hank?" He slid the spatula under the trout and turned it gently.

"He's in Europe, remember?" Was it possible Matt thought there was truth behind the gossip? There was no doubt Matt was her one and only and she didn't want to hurt him. The thing with Hank was just . . .

"I forgot." He lifted the lid off one of the pots. The sweet aroma of steamed carrots filled the kitchen.

"What should I do?" she said.

"I'm on top of it." He replaced the lid. "Then why are you late? You didn't go shopping again, did you?"

"Not really."

"That's not an answer. So you did? You don't need more shit."

"A girl always needs more stuff."

"You look great the way you are. You don't need more paint." He came around the counter and ran his hand through her hair. "Unless you're on the market, why do you need to keep advertising?"

"I'm not advertising anything." She stepped away. She took a sip of wine and walked to the table. She set her glass down and pushed the placemats so they were aligned with the chairs.

"I thought we'd eat in the dining room," he said.

"Okay." She hated what he'd said. It was cruel, said in such a casual way. It made her out to be not much different from a whore. Was she supposed to let herself go? Not wear any makeup, not care about nice clothes, or fitting into current styles? She walked into the dining room. She turned on the light, glad for Matt's insistence they use low-wattage bulbs in the chandelier so it cast a muddy glow on the center of the mahogany table. The dining room set was a cast-off from his mother. She shouldn't think of it in those terms, it was a nice gift and there was no way they could afford a dining room table with eight chairs and a breakfront, but it was still a hand-me-down. She pulled out the chair at the end closest to the kitchen. If he had it all under control, he could set and serve. And then he was going to apologize for that comment. She lit the candles at the center of the table, sat down, and took a sip of wine.

The fish was half eaten before she conceded he wasn't going to take back the words without a prompt from her. "Why are you so mean?"

"What are you talking about?"

"You said I'm advertising."

"Don't over-react."

"I'm not."

"I just think you buy too much stuff. And seeing all that nail polish was weird."

"I like to paint my nails."

"So you need two hundred colors, or whatever it was you have in there? And three of every color? It makes it look like there's something wrong with you. Something doesn't feel right."

"Is that what you really think of me?"

"You get awfully dressed up for work."

"I thought you liked the way I look?"

"I do. When you're with me. The women I work with don't dress like that."

"Like what?"

"All the makeup, high heels."

"I don't think there's something wrong with me because I like to look good."

"Whatever."

"Not *whatever*. I'm trying to talk to you."

Matt put down his fork. His face was partially concealed by the shadows. He picked up his wine glass and swallowed the rest of the contents. He refilled it but didn't raise the bottle in her direction to suggest a refill of her glass. He took another sip.

"Why did you say that?" She placed her fork across the plate and pushed it away from her. The placemat gripped the bottom and it didn't move far.

"I didn't mean anything. I'm just upset by all the crap you buy."

"It's my money! And I don't spend that much." Half of her wanted to shout that she hadn't spent a dime on any of it and demand to know if that made him happy. But telling him would spoil her secret pleasure. And she couldn't imagine he'd be supportive of her habit.

"It's just weird."

"Most women have lots of makeup. It's fun."

"Not like you."

"How do you know?"

"I checked."

"You checked what?" She took a sip of wine. It was getting that dull taste it sometimes acquired after she'd had a bit too much too fast, as if all the fruit and layered textures faded and the alcohol took over.

"I asked some women at work."

"You complained about me?"

"I didn't tell them why. I was curious. It freaked me out. What if you went in my drawers and found three hundred . . . I don't know . . . three hundred condoms."

"That's completely different."

"Okay, bad example. But too much of something."

"This is a stupid conversation," she said.

"I just don't understand why you need it. What you're trying to accomplish."

She stood and picked up her plate.

"Is this something about Hank?" His voice was low, as if he was afraid to say the words. All of his going on about nail polish and too much of something had been the stepping stones to the real conversation.

She put her plate back on the table. It clinked on the wood and the utensils rattled. She picked up her wine and took a long swallow. She had to change direction before she got upset and shouted out something she didn't want to say. There was an uncomfortable mixture of hurt and anger and she couldn't sort out which emotion applied to which insult. Maybe she'd gone too far. It was possible Matt truly thought she was sleeping with her boss, or trying to. He sounded like Laura, putting it all on her. They both had it backwards. Hank was drawn to her. It was so confusing. She loved Matt. She really did. She didn't want to lose him. "If you don't want me on the market, as you call it, why aren't we married?"

"You have that big-ass diamond."

"For six years."

"So. What's the rush?"

"What's the delay is a better question."

"Maybe it doesn't seem like you really love me. You're hedging your bets."

She laughed. "This isn't gambling."

"Life is a gamble."

"Well aren't you good with the clever statements. A little fortune cookie, aren't you." She picked up her plate and carried it into the kitchen. She returned to the dining room and walked to his side of the table. She picked up the bottle and refilled her glass. Matt held up his glass and she added a splash. Without taking a sip, she set her glass next to his. She walked behind him and put her hands on the sides of his jaw. She bent over and pressed her face into his hair. It smelled clean and a little bit like rain. She ran her lips across the top of his head, letting the soft strands caress her skin.

She had no idea what she wanted from him, what she wanted from life, really. Excitement was one thing. Maybe they'd been together too long and there just wasn't anything left to get excited about. That's what made Hank interesting. It wasn't that she wanted an affair, although she certainly felt a subtle melting in her belly when he looked at her, or stood close to her. She liked the not knowing. From one word to the next, one gesture to another, she never knew what was coming. Everything else in her life was delivered as expected — the tasks in her job, her evenings and weekends with Matt. A wedding would be exciting, but only temporarily. Going to a new store had been exciting. More than she'd expected. The intensity grew when more fear was added to the mix. "Are you bored with me?" she said.

"Of course not."

She wove her fingers through his hair but he didn't respond. Finally he said, "I should ask you that question."

"I'm not bored," she whispered. It was a lie. If he would just do something different. Anything. Something shocking would be even better. She knew it was greedy. He was terrific.

How many guys came home and thought about cooking dinner? Yet, she wasn't surprised. Maybe if he stood up right now, slid his hands up her shirt and unhooked her bra, pulled down her jeans, and bent her over the dining room table. That would be exciting. And surprising.

Wasn't she too young to be bored? There weren't any children keeping them in the house every night and most weekends. He was a great looking guy and she was a gorgeous woman. She could picture them in a film, on TV, they'd look fantastic. But there was nothing about their lives that made them suitable even for a reality show. They might be hovering around thirty, but they behaved as if they were fifty. Eating the same meals, watching sports, shopping, drinking wine, going to work. Once a year they took a vacation, but even those were pedestrian — a condo on Maui for ten days, a trip to Lake Tahoe. Once they'd gone to Puerto Vallarta. What a cliché. But what did she want?

She stepped away from him. He reached for his wine glass. The back of his neck looked tender — soft baby hair crept down toward his shirt. She pulled off her blouse and dropped it on the floor. She unhooked her bra and let it fall on top of her blouse, a white streak across the dark blue. The room was warm, but still a cool draft washed across her breasts making her nipples contract. She stepped closer to Matt and pulled his head back. His neck stiffened, resisting her pull. "Relax," she said. She turned his head gently to one side so his cheek touched her skin.

He sat up straighter. "What are you doing?"

"I don't know, mixing things up?"

"I'm not in the mood." He swallowed his wine and eased away from her. He picked up his plate and went into the kitchen.

Without his body in front of her, the cool air bit at her breasts. She knelt and picked up her clothes. She put on her bra and slipped the blouse over her shoulders. It was twisted out of place but she left it alone.

Eighteen

LAURA AND BRENT were supposed to be reviewing the slides for her presentation at the offsite — price changes implemented last fall and how they'd affected sales volume. The offsite was only two weeks away, but she hadn't been able to focus on putting the analysis into a presentable form, couldn't seem to make the key takeaways flow in any coherent fashion, and wasn't even sure what was wrong with the ordering of the slides. She couldn't ask Brent those questions, he'd see that she hadn't put in much effort for the first go around, he'd realize she was in such a fractured state, she couldn't even figure out where to start. She hoped he'd tell her what to do without any prompting.

They sat in a small conference room, the blinds angled toward the ceiling so the sun didn't create glare on the screen at the end of the room where the slides were displayed. It was the first day of full sun in a while and she hated keeping the blinds closed. She was beginning to feel like a sewer rat —

spending all her waking hours in semi darkness. She'd turned into something unrecognizable for sure. Never in her life would she have believed she could kill a man. Not only kill him, but beat him to death. Sometimes she hoped she'd dreamed the whole thing. She hadn't really left his broken body, a skeleton covered in dried skin like discarded chicken bones wrapped in brown butcher paper. When she'd woken at two or three in the morning these past few days, weeks . . . seventeen days, her thoughts were suspended in that moment when she'd realized he was dead. She'd taken a human life, although she preferred to think of him as sub-human. The pieces of her existence floated in silence, like the fish in their tank, oxygen pumped into the environment, sucked in through their gills, but still they remained motionless.

Nothing had been said about the director position. She'd interviewed with Sandeep and the others, and then, nothing. She'd never seen a word about the murder in the weekly paper. The police hadn't come to ask if she had running shoes with a particular configuration on the soles. Yet, those things were all she thought about. Had her life always been this small? Limited to striving for some vague goal line in her career, running miles a day, feeding and watching her fish? Now that the running had been taken away, she noticed how narrow and sterile her world had become.

"Focus," Brent said.

She looked at him, wondering whether her eyes looked similar to the glistening, vacantly staring eyeballs of her fish.

"What's wrong with you?" he said.

"Nothing."

"It seems like you're not here."

"I'm here."

"I don't even know what to say about these slides. They need a lot of work."

"Can you be specific, please."

"You shouldn't need me to tell you. These aren't ready for feedback. Twenty slides with spreadsheets pasted in? Where's the analysis?"

"This is to give a sense of the areas I'm covering. I wasn't going to make charts and provide the insights until I got your feedback on the scope."

Brent stared at her as if she were under water, silently opening and closing her mouth. "You seem distracted. More than distracted, completely out of touch."

"Do I?" Along with telling her what to put in the slides, she wanted him to tell her it was the pressure, it was okay, she wasn't having a breakdown, her brain ceasing to function in a way that allowed her life to continue as it had been. She pressed her thumb and index finger on the bridge of her nose and bent her head forward. "Do you ever wonder if it's a mistake?"

"What's a mistake?"

"Trying so hard to succeed. Making your whole life, or most of your life, about your job?"

"My whole life isn't my job."

"What do you do in the evenings after work?" she said.

"I dunno. Watch a game, catch up on email."

"And what do you do every morning?"

"Read *The Journal* and *The Times*. Work out. Okay, so my week is devoted to Avalon. But I love it. What else should I be doing?"

She shrugged. "What do you do on the weekends?"

"Errands, go out for dinner. Watch a game, go hiking. Play tennis."

"Who do you play tennis with?"

"Ken, from biz school. You know all this, why are you asking me?"

"And you talk about . . . ?"

"Don't make it sound so dull. I love what I do. And so did you, until a few weeks ago. What happened?"

"What do you mean?"

"Did you get bad news about the job? Or is something else going on?"

"I haven't heard a word about the job. Hank is ignoring me."

"I guess it's on hold while he's in Europe."

"That's the point of email. And smart phones. And Skype. And IM. The rest of your work doesn't need to stop just because you're traveling."

Brent grabbed the chair to his left and wheeled it away from the table. He stretched out his legs and rested his heels on the seat, crossing his ankles. Despite the casual pose, he looked every bit the executive with his precisely faded jeans, button-down shirt, and black suit coat. He still wore his silly slip-on shoes with the narrow toes. Black leather. They looked as comfortable as bedroom slippers. If she wore shoes like that she'd look ridiculous. The style was ridiculous, but he managed to achieve an executive air in spite of them.

It was said you should dress for the job you wanted. At some point after he was promoted, Brent had changed the clothes he wore — losing the khakis and polo shirts, adding the suit jackets. A confidence had come over him that made his clothing look completely appropriate. If you took that advice too far, it came across like posturing. She worried that her business clothes gave that impression, but somehow the jeans and jacket combo didn't work as well for women.

"In my experience, the best thing you can do is concentrate on the job you have. Be a star in this job and stop obsessing about getting promoted."

Laura folded her arms. She glared at him but he was studying the slide displayed on the screen and didn't appear to notice her gaze locked onto the side of his head. She waited for him to turn but he was oblivious. She coughed carefully so her voice didn't sound rough, or worse, tearful or laced with hysteria. "Easy for you to say."

He turned. "It's still true."

"Why are you doing this?" Laura said.

"Doing what?"

"I thought you were my friend."

"Exactly."

"Then why are you treating me like I'm crazy?"

"I'm trying to give you advice. You seem desperate."

"I do not."

He raised his hands, palms facing her, and took his feet off the chair.

"Wow," she said. "That is unbelievably condescending."

"I'm the only one who'll be straight with you. And I'm telling you — chill out."

She stood. "Fuck you."

"Calm down!"

"Condescending. Again. What am I, a hysterical female?"

"You said it."

"A guy can get pissed and he's the man. But a woman gets angry and she's hysterical. Desperate. Unhinged."

Brent put his elbows on the table and leaned forward. "Please sit down and listen to me."

"Why?"

"Because I'm your friend. Everyone needs an outside perspective. You don't want to be like the execs who stop listening to input and lose sight of how they're perceived."

"Like you. Condescending. Arrogant." She wondered if those two things were the same. It didn't matter, she needed to drive home her point.

"You can label me all you want, but we've been friends a long time and I'm trying to help you. Getting angry, hanging around Vanessa and trying to manipulate her into giving you information isn't doing yourself any favors. You know I'm always straight with you. You gotta listen."

"Vanessa and Hank are probably doing it, so everything there is all distorted."

"That's what I mean. Why would you say that?"

"It's true."

A look of pity brushed across his face.

"I think it's true," she said.

"It doesn't matter if it's true. It makes you sound petty and not focused on what's important. The director level is a whole new ball game."

"I know that."

"Then act like one." He stood. "I'll go over the slides again. After you fix them. Let me know when you're ready.

"You're just going to walk out on me? Tell me what to do and march out of here like you're in charge?"

"You asked for my input. I'm trying to help you."

"So you said."

"You're on the verge of blowing it."

"Is that what Hank told you?"

"We didn't discuss it."

"Yeah, right. That's why you're such a know-it-all. The guys on the exec staffs talk. It's just like every other layer of the org. You have your secrets and gossip too."

"Maybe. But not that. And it's not all guys. Don't turn this into a gender war."

"That's what it is."

"Only if you make it that."

"Did Hank say something to you?"

"No."

"But you wouldn't tell me if he did."

"That's not the point."

"So he did say something."

He sighed. He leaned on the back of the chair. His weight forced the chair forward. The plastic arms thudded against the edge of the table. The projector shook and the image on the screen tilted to one side. The sound of the projector fan seemed to grow louder, as if the machine had overheated and the fan was racing to catch up. Laura pressed the power button. The light went out but the fan continued to whir.

"It doesn't matter if he said something or not. What I'm telling you is my own advice, based on my experience. Based on how you're coming across to me, and I overlook your flaws because I'm your friend."

"What flaws?"

"We all have flaws."

"I know. What flaws, specifically, are you talking about?"

"All I'm saying is you should put your energy into making this presentation kick ass. Stop harassing Vanessa, stop loitering around Hank's office. Just stop."

"You make it sound like I'm a loser."

"You can't force him to give you the job."

"I deserve that job."

"No one deserves anything. You have to work for it."

"I have. There's no one more qualified."

"You don't know that."

"What did he tell you about the other candidates?"

"Nothing."

"I don't believe you."

He looked at her. His eyes were difficult to read, pale blue shrouded by thick, blonde lashes. It was monumentally unfair that he was a director and she was not. She was six years older than him. They had similar degrees, nearly identical career paths, yet he'd achieved the level he aspired to without any obvious effort. It was simplistic to attribute all of his success to male privilege. That wasn't all of it, but there was still that aspect, even now, well into the twenty-first century, it was not a level playing field by any stretch of the imagination. He did his job, acted like a pro, and suddenly there he was.

At this point, she was in danger of missing it altogether. If she didn't get this job, what were her options? Leave the company. That was always an alternative. But it wasn't necessarily easier to step up by changing employers. Unless she went to a start-up, but she was on the verge of being too old for that, since she wasn't an engineer. Maybe a more established start-up, one with a hundred employees or so, in its third stage of funding, but then, again, seeking a title bump became more difficult.

As if someone outside of herself had been speaking, she heard her words of disbelief echo through her mind. In his eyes, she saw how that sounded. Petulant and slightly crazy. It was one thing to be skeptical, another to essentially accuse a good friend of being a liar, of plotting behind her back, getting involved in schemes to bring her down, to prevent her getting the promotion. Maybe she *was* crazy. How did you even know? She'd murdered a man. If someone had told her two weeks ago she would one day crush a man's throat until he died, she would have been horrified, or laughed.

"What can I do to help? Do you want me to run interference so you can take time off to get your shit together?"

"I'm not an invalid." Suddenly the projector fan stopped. Her voice was unnaturally loud. "Taking time off would make me look weak."

"Then tell me what's wrong, because you need to change the game plan."

A rush of desire to tell him everything surged through her chest. His eyes remained steady, so blue, wise, almost, as if he knew more than she did, as if he really did know the secret to success — a Zen priest of high tech careers. She couldn't imagine what those eyes would do if she told him she was a killer. She laughed.

"Why are you laughing?"

She sounded mad, but she couldn't help it. Thinking about what she'd done gave it the shape of a movie she'd seen, then replayed in her dreams, changing the details and inserting herself. "I don't know. I think I'm tired. I'm frustrated because I haven't been able to run."

"Why not?"

"Too cold, too wet."

"That never stopped you before."

"I guess I'm getting old." She smiled in what she hoped was a self-effacing manner.

His expression remained steady, waiting for her to provide the real reason.

"I need to get back to it, I'm just making excuses. And when I don't run, I get tense, my brain gets off track. It's like I'm not even me when I'm not running."

He squinted. "Not you?"

"I don't know what I'm talking about. Maybe I do need a break. But I just don't think that would help my situation." At the back of her mind a persistent voice whispered that he was looking her right in the eye and lying. He did know more about the job. He knew the reason for the delay and he knew what Hank's hesitations were regarding her qualifications. He knew everything. It was that Zen thing. He was quiet and steady and she was sure Hank confided in him, telling him more than what he let on to the rest of his staff. Brent could get her that job with a simple word. He wasn't just a friend, he was her ticket in.

She closed her laptop. The sound of it snapping shut was like a loud clap, signaling a change of course. She leaned back and clasped her hands, resting them on her knees, a pose of openness and rational thought. "What else do you think I need to do to prove myself to Hank?"

Brent's eyeballs quivered slightly. Or had she imagined it? She waited.

"He knows your track record."

"So, nothing?"

"I'm sure you'll have another interview."

"Then tell me what my weaknesses are that you think I need to acknowledge."

"You need to spin your weaknesses as positives."

"I know that, Brent."

"Okay, just saying. Usually you wouldn't focus on weaknesses, but I guess this is different from a normal interview where you're an unknown."

"Exactly. How many interviews did you have when you got promoted?"

"Only one, really."

"My first one was weird," she said. "Not even a true interview."

"Then just prep with your accomplishments. Figure out how to present yourself in a positive light."

"That's what I'm asking you to help with. What are my flaws?"

"You should know that."

"Clearly I don't."

"Play hard to get."

She laughed. "Are you serious?"

"There's something to it. People want things that seem out of reach. It's human nature."

She thought about Vanessa cutting off access to Hank. Did that make him seem more appealing? The fact that Laura had to beg for time on his calendar? That it was almost impossible to run into him casually because Vanessa fetched his coffees and his lunches? He was locked in that corner office all day, people coming to see him, never the reverse, except when he was huddled in conference rooms with his peers. He left his office and scurried to meetings like a rat running unseen through the HVAC system. There might be something to what Brent was saying.

He leaned forward. "Look," he tapped the table with his index finger. "You lower yourself when you hang around the admin's desk hoping to see him. People that hang out there are perceived as not being busy enough. Chatting her up, drooling over her."

"Well I'm certainly not doing that."

"No, but the effect is the same. Eating candy, talking about BS. When he wants to talk to you, he'll send her looking for you. A contrived encounter is obvious. He's a smart guy."

"I always thought it was good policy to make friends with the admin."

"It is, but not like that. Not actually being friends, just treating her with respect, giving her holiday gifts and that sort of thing."

Brent really was wise. She shouldn't have been so defensive. All she needed to do was figure out how to get him to sell her qualifications to Hank. Like Hank, he was smart. She had to do it in a way that prevented him from seeing through her. Not now. It was best to wait and plan a strategy. She couldn't just sit around watching her whole life disintegrate like a tissue on wet pavement. She stood. "Thanks. You've given me a few things to think about."

He grinned. "Good. Back on top of your game."

"Absolutely. Time to review the slides tomorrow? About one?"

"Yup."

They walked out of the conference room. He held the door open and let her go first. She felt it was symbolic — he had her back.

Nineteen

A BOX OF t-shirts in varying colors and a second box filled with hats bearing the images of wild animals for the team building activity consumed all the available space in Vanessa's tiny trunk. Her medium-sized gray suitcase sat on the passenger seat. Some in Hank's group were carpooling to the resort in Napa Valley, but she preferred to drive by herself. If she couldn't ride with Hank, and he hadn't offered, she'd rather be alone. The three-day offsite promised to be one long, unbroken reminder that she wasn't part of the team. The only upside was she would receive overtime pay for the extended days that started immediately after breakfast and ran through dinner. Even now, sitting in traffic on 580, she was getting paid.

Once she passed Vallejo, traffic was lighter, and she gradually pressed the gas pedal closer to the floor until her Miata was zipping past cows and ranch homes, their small patches of land planted with grapevines. Soon she was going seventy, passing bona fide vineyards with acres of vines. Too bad it wasn't spring or summer and she could enjoy the drive with the top down. She turned onto the road to the deceptively casual Vintner Valley Resort. It featured a hotel built in the nineteen-twenties with a modernized conference room, smaller meeting rooms, and outlying cottages with four units each. Only she and Hank were staying in the main hotel. The others were grouped in teams so they could use the common area of their buildings to plan strategy in the war game activity.

The parking lot outside the main building was uneven, broken up by trees, which gave it a woodsy, tranquil atmosphere but made it difficult to park. By the end of the weekend, her windshield would be littered with pine needles and cones. Probably a fair amount of bird shit, for that matter. She left her suitcase and supplies in the car and went inside.

The old fashioned check-in window appeared inadequate for the size of the conference center, but behind the closed door was obviously a well-connected computer network because everything was ready — coded key cards and a printed list of names. The young guy, maybe not so young, close to her age, but seeming younger because of his blonde-blue-eyed-well-built-surfer look, wore a nametag announcing his name was Alan. Watching his easy smile and untroubled eyes made her feel old. She was only twenty-nine, for god's sake, why did she suddenly feel middle-aged? It must be the difference in their jobs. She was locked in a cubicle, fifteen feet from a sealed window all day, while he jogged around trails and took advantage of his access to tennis and swimming whenever he was in the mood. A job that appeared low pressure, although it probably wasn't. In many ways, his role was much like hers. Simple clerical work. But simple only described the tasks, not the consequences — people exploding over the smallest errors — as if a typo or a double-booked conference room signaled the downfall of the company. She imagined it was worse here. People were very protective of their vacation time.

Along with the keys, Alan handed her a stack of maps. He placed another map on the counter and marked the points she needed to locate — the main conference room and assigned breakout rooms, the cottages Hank's team would be occupying, the various trails, the pool, tennis courts, executive golf course, and the restaurants. There were two — a casual place serving three meals a day, and a place with fine dining open from five o'clock to ten at night.

He sent a high school kid with her to carry the luggage and supplies. The boy stacked her boxes of shirts and hats and her suitcase on a cart. He took the box of keys and the maps and added them to the pile. Vanessa followed him back into the hotel, carrying nothing but her purse. They rode to the third floor in a very slow, but otherwise modern elevator, and walked down the hall to her room. The four-poster bed, armchair, and small writing desk evoked the twenties, although each piece looked more like a replica. She tipped him and he left her alone with her boxes and suitcase. She stood for a few minutes looking out the window at the dense growth of pine trees. The highway wasn't visible, just the tree line and foothills to the west. There wasn't a grapevine in sight.

After she unpacked, she returned to the first floor. The check-in area was in a small alcove. The rest of the space had the appearance of an enormous family room more than a lobby. Sofas and armchairs, low tables, and a few footstools and floor lamps were arranged in clusters that appeared unplanned, but welcomed small groups to stake out their own territory. A stone fireplace filled the wall adjacent to the windows that looked out on a garden area. The fireplace was at least eight feet wide and five or six feet high. Three logs, one the diameter of her spare tire, put off flames that roared and cracked. From where she stood, she couldn't feel the heat, but as she walked closer, the area grew warmer until she reached the armchairs closest to the flames where it would have been impossible to sit for any length of time. She chose a chair further away and ordered a glass of Merlot from a server passing through the room. It was technically a work day, but the only things planned for the rest of the afternoon were check-in, the first team meetings, which didn't involve her, and a dinner at a local restaurant. A glass of wine seemed appropriate — after all, she was in the heart of the California wine country. Some of the best wines in the world were waiting to be squeezed off the vines in the surrounding valley, how could she not have a glass?

The wine was nothing remarkable after all. She wished she'd asked the server for a recommendation. While she sipped it slowly, she thought about Matt. He'd given her a rather limp kiss good-bye. She'd felt he wasn't looking directly at her. His shirt felt cool, as if it stood apart from his skin, failing to absorb his body heat. He'd released his hold on her while she still had her arms tightly around his waist, her fingers pressed into the muscles that ran down the sides of his back. She'd put her face up to his again, but he'd only brushed his lips across hers and lifted her arms away. He said nothing about Hank. "I guess you'll be drinking lots of wine and eating in nice restaurants. You'll like that."

"Not that much wine. It's work, not a party."

He laughed. "In the Napa Valley."

She smiled. "Yes, but that's to ease the sting of working extra hours."

"Working or hardly working."

"It really is work, at least for the others. I'll probably be bored, sitting in the meetings and not understanding half of what they're talking about."

She'd felt their conversation stopped abruptly instead of winding to a conclusion. He walked her out to her car, waited while she got in, and closed the door for her. She started the engine in order to lower the window, but he was already moving away. He waved and went into the house before she pulled out of the driveway. Of course he needed to get to the office, but it wasn't as if he'd had to leave right that minute.

She put her wine glass on the table and closed her eyes. Now was not the time to be thinking about it. Matt would be fine. He loved her, and maybe it would be good for them to have a few days away from each other. Unless it gave him time to think and he decided he wasn't up for competing with Hank. Beyond enjoying sports, he didn't have much of a competitive nature. Normally she liked that about him, but she wasn't sure if it was always a good thing.

She was only half finished with her wine when Hank came through the door. He didn't look around, striding across the room as if he'd known instinctively where she was sitting. He stopped a few feet in front of her and rubbed his palms together. "Everything all set?"

"Yes."

"I assumed the glass of wine meant no problems."

She took a small sip trying to decide whether there was a tone of disapproval, or it was jealousy she heard in his voice. Or neither, and she'd lost her ability to read his mood and his underlying meaning. He seemed to be trying to create an air of artificial professionalism between them. "The agenda says they don't start picking up their hats and things until three. Why don't you have a glass of wine with me." She smiled over her glass, tipped it, and let the dark wine flow up toward her mouth, wetting her lips.

"Not now."

"You're all checked in." She took another sip.

"You relax and enjoy it, I'll get settled."

Her smile felt a little goofy. She couldn't imagine what he had to do. Guys didn't get settled, they pulled their clothes out of the suitcase and shoved them in a drawer, hung the garment bag, and put a shaving kit on the bathroom counter. It took all of four minutes. "The team-building stuff is in my room. I'll bring it down as soon as I finish this. Did you see anyone else?"

"Sandeep's SUV was full. And Brent and two of the PMs who report to him were just pulling in."

She stood. "I'll get everything set up in the conference room."

"Thanks." He turned and went out.

She swallowed the rest of her wine. The room had less oxygen with Hank gone, everything faded and dull, the colors drained out, leaving the non-descript furniture, the fire too hot, too loud, and too overpowering. It seemed as though he hadn't really come in to talk to her or been pleased to see her, just wanted to make sure she was doing her job. She left her wine glass on the low table near a discarded copy of the San Francisco Chronicle.

The conference room was dark. It took a few minutes of fiddling with the control panel to get the lights turned on. She spread the shirts, hats, and room keys on a table at the back. She pulled a chair out of the last row and sat down. She felt like a child with a lemonade stand. She wished she'd insisted the clerk check everyone in at the front desk. Why did she have to be involved?

By the time everyone had come through, she was exhausted from smiling and repeating the logistical information over and over, explaining how the teaming worked. A few had questions about the war game activity and she couldn't answer a single one. She wasn't really sure she understood the rules or the purpose. To her, it seemed pompous. War games? Really? It was just a data storage company, not a mid-sized country with diplomatic engagements they had to be concerned with. She advised them to take their questions to Brent.

Before Hank's refusal to join her in a glass of wine, she'd assumed she and Hank would have some time alone throughout the three days. Their rooms were only a few doors apart, and Hank wasn't part of the teaming activities, so he'd have down time. He'd been traveling for over two weeks and then returned to a week of all day meetings. She felt like she hadn't talked to him in a month. Something had changed and she couldn't figure out what it was or when it had happened.

HANK WAS NOT pleased that the tables in the private dining room at Tallmadge's were arranged as four-tops. Vanessa assured him she could work quickly with the manager to configure the t-shape she'd requested well ahead of time. Everyone could have a drink in the bar while they waited. Hank waved her away. She was not pleased that Hank chose a seat with Sandeep, Brent, and one of the junior product managers. And Laura was obviously not pleased when it became clear she'd ended up at a table with Janelle and Vanessa.

Laura stood with both hands on the chair back. Her fingertips were white, the flesh pressed out around her short nails like the soft pads on the keys of a saxophone. "What is this, the girls' corner?"

Janelle scooted her chair closer to the table. She opened the large leather-covered menu and propped the bottom edge on the table, forming a perfect V between the finely polished utensils. The menu blocked her face, obscuring her opinion of the seating arrangements. She read the menu items out loud as she scanned the left side, biting hard on the T's. "Bru-*schett*-a; La Caprese with basil and *tarragon*; arugula *topped* with *goat* cheese." If there were entrees that included a significant amount of words ending or beginning with T, Vanessa feared she would either laugh or start mimicking Janelle's quirk. She'd never noticed it, but she didn't spend enough time around Janelle to know whether it was a long-standing trait, or something done to mask annoyance — over sitting with the admin, being squeezed out of the male-dominated tables, or watching Laura refuse to take her seat.

Vanessa sat down and opened her menu. She glanced over her shoulder at Hank. It was hard to tell in the dimly lit room if his lips were still tight, hardly moving when he spoke. He refused to let his gaze drift anywhere near her direction. He should have suggested she sit at his table. It made more sense.

Janelle lowered her menu. "Are you going to sit down?"

Laura turned and glanced toward the arched opening that lead to the main dining area.

"Are you waiting for someone?" Janelle said.

Laura's fingers tightened on the back of the chair.

"Get over it." Janelle raised her menu. "If you make an issue out of it, you'll look strident."

Laura turned. "Why are women always accused of being strident?"

Janelle laughed. "We're not *always accused* of anything. *You're* being strident."

"I don't like it that three women are grouped together. Like we're second class."

"Sit down," Janelle said.

Laura turned to Vanessa. "Didn't you make a seating chart? To make sure the teams were dispersed? Sandeep and that PM are on the same team."

"The seating chart was for a different arrangement. They got it wrong," Vanessa said.

"Why didn't you get here early to check? Why didn't you make them re-do it?"

"Laura." Janelle's voice was sharp. "Sit down and decide what you're having for dinner."

"This needs to be fixed," Laura said.

Janelle closed her menu and placed it on the table. She took a sip of water and glanced toward the sommelier who was talking to Hank. "Do you know what wine choices we have?"

"A Sauvignon Blanc, a Cabernet, and a Zinfandel," said Vanessa. "All different wineries, so we can get a sampling."

"Mmm. Can't wait to try them." Janelle took another sip of water. Her hair was calmer than usual, natural and soft. Her make-up was the same as always, too colorful — bright blue eye shadow with a touch of pink at the corners.

Laura let go of the chair. She adjusted her purse on her shoulder, turned, and walked around the table nearest them, along the wall to the doorway, and out into the main restaurant. Brent's head snapped up as she disappeared around the corner. He put his hand on the table as if he meant to stand, then looked at the others. His hand remained on the table. Then, he settled back, picked up his wineglass, and swirled the liquid. It flowed around the inside of the glass, rising dangerously close to the edge. He stopped moving it and took a sip.

"I wonder if she's having some kind of psychotic episode," Janelle said.

"What?"

"Laura. Something's wrong with her."

"There is?"

"She's behaving badly. Very unprofessional."

"I think she's attracted to Hank." For a moment, Vanessa was horrified at what she'd blurted out, but after a pause she realized she was glad of the opportunity. Why not turn the gossip back on Laura? Besides, it was flattering to have a woman in Janelle's position treat her like a girlfriend. Maybe the whole problem with her job was too many men and not enough women, too few opportunities to have a normal conversation with the handful of women who worked in Hank's organization.

"Funny," Janelle said. "She . . ."

The sommelier pushed his cart up close to their table. After introducing himself, he described each wine — the vintner, the variety, and the characteristics of the year.

"I'll have the Zinfandel," Vanessa said.

"If you're going to try all of them you should start with the Sauvignon Blanc," Janelle said.

"I'll stick with the Zin."

The sommelier filled Vanessa's glass a third of the way. "And you, Miss?"

Janelle giggled. "I'll take my own advice."

He poured the pale white wine into her glass. When he moved to the next table, Janelle raised her glass. "To the girl table."

They tapped their glasses together and grinned at each other. Vanessa took a generous sip and a warm rush of pleasure ran over her collarbone and down her chest as if the rich red wine had spilled across her dress.

Janelle continued as if she hadn't been interrupted. "Laura said the same thing about you. Except more."

"I know," Vanessa said. "It's probably just because of the

ops director job, but she hangs around my desk a lot. Like a groupie outside the stage door."

Janelle laughed.

Vanessa took another sip of wine. She flipped open the menu. She shouldn't let wine and a hint of friendship lull her into getting too chatty.

"Do you want to share an order of bruschetta?" Janelle said.

"Sure."

"I hope she's not in the bathroom slitting her wrists."

Vanessa tried not to laugh. It was cruel, and not funny at all, but she still wanted to laugh.

"It's okay to laugh," Janelle said.

Vanessa smiled, but her lips wobbled as if they couldn't quite hold her teeth in place. It was dangerous, this conversation. By no means were she and Janelle peers. Exposing her thoughts, talking trash about Laura, despite how good it felt, might not be a great idea. She wasn't sure how, but she felt it could get her into trouble. She didn't really know what kind of relationship the two women had. It was odd that Janelle was saying such negative things about someone who reported to her.

The bruschetta arrived and their glasses had been topped off with a small amount of wine before Laura returned to the dining room. She stood for a moment in the doorway, backlit by the light from the main restaurant. Her hair glowed like dark walnut and her face was hidden by shadows. She'd taken off her jacket to reveal more of her cerulean cocktail dress with straps as fine as strands of hair. The dress was slightly loose. Her shoulders were slim and muscular, and her skin smooth across her collarbone — she was thin but not boney. Only her breasts, slightly lower than they should be to give the dress full credit, revealed her age. Her arms were also well muscled, her waist slim, and her hips narrow. She looked good but there was nothing truly desirable about her. Vanessa felt a twinge of shame for critiquing a woman's desirability, but it was an impression that had come unbidden. She picked up a piece of bruschetta and took a bite. Talking to Janelle was shifting her perspective. She was smarter and more interesting than she gave herself credit for. Feeling like their slave might have been partially shaped by her imagination. She smiled and took another bite.

Laura walked to the table where Brent, Sandeep, the PM, and Hank were drinking wine and eating off a shared plate of sautéed calamari. She tapped the product manager on the shoulder and leaned down to whisper in his ear. The dress fell low, exposing the tops of her breasts.

The product manager pushed his chair away from the table, an awkward jittering motion since he was holding his wine glass in his right hand. Brent spoke. Vanessa couldn't make out his words, but the tone of his voice was deep and commanding. Laura straightened. Her voice, in contrast to Brent's, was loud, rising above the voices and background music. "It's more appropriate for me to sit here. I think you can see why and I don't think you want me to spell it out in front of everyone."

The product manager froze, half-standing.

In a loud voice, Brent said, "Sit down."

The product manager remained motionless.

"Thank you for understanding." Laura put her hand on the back of his chair.

Sandeep pushed his chair out. He picked up his wine glass and stabbed his fork at a calamari ring. It dangled as if it would slip off but he moved it quickly to his mouth and swallowed it. "I'll change tables. No problem." He strode across the room, pulled out the chair that originally belonged to Laura, and sat down. "Musical tables." He smiled. "Is there a piece of bruschetta for me?"

"Certainly." Janelle nudged the plate in his direction.

Laura sat in Sandeep's vacated chair. She signaled the sommelier to bring her a wine glass. The three men diligently ate calamari. As far as Vanessa could see, no one was speaking. Janelle was right. Something was very wrong with Laura. She had a crazed look in her eyes. Instead of hiding out in the women's lounge, it looked as if she'd gone to the bar and fortified herself with a shot or two, or slipped something mind altering down her throat. Vanessa wasn't sure what was going to happen over the next few days, but she was pretty sure Laura wasn't going to get promoted. And she was absolutely sure that Laura was oblivious to that fact.

Twenty

UNTIL SHE WAS FACED with the utter darkness in the wooded resort, Laura had forgotten how much ambient light there was in suburbia. The pathways and narrow roads winding through the pine trees were lined with small lights close to the ground, the wattage wasn't strong enough to illuminate more than a few scattered patches across the pine needles and pavement. Once she turned off the bedside lamp, she couldn't even make out the shape of the armchair near the window.

She lay curled on her side in the soft queen-sized bed, buried under a crisp cotton sheet and a down-filled comforter. The pillow was cool enough to sooth the inside of her head, dulled by too much wine and rich food. Despite the sensation that her brain had sunk into a can of Crisco, she knew in some inner area where her neurons were still firing correctly, that the evening had gone well. After the initial awkwardness of making sure she wasn't relegated to a table of females, things had gone quite well. She'd been a nimble conversationalist, keeping the rapt attention of Brent and Hank, as well as the product manager, although keeping his interest was a trivial task. Now that she could rest and know her determination to take charge had paid off, she could return to considering her next steps — protecting herself from the unexpected.

That morning, before she'd left home, Charlie had come over with a copy of the weekly paper. Even behind his glasses, she could see his eyes contained a glimmer of determination.

"There's a mention of that man who was beaten," Charlie said. "He died early in the morning. They say anyone with information should contact the police."

Her wrist seemed about to collapse as she took the paper and she'd thought for an instant she might drop it. He let go and her hand trembled violently. She hoped he hadn't noticed. All she could manage was a quiet, "Oh."

"It's strange that you never saw him, since you run there every day. I've always admired your dedication — running in the dark, the rain, when there's frost. But you really need to be careful. Going to a deserted location in the dark like that, it's not a good idea."

"So I've been told." Laura tucked the paper under her arm and started to close the door.

Charlie put his hand out. "Why do you think that is?"

"What?"

"That you never saw him?"

"I don't know. A lot of people come and go. Some people run once and disappear. I don't pay attention to them. I'm in my zone." She smiled.

"I've heard about that zone thing. Still, I'd think you would notice who's jogging at the same time as you. Even in your zone. It could have just as easily been you, murdered in the dark. Doesn't that concern you at all?"

"Not really."

"It should. It concerns Jenny and me."

"Thank you for being worried, but I'm fine."

"You might have tripped over his body when you were walking to the track."

"Don't be morbid." She started to close the door. "I need to get going. I'm out of town for a few days — an offsite meeting for my company."

Charlie nodded. "Be careful. Whoever killed that guy — with their bare hands . . ." he shook his head, ". . . is still out there."

She nodded. "I told you I haven't been running." Why wouldn't he let it go? His mind was stuck in some kind of worry loop, trying to make sense of what happened. It was unnerving to live in a town deemed safe, murder-free, then be faced suddenly with the possibility it wasn't safe after all. "I'm sure it was an anomaly. Someone with a grudge against that guy, not a serial killer or anything like that."

"You don't know that," Charlie said.

"I'm sure I'm right."

"Do you know something you're not saying? Otherwise, how can you be so confident?"

"I don't know anything. Except I know I'm right. Serial killers have different methods."

"What do you know about it?"

"Nothing, I'm just saying, they don't beat people up and leave them under bushes. Look, I really need to start packing."

Charlie backed away from the door. "Be careful. Please."

"I will. Thank you for being so concerned about me."

When he finally turned away, looking reluctant to stop verbalizing his fear, she closed the door and locked it. He couched his fear as concern for her when, most likely, he was worried for himself. Old and watching his strength melt further every year, every month. Upset that his idyllic retirement was spoiled by something as ugly as murder.

Now, everything he'd said echoed in her mind with a suggestion of disbelief. There was no way he could know she'd killed that man. Unless he'd seen her, but then he'd come right out and say so, she was sure of it. She turned onto her left side, facing the wall. Even in the darkness, she could feel the wall was too close to the bed. But looking out the other way wasn't ideal either. The property was open into wild forest. Anyone could approach the cottages unseen. Sleeping alone at a resort, a place that was supposed to be a getaway, made her ache for someone in the bed with her.

There was no one on her side, no one to ease her fears, no one to keep her safe, no one to talk to.

Charlie's questions pricked at her mind, telling her she was in trouble. It was possible, a very remote chance, but not completely beyond considering, that the police might be so thorough they would knock on every door in a ten-block radius. She couldn't imagine them going to the trouble, but it was possible. She'd better think about a story line. It had been easy to deflect Charlie's probing, but the police would be more direct. It was not a good idea to be caught by surprise. In the morning, when her mind was freed of alcohol, sharp with an infusion of caffeine, she'd make a list and think through her options.

With a course of action decided, her muscles started to untwist into the welcoming bed. She rolled onto her back. Dinner really had gone very well. She felt calm for the first time in several days.

IN THE MORNING the trees were almost invisible, the entire wooded area misty and quiet, the fog settled close to the ground. Laura flung off the comforter and hurried into the shower. Before she'd even started shampooing her hair, she abandoned her late night plan to come up with answers for the police. The compulsion to have a story was the result of night terrors, demons stalking her brain, preying on her momentary attack of loneliness when she was too tired to think clearly. And, if she was honest, beyond tipsy. She didn't need a fucking *alibi!* She didn't need a story of any kind. There was no way to prove she'd been running at the high school that day, and there was no way the police would consider putting out that much effort. She laughed.

When she was dressed in jeans, sturdy ankle boots, a turtleneck shirt, and a jacket, she shoved her phone into her pocket and went out. Without a purse and the burden of wallet and keys and all that other crap in addition to her laptop bag, she felt light and eager to start the day. She hurried down the wood stairs. There were more important things to work on than worrying about a dead guy who looked like he'd been ready to keel over anyway. A guy who was mentally disturbed and a huge drain on society. No one would even notice the empty space he'd left in the world.

In the restaurant, a sea of empty tables covered in red cloths, set with white napkins and flatware, spread out before her. Cups and saucers and tiny cream pitchers were all in their places. The only occupied table was in the back corner near the window facing the main building. Hank and Vanessa were seated there. Vanessa's hair looked redder than normal — bright and brassy in contrast to the dark red of the tablecloths. Her elbows rested on the edge of the table and she leaned over the place setting, all that hair cascading over her shoulders and down her back so that her black sweater was hardly visible. Her hands were clasped, her knuckles touching the coffee cup.

Hank sat with his shoulders back, chin lifted. Because his

arms were straight, his hands, palms down on his thighs, he gave the impression his chair was too far from the table, untouched by the intensity that hummed around Vanessa. Neither one was aware of Laura's presence, their heads immobilized, looking at each other, or maybe looking past each other, on Hank's part. Outside, the fog pressed close to the glass, leaving a thin film of moisture. The staff seemed to have intuited the couple's need to be alone because there wasn't a server or even a runner with a pot of coffee anywhere in sight. Orchestrated Beatles music played from hidden speakers, the strings of violins turning pop rock into notes dripping with sentimentality.

Minutes ticked by. Vanessa spoke. If Laura inched her way into the room, they'd catch the movement, but standing in the doorway wasn't accomplishing anything. There was a small amount of pleasure knowing they weren't aware of her presence, knowing they'd be startled when they did see her, wondering what she'd overheard. If she stood here long enough, Vanessa might unclasp her hands and touch Hank's arm. He'd pull his chair closer to the table and relax his posture.

The scene proved she'd been right. She didn't need corroboration. No one believed her manufactured rumor because they didn't want to open their eyes. And she was not projecting her own feelings! That was simply a diversion on Vanessa's part, trying to move attention off herself. There was something between those two that was not a business relationship. It was possible they weren't even aware of it. Maybe they'd never actually done it, but they both wanted to. There was no other reason to be sneaking into the restaurant in a failed attempt to be alone before the sun was fully up. Burning desire wiped out all their self-preserving caution. Now that Laura thought about it, the contrived seating arrangement at dinner the night before had been nothing but an attempt to cover up their relationship, deliberately not sitting together, and putting Laura in a position where she wouldn't catch Hank constantly turning his head, unable to stop looking at Vanessa. Even now, his eyes were locked onto her.

Laura walked quickly toward their table. When she was seven or eight feet away, Hank turned. Laura grinned. "Hi, you two. Sorry to break things up . . ."

"You're not breaking up anything. We haven't ordered yet," Hank said. "Pull up a chair."

God he was smooth. It was as if he had those words in his front pocket, ready at a moment's notice. "Actually, I'm just going to get a coffee and go for a walk."

"You should eat," Hank said. "It's a long day ahead."

"I'll grab some yogurt later. How often do I get to walk in the woods? I don't want to waste a minute sitting inside. And I don't want to interrupt you."

"Then why are you?"

Vanessa pushed her hair over her shoulders. No matter what she did with it, her hair framed her face in looping, tangled curls that gave her a look of yearning.

Laura's heart beat faster. She had walked in on something. It was difficult to read, but it was as tangible as the fog clinging to the trees, moisture turned into something solid. "I just said that to be polite. A little respect would be nice." Laura glared at the side of Vanessa's head, waiting for her to turn and show she realized she'd made a mistake in front of her boss.

"Respect is hard to come by," Hank said. He sipped his coffee. He put down the cup and turned to look out the window.

"I suppose, but it's part of the package when you're an exec," Laura said.

He looked at her and laughed, loud and hard. "Is that what you think? People may respect you to your face, but the higher you go, the more they criticize you behind your back."

He looked genuinely amused. Was the comment a backhanded slap? Had Vanessa told him about the rumor? If she had, it was further proof their relationship was very intimate. She smiled. "Well, I just wanted to say hi." She turned and walked past the doorway to a small staging station. A server stood there filling pitchers with cream. Laura ordered black coffee to go.

When the server returned, Laura took the cup and went outside without looking back at Hank and Vanessa. She'd seen enough. There was no doubt the reason her promotion had been pushed to the side was because Hank was not focused on running the business. It was entirely possible that Vanessa wanted to keep Laura away from him because they'd been found out. He might have even told her to do just that. But if Vanessa had half a brain, she'd remember she'd been caught stealing that candy bar. All Laura had to do was figure out how to leverage that little mistake. A girl who stole a two-dollar chocolate bar possessed a broken moral compass. The same thing could be said about a woman who'd beaten a man to death. But had she really? She wasn't excessively strong. Sure she lifted weights, but there was no way her strength was comparable to a normal male. There was something wrong with that guy — in his head and his body. He hadn't even fought back. He'd wanted to die, might have already been on the verge of death. All she'd done was help him over. It wasn't murder by any stretch of the imagination. In some ways, it proved her ability to take care of herself. If she hadn't beaten him up, he would have shot her. She couldn't let the reversal of their roles, her brutality, erase how terrifying he'd been. Her gut had informed her he was planning to hurt her badly, irrevocably. She'd done nothing but defend herself. She'd never admit it to anyone, but there was a growing flicker of pride every time she remembered that moment. There weren't many people in the world, and especially many women, who could claim they were capable of killing someone. Of taking the ultimate step to protect themselves. She hadn't let him intimidate her or turn her into a statistic — another female victim of violence.

She went back to her cottage and studied the list of teams and the room locations. Brent was two buildings over on the first floor. She finished her coffee and got a bottle of water out of the mini refrigerator. She hurried back down the stairs and took the path to his cottage. The fog was lifting and there were spots of sun on the pavement. The pine needles covering the ground alongside the path already smelled dry, the scent clean and comforting. She needed to get out of the suburbs more often. In her twenties she'd spent a lot of time kayaking and hiking. When had she drifted away from all of that? The same way she'd forgotten the part of herself that loved riding horses. Having a well-balanced life was important. She needed to get more physical, needed to get back to running, for sure, and those other things as well. She really should look into getting a horse and finding a place to board it. Riding every weekend would make her a completely new person. She knocked on Brent's door.

He opened the door quickly, as if he'd been standing right there. He was dressed but his feet were bare.

"Can I come in? I really need to talk to you."

"About last night?"

"What about it?"

"You kind of effed up."

"What do you mean? Are you going to let me in?"

He stepped back and walked to the armchair facing the window. He sat down. She went in, closed the door, and sat on the love seat across from him. "Why did you say that?

Dinner was great."

He laughed. "You acted like a lunatic."

"I did not."

"If you can't see that, you're in trouble."

She twisted the cap off her water bottle and took a sip. She replaced the cap. "I don't know what you're talking about, but I need to ask you a favor."

"What's that?"

"You need to get Hank away from Vanessa and beat some sense into him."

"Is that right?"

"You need to sell me. Get him to move on the job and stop wasting time talking to a bunch of people who aren't half as qualified as I am. He knows I can do it, he knows I'm the best candidate. I think he's just worried he isn't doing his due diligence. That, and he's obsessed with Vanessa. He's not paying attention to running the business."

"You have it all figured out."

"So you'll talk to him?"

"I can't."

"What do you mean you can't?"

"After last night."

"All I did was equalize things. You can't stick all the women at one table. What were they thinking?"

"All the women were not at one table."

"Most of them."

He stood. "I need to get something to eat."

"I'll go with you."

He shrugged. He went to the dresser and pulled out a pair of socks. While he put on his socks and shoes, she sipped water. He stood and put on his jacket.

Outside, the fog had almost completely evaporated, only a few small puffs hung in the air.

"You owe me," Laura said.

"How so?"

"I supported you when you were trying to get promoted."

"I suppose you were a cheerleader. But you didn't *do* anything."

"Don't say that."

"You've been a good friend. And I appreciate it," he said.

"*Been?*"

They emerged from the wooded area, crossed the two-lane road, and walked up the path leading to the restaurant. At the bottom of the steps, Brent stopped. He turned, but didn't look at her. She followed his gaze, out across the crisscross of paths, toward the hotel, gleaming white in the sunshine.

"Just tell me you'll talk to him about me. Okay?"

"Sure. Okay. I'll talk to him."

She led the way up the steps and into the restaurant. Hank and Vanessa's table was empty. The room smelled of bacon and cinnamon. She'd have a full breakfast after all. The chances for that were rare, and the pine-scented air had made her hungrier than she'd realized.

Twenty-one

SITTING AT HER desk surrounded by the walls of her cube was disorienting after three days in Napa Valley. The cube felt foreign yet familiar, as if she'd occupied it in another part of her life and she was returning to the past. How could so much change in so few days — less than a hundred hours? She tried to concentrate on tracking expenses from the offsite, proud of her efficiency in taking care of everything immediately. Until the bills from the corporate cards arrived, she couldn't enter them in the expense reporting tool, but capturing them in a spreadsheet and writing the justifications while it was all fresh in her mind would save time later.

Hank's door was closed. She had no idea what he was doing. No one was in there, and he wasn't on the phone. Possibly he was cleaning out email in preparation for his departure from Avalon. She still found it difficult to believe he'd accepted a position at another company. Her face had been numb, her eyes flat and unfocused since that breakfast meeting in Napa. Two more weeks and a void would open at the center of her working life. She'd asked if he would take her with him but he said there was an admin already in place. Once he was settled at the new company, he'd let her know if anything could be worked out.

All of this had been in process for nearly two months. It should be satisfying, an honor, almost, that he'd trusted her with the information since he hadn't offered his resignation yet. Once he did, he'd be removed immediately. Someone at his level couldn't be trusted after they showed their hand, proved their disloyalty. It wasn't disloyalty at all, but that's how the executives higher up the chain behaved. And maybe they were right. She certainly felt he was disloyal to her. They would shut him off fast. A valued and respected key officer of the company would be transformed, in the space it took to speak six words, into an enemy with the potential to commit corporate espionage. She giggled softly.

"What's so funny?"

Vanessa looked up at the sound of Laura's voice, grating and demanding. The sharpness of Laura's nose and cheekbones, her thin bony form with long, wiry muscles, gave the impression that all the flesh had been sucked out of her.

"Nothing."

"You were giggling. It's unnerving to come around the corner and see someone sitting alone in a cube, laughing."

"How do you think it is to be working and have someone start talking to you without even asking to be excused?"

Laura folded her arms.

"What do you need?" Vanessa put her hands under her hair and lifted it over her left shoulder. She twisted it into a wavy coil so it wound down the front of her arm.

Laura's lips parted slightly. She seemed to be staring at Vanessa's breasts. The effort of raising her arms might have rearranged the neckline of her sweater. She waited for Laura to make a rude comment, but Laura remained silent, her mouth gradually closing until her lips were a colorless pinch of skin. "As I've said before, women need to stick together."

"Is that why you didn't want to sit with me at the offsite dinner?"

"That wasn't it at all."

"Then what was it?"

Laura moved closer and leaned on the counter, pressing her ribs hard against the edge so her shirt bunched up like a half deflated balloon. She rested her chin on the heel of her hand. "You can't put women in a female ghetto."

"It was random."

"Ha! Random that three of the seven females ended up at the same table? That's naive."

"What do you want from me?"

"I wanted to invite you out for a glass of wine after work," Laura said.

"Really?" Just last week, Vanessa would have laughed and sent Laura on her way. But now — her future was not very clear. Of course she hoped Hank would find a spot for her once he was settled, but she couldn't count on that. She shouldn't count on that. Maybe she did need a network of sorts.

"Are you free after work?" Laura said.

"Sure. Why not."

"My treat."

"That's not necessary."

"No, but I think I owe you."

"Why?"

"I know I was a little rude at the offsite. Walking away like that."

Vanessa touched the handle of her coffee mug. She ran her finger around the lip. It was almost time for an espresso to blast out the mid-day brain fog. Laura didn't look like she was going anywhere soon. This wasn't just another way of loitering, waiting and hoping to see Hank. Laura hadn't even glanced at his door. Still. "I'll meet you in the lobby," Vanessa said.

"At five-thirty?"

"Sure."

"What about your meeting with Hank?" Laura said.

"I'll tell him I need to get going. It's no problem." There wasn't any reason to meet with Hank now. Just a bit of gossip, keeping up his routine, but he wasn't actively pushing to get much done. She picked up her mug.

"Time for espresso?" Laura said.

"Yes."

"I'll go with you."

So now they were going to be companions? Vanessa smiled to herself.

THE BAR LAURA chose was part of a restaurant located on a narrow street in downtown Palo Alto. The building was an old Spanish-style house designated a historical landmark. In the summer, diners ate in the central courtyard, or along the balcony on the second floor, feeling as if they were enjoying a balmy Italian or Spanish city, surrounded by adobe walls and tile floors. The bar didn't have quite as much charm once you were inside. It was a bar — a too-large TV and the bar itself. Along one wall was a row of regular tables and near the front windows were three tables that stood four feet high with low-backed stools. Sitting on them meant perching your feet on a rail as if you were a large bird. It was impossible to look attractive pitched forward, straining your legs to maintain your position, your purse dangling from the back, tapping your shin whenever you moved.

Laura sat at the tall table nearest the side wall. Vanessa climbed onto her stool. They ordered two glasses of Chardonnay and a plate of fried calamari. When the wine arrived, Laura lifted her glass, clicked it too hard against Vanessa's, and said, "To the superior sex."

"Superior?" Vanessa took a sip of cool, crisp wine. "I thought men and women were equal?"

"That's what we let them think. But really, we're stronger,

don't you think? We have better endurance, we're more well rounded, not suppressing our emotions. We live longer, we create life. I could go on."

Vanessa smiled. "Well you and I haven't created any lives."

"True, but the possibility is there."

"Why does anyone have to be superior?"

"That's why they try to keep us down. They're scared of us."

"You make it sound like a war."

"Don't be ridiculous."

"That's how it sounds."

"I'm just saying men go out of their way to make sure they keep the power. And they act like they're physically stronger, but really, they're not."

"Every man I know is a lot stronger than I am," Vanessa picked up a piece of calamari, dipped it in the sauce, and bit off a small piece. It was very tasty. She took another small bite.

"See, they've brainwashed us into thinking that. Most of the movies are made by men, showing men dominating women . . . fighting . . . killing. It's all a great big show."

Vanessa laughed. "You're kidding, right?"

"Not really."

"Well I could never beat a man in a fight. And I don't want to."

"Don't you want to feel strong? To be able to go where you want, when you want, without being told you're putting yourself in danger?"

"I don't go anywhere that makes me worry I'm in danger."

Laura took a long sip of wine. Her lips pursed around the rim of the glass as if she was trying to filter out sediment as she drank.

The place was filling up. Only one empty table remained. Five or six guys Vanessa's age clustered around the bar, their heads tipped back, staring at the basketball game. She shifted in her chair so the flicker of the screen didn't distract her. It felt as if Laura was headed somewhere with this line of conversation, but Vanessa couldn't see where, and she didn't want to be tripped up by the noise, the rapidly emptying glass of wine, and the effort of keeping herself securely balanced on the chair.

"I'm just saying it's an act. They aren't always that strong. And I can't believe that in the twenty-first century, men essentially run the whole business world. How many executives are women? Maybe ten percent? And we're more than fifty percent of the population. Isn't that amazing, when you stop and think about it? It's outrageous, actually."

Vanessa shifted her position again. She'd thought this would be relaxing, that Laura would unwind a little and be a bit more like a girl. Instead, she acted like she wanted to recruit Vanessa to an army of female warriors.

Why did it have to be a competition? Vanessa loved men, she liked that they were strong and in charge. She didn't want to be able to beat up a man. Who even thought that way? She sipped her wine.

"Are you ready for another glass?" Laura said.

"In a few minutes." Vanessa slathered a calamari ring with sauce and popped the whole thing in her mouth. They were so good — the batter light and crispy, the calamari firm and sweet, and the sauce spicy but not drowning the taste of the seafood.

"I just don't like feeling as if I don't have any power. For example, the way Hank dangles this job over my head, making me beg for attention."

"He has other things on his mind."

"What other things?"

Vanessa sipped her wine. "You know, the business. End of the quarter. Strategy sessions. Customer meetings."

"I know all that. But part of his job is staffing."

"It doesn't have anything to do with women against men. It has to do with finding the right person."

"But what I'm saying is that nine times out of ten, the *right* person turns out to be a guy."

"There's just more guys who went to college . . ."

"No, actually, that's not true."

"Okay, well more guys who make their career the top priority."

Laura shrugged. She lifted her hand and signaled the server.

After two fresh glasses of wine were sitting near the center of the table, she said, "I just wish he'd make a decision and quit making me feel like he has all the power."

"In this case, he sort of does," Vanessa said.

"Is that what he told you?"

"No."

"What were you two talking about when I saw you having breakfast in Napa? It was all very intense. I was standing there for ten minutes before you noticed me."

"I don't remember talking about anything specific."

"The air almost *smelled* different."

"If you're going to start in with that again, I'm leaving."

"I'm just being honest. It's either that, or you were talking about me."

"Those are the only two choices? Really?" Vanessa laughed.

"Why won't you tell me? I'm not going to get you in trouble."

"I really don't remember."

Laura smirked. She lifted her eyebrows, creating a ripple of lines across her forehead. She tried to turn the smirk into a smile, but ended up with her mouth twisted up on one side so she looked like she was indeed making an effort to get Vanessa into trouble. "As I've said before, you're a very secretive person."

"It's my job."

"I know you know things."

"Not everything is about you," Vanessa said.

"It must be very stressful. Having to keep so much information to yourself."

"Not really."

"The stress can make you do crazy things."

Vanessa wiped her finger down the side of the glass, removing the foggy sheen created by the chilled wine, leaving a clean stripe, wider than the width of her finger. She picked up the glass and took a sip. This was not a casual girls' night out. Laura was after something. Had she seen Vanessa take the candy bar after all? She'd acted like it at the time, and now, it seemed that she'd hung onto that sliver of knowledge, biding her time, waiting until she could use it to force Vanessa into betraying Hank. "It's not stressful. I find it easy to keep things to myself."

"Now that you say it, I can see that about you." Laura smiled. Her teeth were perfectly straight, but longer than average, drawing more attention to themselves than they would have if they weren't so thin, like bones, the teeth of a skeleton without the covering of pink, fleshy gums.

Vanessa looked away. When she turned back, Laura was still grinning.

"You make it sound like I'm sneaky," Vanessa said.

"Do I?" Without waiting for Vanessa to speak, Laura changed the conversation to their co-workers. Barely pausing for a breath, she ran down the strengths and weaknesses of every person on Hank's staff. After a while, the server came by and asked if they wanted a third glass of wine.

"No thanks," Vanessa said.

"I think you should." Laura turned her grin on the server.

"Two more glasses. And crab cakes."

Vanessa wanted to argue, she should be more firm, but it was Laura's agenda. If Laura had seen the theft, it would be better to know about it. "I'm not sure I should drink three glasses and drive."

"We'll drink it more slowly. And the crab cakes will absorb the alcohol. You'll be fine."

"That's not how it works."

"I do it all the time. It's no problem. You just need to drive carefully, be hyper alert. Focus."

The server returned with two glasses of wine and let them know their food would be up soon. Vanessa ordered a bottle of sparkling water.

"Sometimes secrets have a way of leaking out. You get caught off guard. People know things that you think they couldn't possibly know."

"What are you talking about?" Vanessa said.

"Just thinking. Rambling a bit. White wine does that to me." Laura laughed. "We have to stick together. If someone asked you questions about me, you'd make sure I looked good, right? Now that we're friends?"

Vanessa opened the sparkling water and poured it into the glass the server had provided. The ice crackled. She dropped in the lime wedge and took several long drinks. She couldn't follow Laura's train of thought. She wasn't sure if this was about Laura witnessing the theft, more of her speculation, or angling for Vanessa to influence Hank's decision over the director position. "We're friends?"

"Of course we are. You'd only say good things about me, even if you weren't sure what the questions were about. And I'd do the same for you, of course."

"Are you talking about the interview? I doubt Hank will ask for my input."

"I'm talking in general. Having each others' backs."

"Then why would you spread rumors about me? How is that having my back?"

"I wasn't spreading rumors. I just asked Janelle if she'd heard anything. It wouldn't be good if you and he were having sex. You can see that, can't you?"

"We're not."

Laura glanced down at Vanessa's diamond ring.

Vanessa pushed away her empty wine glass and picked up the fresh one. She knew she should stop. It was not okay to drive, but it wasn't as if she'd never done it. She broke off a piece of crab cake, dipped it in rémoulade, and took a large bite. She chewed slowly.

"Don't act like you're flawless," Laura said. "I saw you steal that candy bar."

There it was. Next, she'd make a demand. Vanessa put her fork on the edge of the plate. She should drink more water. She took a sip of wine instead.

"Aren't you going to say anything?"

"There's nothing I can say."

"I think it's clear that you owe me."

"What do I owe you? I can't make Hank offer you the job."

"You can make Hank do whatever you want."

"No, I can't. And why do you make everything about sex? It's not very professional."

"I don't."

"Yes, you do."

"Only when it's obvious."

"It's not obvious. That's what I'm trying to say. You see it where there's nothing."

Laura grinned.

"Why are you smiling?"

"I'm not."

"There's nothing between us," Vanessa said. "You're imagining it."

"I see how he looks at you."

"He doesn't look at me any differently than any other girl."

"It's okay to admit it. Men and women get thrown together in high-pressure work situations all day every day. Half of them have unhappy relationships, or no relationship at all, and it's guaranteed there will be some attraction. Anyway I'll keep your secret about the candy bar. But you have to promise you have my back."

"That's a very generic promise," Vanessa said.

"Do you?"

"What?"

"Don't be cute. Do you have my back?"

"I don't know what you mean."

"You'd defend me, just like I'm defending you. And defending sometimes means keeping your mouth shut. Like if I needed you, or Hank, to say I came into work super early."

"What are you talking about?"

"Never mind. Just promise you have my back. I don't think you'd be employed here any more if they knew you were a thief. And I wonder what your fiancé would think of that. So I have your back and you have mine."

"Fine. I have your back." Vanessa finished the rest of the wine. She felt queasy and very unclear about what she'd just promised.

Twenty-two

THE MINUTE SHE BECAME conscious on Saturday morning, Laura decided she had to join a gym. She'd delayed too long already. Her body was screaming with rage, atrophying right before her eyes.

She took a shower and studied herself in the mirror on the back of the bathroom door. Five months before her fortieth birthday was not the time to give up a lifelong pursuit of fitness. It was showing more every day. Her thighs looked less firm. She jumped. Yes, they jiggled much more than before. She wanted to turn away, but forced herself to keep looking. All the soft areas of flesh were looser, the skin like bread dough that hadn't been pummeled down, spilling out of the bowl. After she covered herself with cotton bikini briefs and a spandex bra, navy blue leggings and a small white t-shirt, she looked good. Fantastic, really. But she couldn't go another week without a good, solid cardio workout.

She made coffee, drank two cups, ate a container of plain

yogurt and an apple, and fed the fish. She waited impatiently for them to grab the lance fish off the feeding stick. It had been weeks since she'd sat in the chair and let their dancing bodies sooth her. Soon. Maybe tomorrow. She put on a sweatshirt, sport socks, and trainers and stuffed her phone and wallet into a tiny purse.

Outside it was cold. It would have been tolerable if the sky was blue and clear, but it was bathed in high white clouds, a wash of nothingness that made the trees look more barren, and covered everything with a dingy shadow. She put her key in the deadbolt and snapped it to the left.

"Oh good, I wanted to talk to you."

Charlie's voice reverberated through her arm, rendering it motionless. She tried to pull the key out of the lock but the teeth had turned a fraction of an inch too far and it didn't want to slide out easily. She jiggled it back to the center and removed it. She turned to face Charlie. He wore red track pants with a white stripe down the outside of each leg. The waist sagged, allowing his t-shirt-covered belly to droop over the edge. He gave the pants a tug and stepped closer. There was a reflection on his glasses that prevented her from seeing his eyes, always unnerving but more so now that she knew they were boring into her, accusing. He'd always had an arrogant cast to his face. It was something midwestern, moral condescension not just in ethics, but also in a simpler, more open view of life. As if people in more sophisticated suburbs, on the west coast in particular, were inherently superficial and lacking in scruples.

"I'm heading out, what do you need?"

"Are you going jogging?"

"No."

He waited as if she'd left the sentence hanging and planned to say more. She smiled.

"Well . . . I don't need anything." He tugged at the waist of his pants then folded his arms across his ribs, pressing them close, as if that would keep the pants from sliding to an awkward spot on his hips.

"Then what's up?"

"The man who was killed at the track . . ."

"What about him?"

"Jenny and I were talking. You must have seen him. We think there's a very good chance you saw his killer at some point — since you were there every single day, rain or shine. We let the police know you were there all the time. If they talk to you, they might be able to jog your memory. No pun intended." He laughed. She stared at him. He laughed harder. "That's not funny. Sorry," he said.

"Why would you tell them that? I said I didn't see anything. I didn't know the guy."

"It's not possible. You were there every day."

"How do you know?"

"We hear you go out. You're like clockwork. So much that we joked we didn't need an alarm clock. Your feet on the stairs were enough."

"I didn't mean to disturb you."

"You didn't. I'm only making a point."

"You shouldn't have spoken for me."

"Communities fall apart when people don't watch out for their neighbors."

"He wasn't a neighbor!"

"Then you did see him?"

"No. I don't know. You said they hadn't identified him, so I figured he wasn't."

"Neighbor is a relative term. The only thing required for evil to prevail is for good men to do nothing."

Laura pressed her teeth together, forcing herself not to laugh at the idealistic view, trying to avoid blurting out more unfortunate words. "As I told you, I never saw the guy and I never saw anyone who looked out of place. In fact, I hardly ever saw other people during the winter. It's too cold and dark that early in the morning. Someone has to be very dedicated to go running."

"Like you."

"Yes."

"Why don't you go any more?"

"I guess knowing someone was killed spoiled it. I don't want to be looking over my shoulder."

"I'm glad you took our advice."

She smiled. Let him feel fatherly and protective. It didn't matter to her if he was wrong, if he thought she needed looking out for.

"We worry about you," he said.

"That's not necessary."

"A young woman shouldn't be running around in the dark. That could have been you who was beat up and left to die."

"Not likely," she said. She took a few steps closer to the railing. "Something else must have been wrong with that guy. It's not like it's easy to beat someone to death."

"It's easy to hurt a woman," he said. "You should be more careful. Even in a quiet town like this. Especially since you don't have a man to look after you."

She wanted to punch him. As if he offered any solid protection to Jenny? She didn't need a man. She was sick and tired of that attitude. How could people still parrot archaic beliefs as if nothing had changed over the past fifty or sixty years? The same rage that surged in her when that awkward, creepy jogger spoke to her, spilled into her throat. She couldn't let it gain control — she had to stay calm. Charlie could interfere all he wanted, but she had her story. There was nothing to worry about. She'd never seen the guy. She'd never seen anyone else. Who could prove otherwise?

If the worst happened, and it turned out someone had seen her running in the dark, the monster close on her heels . . . if they somehow found that newbie runner, she'd turn to Vanessa. She was relieved she'd set that up after all. It would be easy for Vanessa and Hank to say she was in the office early that day. She could explain that she didn't want to waste time with police questions, looking at pictures, getting dragged into something sordid. Vanessa was scared. Laura had seen it all over her face. Vanessa would get Hank to back her up, no matter what it took. It wasn't that much of a stretch anyway. She was usually one of the first in the office. There'd been many times when she'd arrived before Hank or Vanessa. Confirming she'd done the same the week of the killing would be a no-brainer. "I really wish you hadn't said anything to the police." She passed her keys to her right hand and put her left hand on the railing.

"It's your responsibility."

"I work long hours, I don't need to get dragged into a dead-end investigation when I have nothing to offer."

"You don't know that. This is the one thing I don't like about Californians, or at least the Bay Area. No one wants to get involved, everyone thinks they're too busy."

"Well we are."

"For what? Before you know it, you'll be my age. You should slow down. You should think about what really matters in life."

He hoisted up his pants. He moved closer to where she stood, stepping sideways so he was at the center of the top step. There was room to move past him to descend the stairs, but she'd have to brush against him, possibly push him to one side. There was a frailness about him. His body no longer seemed slim — frail was a more accurate description. Nothing but bone and a small strip of aging muscle held the elastic waistband of his pants in place. A gentle bump from her shoulder and he'd lose his balance, grabbing first for his unstable pants, further losing his footing. In the space of a breath, he'd tumble down the stairs, rolling shoulder over hip. She could hear the bones snapping, the grunt as the wind was knocked out of him, landing with a thud on the pavement below. She could hear Jenny screaming. Or maybe not. There was nothing about a tumble down the stairs that would immediately bring her to the door.

Laura moved closer to the edge of the step. Charlie shuffled out of the way. He leaned his hip on the opposite side of the railing from where she stood. She swallowed. "I have things to do," she said. "You need to get in touch with whoever you spoke to and tell them you were mistaken."

"It's your duty as a citizen to talk to them. You honestly can't spare ten minutes for public service?"

"I don't know anything about it. Talking to them would be a waste of my time. And theirs. You need to respect my request for privacy."

"You owe it to your other neighbors, to that dead man, to Jenny and me."

Laura folded her arms. "I don't owe anything to anyone." She pushed past him and walked down several steps. She turned and looked up at him. "You give them too much credit. I never saw the guy and I never saw anyone who looked even remotely like a killer. I need to get going. Please do what I asked and admit to them you didn't know what you were talking about." She turned and jogged down the stairs.

At the bottom, she ducked under the balcony that ran along the second floor. She went through the small alley to the garages along the back of the property.

It was doubtful Charlie was going to follow her instructions. He seemed very intent on manipulating a tenuous connection to a crime into a scenario where he was a hero, helping the police catch a killer, but he knew nothing. She was the only one with any knowledge. As long as she kept her cool, everything would be fine.

WHEN LAURA RETURNED from the gym, a white sedan with a government license plate was parked prominently at the curb in front of the four adjoining lofts. As she turned into the driveway, she glanced into the sedan. No one was inside, which meant that if it belonged to police detectives, they were hovering around her front door. Nice.

She picked up the gym information packet off the passenger seat, popped open the trunk, and dropped it inside. It wasn't until the trunk thudded closed that she recognized what she'd unconsciously done — avoided letting them know she was changing her running routine. Although she would likely be required to address that so she'd better think quickly. Still, it was important to remember they knew nothing. Just the rambling fantasy of an old man. A man who wanted so badly to help make his community nice he was seeing things that weren't there. Well, they were there, but he didn't know that.

Her routine was none of Charlie's business. She was busy at work, interviewing for a job with an order of magnitude more responsibility. The effort consumed all her cycles and drove her into the office as the sun rose every morning. She'd been doing it for weeks.

By the time she reached the end of the front path, she believed it herself.

A woman with shoulder-length dark brown hair, dressed in khaki pants, a white shirt, and a dark brown suit coat leaned on the railing. A female detective was a surprise, although it shouldn't have been. She wasn't sure if that would work in her favor, or the opposite. At least she'd seen the detective before the detective saw her.

The woman turned as Laura started up the stairs. When Laura was a few steps from the landing, the woman said, "Laura Bachman?"

"Yes."

The woman held out a case with a badge. "Detective Horowitz. Sunnyvale police."

"Hi."

"I'd like to ask you a few questions about a man who was beaten to death recently at the Carlton High School track. Have you heard about it?"

"My neighbor mentioned it."

"Charlie Woodard?"

"Yes."

"May I come inside?"

"Sure." Laura stepped up to the door. She put her key in the deadbolt. This was good. She was calm, eager to help, welcoming. Ten minutes, tops. She stepped back, gesturing for the detective to go first. As she followed Detective Horowitz inside, she realized the woman had taken control of the situation. The way the questions were piled on each other, there'd been no opportunity for Laura to say she knew nothing about the crime. She dropped her keys on the table near the door. "What did you want to ask me?"

"Can we sit down?"

"I don't think I'll have anything useful to say."

"Let's sit down."

Laura turned and walked to the couch. She did not feel guilty. The jogger was a monster, planning to harm her — kill or be killed. She'd done nothing but defend herself. She'd already done a favor for the community, if Charlie wanted to look at it correctly. She settled back into the buttery leather of her couch. The detective looked more comfortable than she should have, seated on the armchair placed at an angle to the couch. The detective looked at the fish tank for several seconds, then turned to face Laura.

"I understand you jog at the Carlton High School track."

"I used to."

"You don't any more?"

"I have a lot going on at work, so there hasn't been time lately."

"When was the last time you used the track?"

"Hmmm." Laura glanced at the lionfish. They stared back at her. She took a slow breath. "I think around the first week of January. Maybe the tenth or so."

"You aren't definite about the date?"

"No. Work has been so intense, I've lost track of time." She tucked her hair behind her left ear. That might not have been a good answer. It made her estimated date sound uncertain.

"You're sure it was around the tenth? That would be the second week of January."

"Okay, right. Yes."

"Yes, the tenth?"

Laura nodded.

"Did you ever see this man?" The detective put a small photograph on the coffee table.

Laura picked it up and studied it. The image looked nothing like the monster that had followed her. The long thin beard wasn't there and his hair was cut in a normal business style. His face had none of the gauntness that had sickened her, the bulging eyes. Terrified her, actually. She hated him for that, hated him even now for making her feel she was fragile and female. Well, she'd certainly gotten the upper hand with him. She smiled.

"You recognize him?"

"No."

"You smiled, as if you were recalling something."

"Did I?" Laura stood. She stepped around the coffee table

and handed the photo to the detective. "I don't recognize him. Is that all?"

"We have other witnesses who saw him at the track on a semi-regular basis. Very early in the morning. Which I understand is when you go running."

"Did. I did go running early, but I haven't been able to lately."

The detective held the edge of the photograph, her arm outstretched. "Can you please take another look."

"I don't have to. I've never seen him."

"Who did you see at the track? It's possible he looked different. This is several years old. He was laid off from Lockheed. He'd become borderline homeless after his wife and children moved to Michigan. His state of mind was on the fragile side."

How ironic that the detective chose that word — fragile. Well too bad. He wasn't fragile at all when he was breathing down her neck, dogging her steps, whispering threats in her ear. Laughing at her! Maybe that's why his wife abandoned him. "I'm sorry, I don't recognize him. I wish I could help."

The detective put the photo in her pocket and stood. "I'd like you to give it some more thought. Think through the people you did see at the track, or anyone you saw in the area."

"It was dark when I ran."

"Even in the summer?"

Laura opened her mouth. A sound came out. She coughed,

hoping to cover it. She'd been on the verge of blurting it out — the monster hadn't been there in the summer.

"What did you want to say?"

"Nothing. Just a lingering cough."

The detective stared at her for several seconds. She reached into her jacket pocket and pulled out another photograph. "Here's an autopsy photo. I'd hoped not to have show this to you."

Laura's stomach convulsed as she looked at the image. She shivered. That was a natural reaction, she thought. Nothing she had to hide or explain. She handed the photo back to the detective.

"You've never seen him?"

Laura shook her head.

"Please give it some thought."

Laura put her hand over her throat. When she swallowed it felt unnatural. She let her hand fall to her side. "I will. Give it some thought." They couldn't force her to say she'd seen him. How would anyone know? She was safe. It was important to stay calm and then they'd realize she was a dead end. She walked to the entryway. She turned and waited for the detective to catch up. The loft was silent except for the sound of the aquarium pump, its low rumble filling the space like a heartbeat, her loft a living thing.

The detective turned and studied the fish for a moment. "I've never seen fish like these. What are they?"

"Lionfish."

"They look . . . frightening."

"I suppose they are. They're poisonous. Their spines will sting you."

The detective put her face closer to the tank. "Have you been stung?"

"No. I'm careful."

The detective turned. "What made you choose such large fish?"

"They're beautiful."

"In a horrifying way."

"They can't hurt you. I use a stick to feed them. They're actually quite fragile, don't you think? A creature that can't survive out of the water, that has very few resources to protect itself. Except for its venom."

The detective buttoned her coat. She reached into her pocket as if she meant to take something out, but left her hand there. She glanced at the fish, then walked to where Laura was standing. "Thank you for your time." She pulled her hand out of her pocket and handed Laura a business card. "Call me if you remember seeing him. I'll be back in touch."

"Absolutely." Laura opened the door.

After Detective Horowitz went out and the door was closed and locked, Laura wrapped her arms around her waist. Her shoulders trembled slightly. Her throat ached and her hands were clammy and cold. That monster planned to haunt her from the grave. Well she wouldn't allow it. She did not need police stopping by, searching her place, wondering about her new running shoes, finding the gun and the knife tucked in her dresser drawer. The detective was not going to win this.

Twenty-three

HANK WAS ALONE in his office with the door closed. Vanessa dribbled water from her bottle into one of the snake plants on the credenza. She plucked off a thick dead leaf draped over the edge of the pot like a piece of wet felt. She'd knocked on his door at five-thirty, but he'd waved her away, indicating he was on the phone. Last week, he'd left at five every day but Thursday. Now that he was on his way out of the company, he no longer saw a need to spend the final thirty or forty minutes of his day talking to her. Did that mean their relationship had been a farce all these years? She refused to accept that. It was too humiliating. It implied she was needy and unwanted and downright stupid. Of course, she was refusing to accept he was leaving at all — it seemed like something she'd dreamt. Since he still hadn't given his resignation, maybe he'd changed his mind.

She turned her chair back around and opened a browser window. She went to the site for Bloomingdale's. For several days now, she'd been unable to stop thinking about a shoplifting expedition to the Bloomingdale's at Stanford Mall. They would have first class security, of course, but the pressure to get adrenaline shooting through her body was becoming unbearable. For a day or so, knowing Laura had seen her steal the candy bar had been a perverse pleasure that kept her on the delicious edge, but it had faded more quickly than she'd expected. For all these years she'd received a steady jolt of energy from taking cosmetics and lingerie from discount stores. The trip to Old Navy had whetted her appetite for bigger things. Bloomingdale's was a huge leap. Yet, she had large anxieties to quiet, so it might be necessary. She turned back to the plants and poked her finger in the soil of each one. They all needed a drink. She unscrewed the cap on her water bottle again and poured a small amount into each of the other pots. It was a waste of expensive water, but she was not leaving her desk until Hank opened his door.

The latch on his door clicked. She spun her chair around. He was standing in the doorway.

"Are we meeting?" She stood and picked up her notebook.

"Oh, right. I don't think I have much to talk about."

"We should still touch base. So I can understand your plans."

"Right. Sure. Come on in." He turned and disappeared inside.

Without bothering to lock her computer screen, she grabbed the water bottle, a pen, and her phone. She crossed the hallway in three strides. She stopped and tipped her head back and shook it. Her hair fell away from her face and spread across her shoulder blades and down her back. She pressed her lips together to make sure her gloss was evenly applied, glad that she'd taken time to refresh it while she'd been waiting. Always waiting. Her entire job, her career, her life was waiting for him, responding to him. She walked into his office and closed the door. She pulled out a chair from the conference table and adjusted it to face his desk. "Have you changed your mind?" she said. She put her notebook and pen on the table near her water bottle. She didn't really need them. They were props most of the time.

"Changed my mind about what?"

"Leaving Avalon."

He pushed his chair away from the desk. The darkness outside cast shadows around the edges of the office, making the areas touched by the florescent lights seem brighter in comparison. The light above his head shone on his hair giving it an inky hue. The ever-present shadow of his beard was darker as well. He looked tired. "Why would I change my mind? This is the height of my career. I have about five more years to continue the upward trajectory. If I'm ever going to be recruited as a CEO, I need to make a move now."

She nodded. Her career trajectory was in the opposite direction — a nosedive to the ground, plowing into the earth below. When she'd gotten her first job as an admin, she'd been so proud. Not many of her friends made the money she had back then, enabling her to move out of her mother's place immediately after high school into her own studio apartment, even though her stay there was short-lived. Back then, her salary and her job description were enviable. Now, not so much, and she'd never thought beyond. Never considered how she was going to spend her whole life. It was as if she'd grown up with the unexplored notion her life would stop at thirty. She'd never imagined herself with children, although she'd never imagined herself without them.

"I know it's an adjustment for you," he said. "But don't be concerned. Whoever replaces me will utilize your skills."

"I thought you were going to see if there was a position for me at QualData?"

"And I will. I will. But that takes time."

She nodded. He was telling her what she wanted to hear. She wasn't sure how she knew that, but she knew. The cords between them were unraveling, as if he were on a small boat, pulling away from the dock, and she was leaning over the widening gap, trying to keep her grip on the side of the boat and the slippery planks behind her, straining to pull him back, in danger of sliding off. All these years, she'd thought they were friends, that there was a special connection. Something exciting between them, a reason to dress up and come to work every day. Now, he acted as if she was nothing but an object to be discarded along with his office and company-owned computer and furniture. A piece of equipment —

maintained in excellent condition — to pass along to his successor.

"Why can't you get promoted here?" she said.

"We went over this."

"I know."

"It will be good for you too. It will stretch you."

"Yes." She didn't need stretching. She needed . . . she needed excitement. Stimulation. What if his successor was a woman? She shivered.

"Are you okay?"

"Yes."

"You look like you're not feeling well."

"No, I'm fine." She stared at him. His lips were soft and pale, the dark contours of his face like the face of a rock, inviting and challenging her to find a crevice, to get inside and learn his secrets. The cuffs of his white shirt were rolled back, revealing his well-formed forearms covered with dark hair, but not so thick he looked beastly, just manly, as silly as that sounded, even in her own head. She crossed her legs. "We've had a lot of good times."

He nodded.

"Lots of good conversations."

"You're an interesting person." He smiled, although his eyes looked past her.

"Not interesting enough, though."

He continued staring at the window behind her with such intensity she was compelled to turn and look. There was nothing to see. Past the blinds, the sky and edges of the bay were dark. No light glittered to indicate there was human life somewhere on the horizon. She turned back.

"Come again?" he said.

"I'm not interesting enough for you to stay. Not a good enough friend for you to make sure, before you accept the position, that there's a place for me."

He rubbed his temple then dragged his fingers along his jaw. "I don't know how I gave the impression we're friends. Yes, we've had a strong working relationship, but you're not my personal assistant. I said I'd scope out the situation when I got settled. That's all I can promise. I can't possibly guarantee you a job at a company where I'm not yet employed."

She folded her arms. It wasn't an attractive look. Pressing her arms across her middle transformed her into a stern, unwelcoming person, but she felt the need for some tangible sign she was protecting herself from his words, holding herself together, gathering strength. "I always thought there was more between us than just work."

"I'm your manager."

"Yes, but I do an excellent job. It's not like you have to actually manage me or correct my behavior or anything like that."

"I'm still your boss, not your pal."

"We talk about a lot of things."

"Possibly some things we shouldn't have. That's my

mistake, and I'm sorry if that gave you the impression we have a relationship beyond our professional interactions."

"It's not just talking that gave me that impression." She smiled and unfolded her arms. She'd been too reticent. Now was the time to remind him of their real connection. She would not allow him to pretend he wasn't drawn to her. Every day she'd felt his eyes on her, for years. It was what drove her when she showered and shaved her legs every morning, when she dried her hair into a silken drape, when she applied her makeup, outlining her eyes in shadows that were more dramatic than what was called for in the office. She wasn't trying to break up his marriage, wasn't trying to do anything. Just have a little fun, flirt a bit. And they did. She shifted in the chair, trying not to look stiff. She took a deep breath and let it out slowly, relaxing her shoulders. She moved them slightly so her hair fell forward, spilling over her upper arms. As if she'd planned it, one strand separated itself and tumbled across her breast.

His posture remained unyielding.

"You know what I'm talking about," she said.

"No." He glanced at his watch.

"Do you have somewhere to go?"

"I don't want to belabor the fact that I'm leaving and that I can't offer you a job right now. I think it's best for you to plan your career here, or at another company, if that's your choice, but don't rely on me. No promises."

"You've said that several times."

"And I mean it."

"So you feel nothing at the thought that you might never see me again?"

"Don't dramatize it."

"It's true though. If you leave . . ."

"When I leave."

"If you can't hire me as your admin, or a project coordinator, which we talked about, remember?"

He nodded.

"If you can't do that, or you forget about it, or can't be bothered, we'll never see each other again."

"It's a small industry. You never know who you're going to run across. We have a lot of years left, especially you."

It seemed as though he was deliberately changing direction, diverting her from what he feared she might say about the past. He did know what she was talking about, but he was forcing her to spell it out. If he thought he could intimidate her, shame her into pretending it never happened, he didn't know her at all. "I think you're trying to change the subject."

"I wasn't aware there was a subject, except you wanting me to offer you another job, and I've been straight with you."

"I'm not talking about the future. I'm talking about our past. What we've had."

The lights hummed so faintly she could only hear it when her breathing paused after she exhaled. "At the show in New Orleans," she said.

He raised his eyebrows.

"You remember."

"What's that?"

"We danced."

"Vaguely. It was a company party."

"But I'm not just talking about dancing. I'm talking about when you walked me to my room. When you came inside. When you touched me, and kissed me. And we almost didn't stop."

He wheeled the chair away from his desk. "What are you doing?"

"I'm reminding you of what we have between us," she said.

"I have no idea what you're talking about. Don't try to create something ugly."

"It's not ugly at all. It was beautiful. And exciting."

He stood. "Is that how the rumor about us started? You fabricated it yourself?"

"No! Of course not. But it happened. I know you remember." He'd had a lot to drink that night, but he wasn't passed out. He might have a foggy memory, he might not want to examine the memory, but she knew it was there. She could feel it.

"Nothing like that ever happened."

"Yes it did. I know you're attracted to me. And I'm not saying I want to get something going. I love Matt. But we've had a lot of fun thinking about what almost happened that night, knowing those feelings are there. It's exciting. I know you feel it too."

"This is my career. This is what makes me excited. If you think I've been inappropriate, I'm very sorry for that. It wasn't my intention to make you uncomfortable."

"You didn't make me uncomfortable at all. Sit down so we can finish talking."

He looked shocked. She'd never told him what to do before. It felt good, another layer of uncertainty. Not knowing what was going to happen made her body feel alive.

"We should both get home, Vanessa."

"But you aren't going home. You don't have a home except on the weekends. This is your life. Avalon, this office." She looked at him, widening her eyes, unblinking. "Me."

"I don't know what you remember or what you think this is, but I'm your manager, you're my admin, and that's the end of it. I really need to get going. And so do you."

She settled back in the chair. "Are you going to grab me and pull me out the door? Carry me down the stairs?"

"Stop it." He went to the coat rack and lifted off his jacket. Without turning, he put on the coat and tugged the collar into place. His back was more impassive and straighter than ever. He finally turned toward her and opened his desk drawer. He pulled out his keys and sunglasses and closed the drawer. "Let's go."

She tried to breathe. Was he leaving Avalon because of her? Was this not about his career at all? It was possible she'd pushed too far. But she was certain he remembered. In fact, it was his overreaction that proved he did. Otherwise he'd laugh it off. He was unnerved, scared, maybe. She smiled. She stood and tossed her hair over her shoulders. There was time to continue this conversation later. He wasn't gone yet.

Twenty-four

LAURA WALKED WITH long, rapid strides, passing Brent's office and one of the smaller conference rooms. She turned the corner and darted past Vanessa's cube. She tapped one knuckle on Hank's door. Before Vanessa could speak or Hank could look up from his computer, she pressed down on the handle and opened the door. Vanessa didn't say a word or make a move to object. Maybe she wasn't even there. Laura didn't turn to look. It didn't matter whether Vanessa had anything to say. Nothing mattered but getting in front of Hank. She closed the door quickly.

Hank's fingers tapped at the keyboard. He glanced at her but continued typing. "I'm busy. If you want an appointment, arrange time on my calendar through Vanessa."

"Vanessa can never seem to find an opening. I'll only take a minute." She pulled a chair out from the table and turned it to face his desk. She sat down and crossed her legs. She smiled, striking a perfect balance of confident, charming, and casual.

"I never had my second interview," she said.

He lifted his hands away from the keyboard. "Things have changed."

"What things?"

He folded his arms and leaned back. He tipped his head up and looked at the ceiling. After several seconds, he brought his head forward slightly and bent his neck to the left then to the right. Cartilage in his neck cracked. He lowered his chin and looked at her. "I'm writing the email now, but I guess there's no harm in telling you, if you can manage to keep it to yourself for thirty minutes."

"Of course."

"Your track record says differently."

"When I'm asked to keep a confidence, I do."

He nodded. "Hm. At any rate, I've accepted a position at QualData."

Laura gasped — a soft, sudden intake of cool air that stung the back of her throat. She hoped he hadn't heard. "Is it a promotion?"

"Yes. Senior Vice President of corporate strategy."

"Congratulations." She smiled and all of the confidence and charm she'd managed to inject into her expression a moment earlier slid like something heavy and wet off the sides of her cheeks, leaving behind the sensation that she'd endured several shots of Novocain.

"Thank you."

"When is your last day?"

"Next Friday, but you know Avalon will ask me to leave immediately. Shut off my email access."

"Don't you have to wrap things up? Get your staff up to speed? What about . . ."

"You know that's not how it works. And the beauty of a well-developed staff is they'll keep the ball moving down the field while my successor is identified."

"Any idea who they might consider?"

He shrugged.

"I assume you'll make the offer to the Operations Director before you resign."

"No. It's more appropriate for the new guy, or gal, to do that."

"The position's been open for months. It needs to be filled."

"There's no rush. We don't want to simply plug in a warm body."

"I know that, but I think it's important to have it locked down."

"Do you?"

"Let me be blunt."

"Always."

She grimaced. "I think we can agree I'm the perfect fit. It would be better for the company if it's taken care of before you resign. It could be months before a new VP is in place, and more delays while that person decides how to structure the group."

"It's not appropriate for me to hire someone when I'm on my way out the door. The offer wouldn't be approved anyway."

"Since when are you worried about what's appropriate?"

He leaned his forearms on the desk. "You'll have to interview with my successor. That's the way it is. Are there any other complaints you wanted to bring to my attention?"

"I'm not complaining." It was difficult to breathe. Her hands were hard knots of bone and twitching nerves, tiny flesh-made bombs ready to detonate in her lap. "I'd be disappointed if that's your final call, of course. I hope I can change your opinion."

"It's not an opinion."

She managed to untwist her fingers. She leaned forward, pinning her elbows to her thighs. There must be a way to surprise him, get him thinking in a different direction. In all of her fretting about the promotion, the battle to schedule interviews, she'd never once considered the possibility he might leave the company. This was Vanessa's fault. He could talk all he wanted about process and change, but if Vanessa hadn't blocked Laura from seeing him, told him she was a gossip, things would not have reached this state.

The shelves behind his desk were nearly empty. No packing boxes were visible, so he must have already taken his personal things to his apartment, or shipped them home. All that remained was the Japanese sword, as if he thought he might need to use it before he left Avalon. Laughter tickled her throat. She took a deep breath and held it for a moment. Bursting out in a gut-boiling laugh would make her look like a mad woman, although her thought was legitimate. No one ever knew how close they might be to committing murder. All it took was the right set of circumstances, the right emotional storm. In the end, it gave you a strange sense of control over the world. She sat up straight again. He hadn't moved or altered his expression. He was going to force her to argue with him. "I put a lot of effort into developing my career here."

"I know."

"I assumed the position would be mine."

"I know that too."

"Then why are you doing this? I think I've proven I'm qualified. I think I deserve the job. I don't think there's anything inappropriate at all in offering it to me, in letting the guys above you know that you left things in capable hands. Then the new VP can start with a fully staffed team."

"If I wasn't leaving, I wouldn't have offered you the job, Laura."

"What?"

"You need further development before you're ready for the next level."

"I don't need anything of the kind."

"It's statements like that which prove you do. You're too impressed with yourself."

"What does that mean?"

"You do good work on paper, but you need more polish, more leadership skills. That's critical for a director." He paused. "I'm doing you a favor here. Do you want some input to help you in the future or not? If you're going to rise to the next level, you need to accept some coaching."

"I think I do all those things. And I have shown leadership, I drove that project . . ."

He held up his hand. "Don't be defensive. You let your emotions prevent you from taking charge of situations and getting things done, even when it's unpleasant."

"Give me one example."

He put his hands on the desk, palms down. "It's a general impression."

"That's completely unfair and not true." She could hardly think, watching his face. He refused to give any hint that he had some respect, much less admiration, for her. She'd given this man dedication and passion and high quality work for years. She had an MBA and a solid career filled with positive performance reviews and he treated her like a delusional new college grad filled with self-importance. He was treating her like his admin, for god's sake.

"Don't get worked up," he said.

She knew her exterior was as smooth as his. There was no way he could sense the rage pouring through her. He was assuming she was upset, pegging her as female and therefore automatically less capable, lacking self control.

"I'm giving you my impressions as a senior manager with

more experience and more insight into what the business requires."

"I've done lots of things that were unpleasant."

"Such as?"

"You might not be aware of all of them. They weren't necessarily at Avalon. I removed someone who was a threat."

"What does that mean?"

"Take it at face value." She couldn't say more than that, but it was a perfect example. There was no way he'd find out. As long as she used business terminology to describe it. The situation was almost funny, because that's exactly what she'd done. An unpleasant task to take care of a problem.

"You terminated an employee who was a threat to the company?"

"I terminated a man who was not behaving appropriately, yes."

"At Avalon?"

"I can't say."

"Being a manager isn't about terminating people."

"Being an *effective* manager . . ." She paused to let him absorb the dig. "Being an effective manager means getting people to perform. That's one of the biggest problems here, at all large companies, really. It's the eighty-twenty rule. If companies are able to shift that proportion, if they can staff the organization so that even fifty percent of the employees are doing eighty percent of the work, think about how productivity would increase. It's actually a very important part of being a manager."

"That's a good insight." He cupped his chin in his hand, his fingers extended so they touched his temple. He drew his hand down his face. If he had a beard, he'd be stroking it, tugging the hairs so they stretched the skin like a piece of canvas being fitted over a wood frame.

There was an open door, she could feel it. He hadn't smacked her down, hadn't ended the conversation. She straightened her shoulders and unbuttoned her jacket. She put one hand on the table, touching her phone, anchoring herself for the next step — a high wire artist sliding her foot along a cable, curling her toes, feeling her way out into the middle of space, confident she couldn't possibly fall sixty feet onto hard-packed earth. "You have no idea what I'm capable of, when it comes to taking care of problems, of threats, if you will."

"Why are you using that term? It sounds like hyperbole."

"When I see a serious threat, I don't hesitate to do what needs to be done. To take care of business." Never in a million years would he guess she was talking about killing a man. There was no way his mind would leap to such an outrageous possibility. She was safe. And it was fun, a little dangerous, to brag about what she'd done, to describe the situation without giving any information. It was remarkable what she'd managed to accomplish.

Hank laughed, although he didn't sound amused. Nervous, if she was reading it right.

"You sound like you're with the mafia."

She smiled. "That's a good way to put it."

"I didn't mean it as a compliment," he said.

"Well I'm taking it as one."

He stroked his chin again. "Anyway, this is all just so much theory. The fact is the position will remain open until the new VP comes on board." He leaned forward, typed a few strokes on the keyboard, and clicked the mouse. He pushed back his chair and stood.

"I thought you were coaching me." It was a frantic, last minute toss, but she couldn't let him dismiss her. If there really was a solid reason he hadn't offered the job, she supposed she needed to know what that was. She was sure anything he said would be incorrect, but she needed to know what he was thinking in order to plan her next move.

"That's right," he said.

It wasn't clear what he was referring to. She folded her hands but he didn't speak. The room was colder than earlier. She shivered, wishing she could control the involuntary response that raced through her body, but it was impossible. "What else?" she said, twisting her legs toward the table, hoping her movement covered the shivering.

"You have questionable judgment."

"Such as?"

"Repeating baseless rumors."

She didn't have to ask what that referred to.

"Look . . ." He turned and lifted his coat off the rack. "I

need to get going."

"Without giving me a chance to defend myself?"

"This isn't a debate. You have questionable judgment. You said you wanted coaching, you got it. Think before you speak and don't get involved in petty rumors and politics. Learn to show more leadership."

"Everything in the workplace is political."

"Only if you make it that way." He walked around his desk. "Let's go."

"We all make mistakes."

"Some mistakes are more egregious than others."

"You're angry because it involved you."

"You took advantage of a woman in an inferior position."

He stood only a few feet away now. She should stand up, not allow him to look down at her like this, but if she stood, the conversation would be over. He'd win. He walked past her and opened the door. She stood and picked up her phone. She wanted to take his sword and slide it through his throat, stop those condescending words from spilling up out of his gut without any recognition of her accomplishments and capabilities. Or maybe Vanessa was the one that was more deserving of the business end of that fancy sword. It would be so easy. More than she ever would have guessed. "I didn't take advantage of her. I was concerned she was taking advantage of you. An atmosphere charged with sex is not good for the business and you know it."

"Then you should have focused your gossip on me. I can

take it. You went for the weaker player."

"I didn't start the rumor." It was a flat out lie, but he'd never figure that out.

"Doesn't matter. Anyway, next time, think about what you're doing. It doesn't indicate leadership potential when you attack lower level employees, trying to ruin reputations."

"It wasn't directed at her."

"Bullshit."

She walked out the door. He closed it and locked it.

"I'm going to talk to Janelle," he said. "Have a good evening." He walked down the short hall and turned the corner. She heard his footsteps moving rapidly away from her.

The seating area in the alcove was dark. Vanessa's cube was also dark. Laura tugged her jacket around her waist and shoved her phone in her pocket. He'd won this round, but she could still turn things back in her direction. She was in control here, not Hank.

Twenty-five

HANK HAD BEEN gone from Avalon for over two weeks and Vanessa hadn't heard a word from him. He'd been replaced by a woman from Engineering — Margaret Meadows. Margaret was crisp and efficient. She was overjoyed to have an experienced admin, and couldn't see any reason to make changes, but the mere mention of changes, created a pinch of loss at the base of Vanessa's throat.

Within a few days of Margaret's arrival in Hank's office, it felt as if he'd never been there. The days were now bland routine — scheduling meetings, filing expense reports, answering Margaret's phone when she wasn't in her office, which was all the time as she got up to speed on the issues and status for the products under her domain. A life of boring administrative tasks.

By now, Hank should be equally settled in his new position. Even if he wasn't, he could have at least sent an email or a text letting her know how things were going. She'd texted him twice and he hadn't replied. Her first message read — *Hey, how are things?* After thinking it over for a few days, she decided the message created the expectation of a lengthy response, so her second message, four days later, read — *Free for lunch this week?* Nothing. Not even a — *Will get back 2 u.* Several times she could have sworn the phone, tucked into the front pocket of her jeans, had vibrated against her hipbone. She'd pulled it out and stared in disbelief at the lifeless screen. The urge to send a third text was overwhelming, but she resisted by surfing the web, without success, for a floor plan of Bloomingdale's.

It was eleven-forty. She glanced at the desk phone. The light for Margaret's line was dark. She stood and shook her hair back from her face so it fell loosely across her shoulders, a habit that was difficult to break. As if he were still there, waiting for her behind the closed door, she wore skinny jeans and high heels with a white silk top. She was pretty sure Margaret didn't like the skinny-jeans-high-heels look, but she'd never said anything. Margaret shot occasional glances in Vanessa's direction, sharp and knowing, then turned her attention toward the window, as if redirecting her attention kept her tongue securely lashed to the back of her teeth. Vanessa tucked her left hand in her pocket up to her knuckles. The diamond caught on the edge of the fabric, pressing into bone. She pulled her hand out half an inch and crossed the hall. She tapped on Margaret's door and opened it.

Margaret looked up from the computer screen. She tucked her too-short hair behind her ears. "What can I do for you?"

Every time Vanessa entered the office, Margaret asked the same question. Vanessa was the one doing things for Margaret. What Margaret should have said was, *what do you need* or *what's your question?* The funny thing was, Vanessa couldn't remember what Hank used to say when she entered his office without an appointment. Margaret appeared to be staring at Vanessa's belt. Vanessa pulled her fingers out of her pocket. "I'm going to take an early lunch."

"That's fine."

"I might be gone longer than usual."

"How much longer?"

"Maybe two hours total, or a little more."

Margaret nodded. "That's fine. Thank you for letting me know."

"Sure." Vanessa should also be the one saying thank you for the extra time allowed. Now she was left not knowing what else to say. "Okay, I'll see you around one-thirty."

Margaret nodded and turned back to her computer.

Vanessa closed the door. She grabbed her coat, umbrella, and purse. She hurried down the hall and along the landing to the stairs. She descended slowly. The lobby was empty except for a man in a dark brown suit with a white shirt and tie, obviously waiting for an interview. He wasn't there to see Margaret. She'd said nothing about the open position Laura was trying to claw her way into. Although since Hank left,

Laura hadn't stopped by once. So much for women sticking together and their supposed friendship.

Outside, she popped open her umbrella. There was a delicate drizzle, the raindrops like snowflakes. As she stepped out from beneath the overhang, they fell on the umbrella without a sound. She walked to the car and got in, managing to keep her hair dry, although the backs of her hands and wrists were covered with moisture when she closed the door.

Hank's new company was three quarters of a mile away, a straight shot up Winton Avenue, over the freeway, and a left turn onto Fairoaks. The building was five stories, made of concrete. The windows had a bluish tint. Avalon was all glass, giving it a fragile appearance, as if someone could toss a rock and the entire structure would shatter into billions of glittering fragments. If you ignored the narrow windows, QualData, with its beveled concrete corners, looked like an enormous bar of soap.

She parked in a visitor slot near the lobby door. She studied her lips in the rearview mirror. A touch-up of tinted gloss would be good, but she risked over-doing it and ending up with sticky-looking lips, too wet, as if she'd just pressed her mouth into a swirl of frozen yogurt. It was better not to look overdone. She shoved the lip gloss back in her purse. This whole effort was a risk. Hank might not be there. However, if his history predicted anything, he rarely made lunch plans, preferring a sandwich at his desk. The other, greater risk was that he would refuse to see her. It was still early — five minutes to twelve. But by the time she fumbled with her umbrella and spoke to the receptionist, it would be noon. The umbrella was a hindrance, but she couldn't meet him with wet skin, her hair drooping. She planned to leave the umbrella in the lobby, tucking it under a chair and hoping it went unnoticed until she was finished.

As it turned out, getting in to see him was shocking in its simplicity. The receptionist called Hank, he answered, and granted Vanessa permission to check in and receive a visitor's badge, indicating he'd be down to escort her to his office in ten minutes. While she waited, her hands turned icy cold, shrinking into themselves. Her ring was loose, sliding toward her knuckle, making her worry it would slip right off her hand.

It was possible Hank felt guilty for ignoring her. It was also possible she'd arrived at the perfect moment in time, that he'd realized this very morning he missed her terribly, that he was bored without their flirting looks and daily gossip sessions, that she had far more to offer than whatever admin was currently supporting him, and he'd do whatever it took to get the girl moved to an alternate role, making a place for Vanessa. Her heart started to beat faster, which should have warmed her hands, but failed to have an impact, as if the steady rhythm wasn't capable of moving blood throughout her body. Her fingertips were white. She hoped it wouldn't give away her fear.

When he appeared at the opposite side of the lobby, he

looked different. As he walked past the reception desk, she approached him slowly. He did not shake her hand, but asked how she was doing and led the way to the elevator that had already raced off to another floor. While they waited for its return, he said, "Nice of you to stop by. How are things going at Avalon?" They chatted about Margaret's management style. The chill left her hands and she felt her body settle down.

His office was on the fourth floor, a corner spot, but not as large as the one at Avalon. It was much darker, with the smaller windows, the tinting, and the darkness enhanced by the wood stain on the furniture. That, too, was different. At Avalon, the only wood had been his small conference table. Here, there was wood everywhere — shelving, desk, a small sofa with wood trim. Thickly cushioned chairs with wooden arms and legs surrounded the table. The solid furnishings looked crowded in the smaller space. Hank pulled out a chair for her. He sat behind his desk and glanced at his computer. "So, what can I do for you?"

She wanted to laugh at the phrase, as if it had been passed around to all Silicon Valley vice presidents. She crossed her legs and smiled. "I hadn't heard from you. I decided to take the initiative, since you always said that's one of my strengths."

He didn't smile. He settled back in his chair and placed his fingertips on the edge of the desk. To the left of his hands was a wood in-box, an empty relic from the past. Lying next to that was his leather-covered calendar and on top of it was the dark red Montblanc pen. Hank had lusted after that pricey pen for years before he'd purchased it. She'd never understood the attraction. It was beautiful, a classy status symbol, but there was hardly any paper around the office, and he rarely used the datebook. There was no need for a pen of any kind.

"I can't offer you a job, or even discuss the possibility right now. Just so we're clear," he said.

"We never finished our last conversation."

"I just told you . . ."

"You pretending you don't remember what happened in New Orleans."

"I invited you in here because I thought you'd act like the professional I know you are."

"What did you think I wanted? You should have known I was here either for your promise of a job or to close off our unfinished business."

"I can't read your mind. I imagined you wanted advice on your career."

Vanessa stood and moved the chair back to its place at the table. She walked around the end of his desk. She sat on the edge, extending her legs. Her jeans rode up slightly, exposing her ankles. Hank pushed his chair away from her. He folded his arms across his chest, gripping each bicep with the opposite hand. The skin around his eyes and lips was dark, either from the absence of sunlight coming through the windows or something brewing inside of him.

She smiled. "We've been friends a long time. You know something happened in New Orleans. I need to get closure."

"That's an overused term and an overrated idea."

"I treated you with respect that night. I never told anyone. Not one single person. And I think you should give *me* some respect and not act like there isn't anything between us. Because there is." She scooted along the desk. It was easy to slip across the polished wood. She pressed her heels harder into the carpet to prevent sliding so fast she flung herself at his feet. Her toes were inches from his. She waited for him to adjust his position. He stared at the floor. The carpet was an odd tan color with a gray undertone. The inadequate light it make it look like sickly skin, badly in need of vitamin D and the other life-giving properties of sunshine. It swam before her eyes. She was staring too hard. The silence was going on too long and it made her unsure of her next move.

"What's to be gained by talking about the past?" he said.

She moved her gaze from the floor to his chin, not yet ready to look at his eyes. If she waited long enough, he might come around, but if she looked up too soon, she might see coldness there. She was not leaving this office until he admitted he was attracted to her. That's all she wanted, an honest statement that there was more between them than admin and boss. If he couldn't acknowledge they had a friendship, at least he would confess his desire, because there was no doubt about that. He could protest all he wanted, but she knew the truth. She was going to wait until he stopped acting as if it were all her. He owed her that. "You kissed me and it's insulting that you pretend nothing happened. That you don't appreciate how I kept you from doing something dangerous. That you act as if I'm a crazy girl with a crush on her boss. It was you. You wanted me. You want me now. I can feel it."

"What are you trying to do?" His voice was low, tight with anger. "Are you trying to punish me for leaving Avalon?"

"No."

"I think you are."

"I want you to admit you want me."

"Why?"

"Because it's the truth."

"What difference does it make? We don't have a relationship. We never will."

"I don't want a relationship. I just want you to stop pretending."

"So you *are* the one who started the rumor. Is that what it was all about, to get to this?"

"No." She stood. She moved to the side of his chair. "It wasn't me." She put her hand on the side of his face. His jaw stiffened under her fingertips. His chair was pressed against the short edge of the L in his desk, preventing him from moving away. She slid her hand around the back of his head, weaving her fingers through his hair. She bent over and brushed her lips across his, glad now that she hadn't reapplied her lip gloss. She ran her hand down his chest to his belt. She inserted her first two fingers behind his waistband.

He grabbed her wrist, and yanked her hand away. "Stop it." Holding her wrist in a firm grip, twisting hard, he stood. "I'm going to get some coffee. Pull yourself together and then go outside and ask my admin to escort you out of the building. She's two doors down."

"Wait."

"No. I don't know what you want from me, but you're not getting it. You can imagine all you want about the past, but it's irrelevant. Nothing happened."

"It did."

"It doesn't matter."

"But . . ."

"You're not going to sabotage my career."

"Is that what you think?"

After he walked out and closed the door, more softly than she would have expected, she settled herself in his chair. It was just a chair, but it represented a position she'd never have. She would never be in charge, never be the one with the power, not even close. Right now, she wasn't sure what she'd ever be, period. She leaned back and put her feet on the desk, crossing her ankles. He hadn't relaxed his body for even a moment, yielded to her hands or her lips on his face. He sat in this chair and saw the thin blouse clinging to her breasts, her jacket falling open to show the denim hugging her thighs and hips. Nothing. Was he right? Had that moment in her hotel room existed only in her imagination? She removed her feet from the desk and stood. No. She remembered every detail perfectly. But it was lost forever. She felt sad that the flirting and good times might have been more on her side than his. It was insulting that he could ignore her like this. There was no doubt he desired her, his glances every day for the past few years told her that, but apparently his career mattered more. She reached over and moved the mouse to wake his computer screen. All that appeared was the small box for entering a password. He didn't trust her. She typed her name in the box but it returned an *invalid username* message. She straightened. It was time to get going before his new admin came knocking.

The arms of the chair bumped against the desk as she moved behind it. The Montblanc pen on the day timer jiggled, as did the coffee cup near his keyboard. She walked to the end of the desk and picked up the pen. It was heavy. She imagined the beautiful script it would create on an acid-free sheet of paper. She removed the cap and wrote in the air, signing her name starting with a flourish for the *V* and ending with an upward sweep on the tail of the *a*. She replaced the cap and extended her hand, letting the pen rest across her palm. The heft spoke of the cost involved in creating something designed to last. She walked around the desk, picked up her purse, and dropped the pen inside. She buttoned her jacket and went out of his office.

Twenty-six

IF HANK THOUGHT he could brush Laura aside, leaving the company without bothering to finish their conversation, he was in for a surprise. In some ways, his leaving might have opened another door. There was no reason he couldn't give her the inside track for a director position at QualData. Leaving Vanessa behind like the lackey she was might suggest he had a whole new attitude. She shouldn't go in assuming that, but it was a possibility. The point was, she would not allow him to just walk away.

She settled back on the couch and lifted the wine glass to her lips. She took a sip of smooth, dark Barbera. All the lights were turned off, except the one illuminating the fish tank. The water glowed with a green tint caused by the lush seaweed filling the space, giving the fish plenty of room to hide when they needed down time. The Volitan hovered at the front, watching her. She'd fed them dinner earlier and both of them had consumed more than usual — four good-sized chunks of lance fish each. The Volitan's spines waved and flicked at her. He was trying to look tough. He didn't recognize how completely helpless he was. Their lives would come to an agonizing end without Laura supplying food and ensuring the tank was kept clean. If there was an earthquake and seventy-five gallons of water gushed across her loft, they would suffocate on the damp floor. Or if the tank simply cracked, and water seeped out over days, and she wasn't there to notice.

She took another sip of wine. It was sending calories right to her fat cells, layering on another unwanted inch to her belly. As soon as she got this job thing settled, she'd double down on her running. The gym was okay for now, but she needed to find a new track or overcome the paranoia that returning to Carlton High School would somehow expose her guilt. Maybe, for the short term, she'd run on pavement.

She put the glass on the table and leaned her head back on the cushion. The detective hadn't returned. The police had no idea what questions to ask. There was nothing to be found out. No one had seen her. She'd been right all along.

She finished her wine and went upstairs.

SHE WOKE AT three a.m. She lay on her back and stared at the shadow of the exposed beams above her bed. In her dream, she'd been sitting on a metal folding chair in an empty room. A detective stood under a high, narrow window, asking her questions. It had gone on for hours — the same questions over and over until Laura wanted to scream with boredom, and maybe she had. Maybe that's what woke her. The detective seemed to think Laura wasn't smart enough to maintain her carefully constructed lie, that the repetition of rephrased questions would trip her up. The detective was wrong. The lie was simple. The best lies always were. It wasn't as if she had to remember a complex series of events. She'd never seen the guy. That was it. When she ran, she was in the zone.

After another fifteen minutes flat on her back, eyes open, the cool air and the darkness settling over her eyeballs, soothing them at first, then drying them so that they itched, she decided sleep was over for the night. She got up, went downstairs, and spread out her yoga mat facing the aquarium. The light was off. She heard the rumbling of the pump but the fish were shrouded in darkness. She was often surprised by their invisibility when there was no light. It seemed their colorful, intricately featured bodies, especially the white stripes, should somehow reveal themselves as they glided through the water. She reassured herself that the rumbling of the pump, creating an artificial current and moving oxygen throughout the tank, indicated they were alive, either sleeping or hovering in their limbo state, almost as if they ceased to exist when she wasn't watching them.

Starting with a sun salutation, despite the lack of sun, she did an hour of yoga, pushing herself to maintain each pose a few counts longer than usual, staying in the warrior pose until her shoulders ached and the quadricep of her forward leg trembled with the effort of remaining parallel to the floor. When she was finished, her body was warm, the back of her neck damp, and her muscles calmed by the exertion. It wasn't like running, but it helped drain the pent-up energy. She rolled up the mat, tucked it under her arm, and walked to the aquarium. She turned on the light. The Radiata emerged from the plants and swam past her, moving slowly along the front of the tank, then turning as if it wanted her quiet admiration. She wondered if they felt her attention, her devotion to them. If it was true what they said, that everything was energy, maybe even simple creatures like fish absorbed the vitality of the life pulsing around them. She certainly absorbed theirs.

She went upstairs to the bathroom and turned on the faucets in the shower. While the water heated, she put a new blade on her razor. After she washed herself, she soaped her legs and ran the razor from her ankle to her hip, in slow, careful strokes, making sure to overlap each one until her legs were as soft as an infant's. She dried her hair and put on makeup and dressed in black slacks, flat-heeled ankle boots, and a black long-sleeved t-shirt. She fed the fish, made coffee, and answered emails while she waited for the sun to come up.

The sun didn't actually come up, but the sky behind the thin covering of clouds slowly grew lighter. At seven she went out and locked the door.

The QualData parking lot was nearly empty, but just as it was at Avalon, a few cars were scattered at the far edges, some hunkering down for a long stay with protective canvas covers. Whether people who had to pay for parking at their condos utilized it for second cars, or those traveling overseas had the transportation service pick them up on site, those scattered cars were like fixtures. There was an older white Carmen Ghia at Avalon that Laura could have sworn had been parked there for three years. It wasn't particularly dirty and it didn't have a look of abandonment about it, but it was there day in and day out, no matter what time she arrived in the morning or left at night.

QualData was a monolithic building, not a campus-like spread of several structures like Avalon, so she didn't have to figure out what building Hank worked in. She parked near a large pick-up truck that hid her Porsche, if Hank even knew what kind of car she drove. The angle of the truck allowed her to see the entrance to the building. The added benefit of a medium-sized tree hanging over the hood of her car prevented anyone from noticing it was occupied if they stood more than fifteen feet away. She reclined the seat slightly and settled herself more comfortably.

Watching people arrive for work was more entertaining than she would have thought. She'd never noticed before, always caught up in her own destination and plans for the day, just like the QualData employees. Some scurried to the building as if a pack of dogs was chasing them. Others strolled while scanning the lot as they walked. If they happened to see a co-worker, they zeroed in like they were conducting man-on-the-street interviews. The women wearing heels took small steps, and one guy wearing hard-soled dress shoes also walked with a mincing gait, staring at the ground to ensure he didn't slip. A few were bent forward, faces twisted into scowls of pressure, racing to the front doors, only to turn around and jog back to their cars seeking forgotten laptop bags or coffee cups left on the roof.

Hank arrived at seven-forty. As always, he parked as far as possible from the building, in a sea of empty spaces, his car in an end slot to ensure there wasn't the remotest chance of a ding to the black paint of his Mercedes S-class. There was nothing about him indicating it even crossed his mind that someone might be watching him.

At the CEO level, most men, and the occasional woman, had protection of some kind. In large corporations, senior executives often warranted that as well, but at Hank's level, there didn't seem to be any concern with his personal safety. It was kind of funny because someone of his rank could just as easily piss off an employee. Maybe even more so, because the lower you were in the pyramid, the thinner the cushion insulating you from direct consequences. You'd think they'd be scared.

There were all kinds of precautions inside the building to avert workplace violence — trained security guards at the reception desk who specialized in defusing tense or potentially dangerous situations, doors accessible only with ID cards. But in the parking lot, there was only the periodic passing of white security trucks, mostly watching for car break-ins.

Even people delivering flowers weren't allowed past the front desk. The recipients had to come to the lobby, pursuing their own gifts, which deflated the surprise and took some of the luster off being doted on. That's how it had been when Tim sent her flowers that time. Except worse. So much worse. Tim managed to take the smallest humiliation and ratchet it up unmercifully.

It was after her striptease. As if that hadn't been soul-shattering enough, the next day he had an enormous vase containing eighteen red roses delivered to her office. The bouquet sat there for over three hours because she'd been in a meeting and hadn't received the voice mail notification until late afternoon. The flowers were breathtaking, and the scent was like music, so sweet, so rich and fresh. They came with a rather large card bearing the shadowy sketch of a woman's profile. Being the cruel man that he was, the card was not in an envelope. It stood right in the center of the bouquet for everyone to read — the receptionist, people stopping to wait for visitor badges, her co-workers.

When she arrived in the lobby, there was that card, bearing Tim's large, child-like script: *I'm sorry I laughed at you. Watching you strip was amazing. Please don't worry you aren't sexy, because you are!!!* She wanted to rip out his fingernails, even now.

At the time, she'd thought his twisted behavior was all about sex. She'd thought he wanted to force her to recognize how much she desired him. It wasn't until the incident with her DKNY shirt that she'd understood it differently. She'd tried to fight him that day, demanding he let go of her, screaming at him for ruining her shirt. His hands had grown tighter around her breasts, squeezing until they ached. She whimpered involuntarily. To get him to stop, she'd lowered her voice, made it soft and meek, but he'd interpreted it as desire. He released his grip and she'd slipped out from between him and the counter. She knelt on the floor and picked up two of the buttons. Another button lay just under the table. She crept toward it and suddenly he was on top of her, pressing her against the floor. His body was as unyielding as the tile beneath her.

"You're my wife. Marriage is a contract, fifty-fifty, and you're not contributing your fifty percent. You give everything to your job and there's nothing left for me." He grabbed her hair and yanked her head close to his chin. "We haven't had sex in twenty-three days, but you have time to run ten miles a day, time to stay at work until seven o'clock at night, time to spend Sunday evenings in front of your computer." He pinned her shoulders and upper arms to the floor with his forearm, shoved his knees into her legs, and slowly removed her shoes. He reached beneath her to unbuckle her belt, and pulled her pants down to her ankles. With his one free hand he'd ripped her underwear, not difficult with the thin lace panels at the sides. Then he'd stopped moving, breathing hard. She had no idea what he was waiting for. They remained like that — neither one speaking — for a long time.

Finally, he released his hold on her arms, and stood. He'd gone to the dining room, poured a shot of whiskey, and a moment later she heard the commentary of a baseball game come on.

Tim had started out wanting sex, but she'd learned that was only a small part of it. He simply wanted to humiliate her, to prove, maybe only to himself, that he had all the power. Not terribly different from Hank, making sure everyone noticed he was the VP, smiling as he watched her squirm in her effort to deliver perfect work all these years, hoping to demonstrate her worthiness. It had nothing at all to do with worthiness or her qualities as an employee. If it did, Janelle and Brent would not have beaten her to the next level.

She watched the front door of QualData for four days. Over the course of the week, her views began to change. Each day she took her place near the pick-up truck. Every day Hank arrived at seven-forty. Each evening she returned, observing him leave any time between six-thirty and eight. If he ever stayed later, that might give her an opportunity to confront him, but as it was, the parking lot was too busy at both ends of the time spectrum. She wasn't sure what she planned to do with the information about his coming and going. Watching him made her feel she was formulating a plan. But she had no plan. No idea how to get to him, or what she would say when she managed to pull it off. All she had was a hot, steady rage that wanted to make him deliver what he owed her.

THURSDAY MORNING AFTER her final vigil, she stopped in the Avalon coffee shop for a latte. In some ways the vigil had been useless. The more she thought about it, the more she realized there was no way she could confront Hank in that parking lot. Even when it was deserted, it wasn't deserted. The security trucks roamed around the clock without a measurable pattern. Random engineers, eyes glowing with the thoughts racing through their minds scuttled out like roaches, long after dark.

She waited in line, rubbing her thumb, stroking the nail like a worry stone, trying to figure out what she should do next.

Watching Hank had calmed her, made her realize there was only one sure way to punish him for the way he'd strung her along all these years. She wanted to kill him. She really did. The idea was intoxicating. Her life and her career and everything she wanted no longer rested in the hands of other people and their whims. There was no man draped in power, unilaterally in charge of hiring and firing, a man with no one to answer to for his capricious decisions. Killing a man, and not getting caught, was easy. All she needed was a creative plan to pull it off. She didn't need any team player bullshit — coming to consensus with a group. And that gun. What a gift that had been. Everything she'd suffered at the track, stripped of her ability to run, had been worth it for that lovely, shiny, perfectly engineered weapon covered right now by layers of lingerie. It stood out among the black and ivory, the mauve and white and coffee-colored silks and laces. An iron-hard container of the ultimate power. Well, maybe not ultimate, certainly not like automatic or nuclear weapons, but still, an object designed to deliver the ultimate punishment.

She no longer had to think about interviews or trying to work her way around a stubborn, seductive administrative assistant. It had been a cathartic, life-changing week. One in which she'd gone from a victim to a woman ready to take back her power. The more she thought about it, the more she realized a way forward was being laid out for her. She hadn't asked for that monster to harass and terrify her, but she'd taken care of herself and the reward had been the gun. The next piece would be gifted to her just as smoothly. She simply needed to let go and observe the flow of events that crossed her path.

She reached the front of the line. Instead of her usual non-fat latte, she ordered full up milk steamed into creamy foam. She walked to the stand with its supply of heat protective sleeves and caps. She slipped on the cardboard sleeve and pressed the lid into place. As she walked back to her building, she popped the top a bit and let the latte cool in the morning air. Just outside the lobby, she paused for a sip, satisfied and soothed by the rich taste.

"Hi, Laura." She recognized Brent's voice before she looked up. He sounded friendly, warm, almost. She took another sip and turned. He had a new laptop bag — small and compact, indicating he was carrying a new, slicker laptop. He wore an overcoat. Everything about him screamed executive wannabe. She was no longer bound by that world, the attempt to dress the part, to promote your skills every fucking time you opened your mouth, to demonstrate your value and leadership. She felt she was soaring above the earth, looking down on him in his simplistic, pointless, small-minded pursuit.

"I haven't seen you in a few days," he said.

"I've been busy."

"Interviewing outside the company?"

"Maybe."

He smiled. "Aren't you mysterious."

"Not really." She sipped her latte and studied his face. He seemed to want to talk, no longer judging her for whatever imagined inadequacies she had. It seemed as if her confidence, her determination to succeed in this new arena was creating an aura around her that altered his perception. His look of pity and condemnation was gone. His expression seemed anxious, his lips not pressed together with their usual determination. There was a small sprout of stubble on his jaw that he'd missed shaving. It was possible he wasn't so sure-fire confident now that Hank was gone. Who knew what changes Margaret would implement. The good old boys club had splintered. Maybe he was worried about his own career now.

He took a step toward her. "We should catch up."

She moved out of the path of the cold breeze sweeping through the space between the two buildings. "We should." And it came to her. A door opening right in front of her, welcoming her inside. "How about meeting up for a drink tonight?"

"Sure. That sounds good."

"The Four Seasons? At seven?"

He nodded.

She shifted her cup to her other hand, seeking the gentle warmth that had made its way through the cardboard sleeve. "Why don't you ask Hank to join us. It would be great to hear how things are at QualData."

He nodded, longer than necessary, his head bobbing up and down as if he couldn't agree fast enough. "That's a great idea. He's building a team there, it's always smart to keep our options open."

"I agree."

"I'll call him. We can probably count on him being free on a weeknight."

"Don't mention I'm joining you."

"Why not?"

"It might look like I'm hoping to get another opportunity for a promotion. And I'm not. Truly. I have other plans."

He nodded. "Okay. Sure."

She took a long drink of her coffee.

"I'll text you to confirm the time," he said.

She passed the coffee cup back to her left hand. She

stepped around him and opened the door, pulling back so he could enter first.

"Thanks." He walked into the building.

They went up the stairs without talking and parted ways on the landing. She glanced toward Margaret's end of the hallway. Vanessa's cubicle wasn't visible from where she stood. It might be interesting to drop by and wield her newfound power, but what was the point? It seemed like another lifetime when she'd lingered in front of Vanessa's counter, eating chocolates, a peasant at the gate, waiting for Hank to grace her with his presence.

LAURA SAW BRENT'S BMW right at the front of the smaller lot reserved for restaurant and bar guests of the Four Seasons Hotel. She drove all the way around to the back parking lot before she saw Hank's Mercedes, predictably parked far from any other cars, angled outside the lines so no one could get close on either side. She often thought that was the opposite of what he hoped — an invitation for malicious keying — but it seemed to work for him. It worked even better for her. Now she could proceed with plan A rather than the less-certain plan B.

Hank did not look at all surprised to see her when she walked into the lounge, her purse strap tugging at her shoulder with the weight of the gun. His lack of surprise meant Brent had done a good job paving the way. Her former self would have wondered what Brent had said, worried he'd made her look weak or needy. She might have hesitated before joining them, over-analyzing the expression on Hank's face, prepping for what she intended to say. Now she'd say what came to mind. What he thought of her didn't matter at all.

As she strode across the room, she felt people watching. It wasn't her thick leggings with riding boots, her tight, low cut sweater drawing their attention. All her clothes looked good on her. Always. Her hair was consistently well cut, swinging around her neck as she walked. This was something coming from inside, as if an enormous emerald glowed beneath her breastbone, emanating from her skin, drawing people to her, none of them entirely sure what the attraction was. It was the allure of freedom, of not giving a shit what anyone thought of you. That attitude of not caring alchemized into a seductive, irresistible power.

"It's good to see you, Hank." She nodded at Brent, set her purse on the floor in front of the chair, and settled down. The cocktail waitress appeared immediately. Laura glanced at the drinks on the dark wood block that functioned as a table. A beer for Brent and a glass of red wine in front of Hank. Without looking up, she said, "I'll have a martini. Sapphire gin, three olives."

The waitress left and Laura settled back in her chair.

"Did you cut your hair?" Brent said.

She shook her head.

"Change the color?"

"No." He sounded like a girl with his silly questions. She smiled. A moment later, the waitress returned and placed the martini in front of Laura. It had come so fast, the girl must have run to the bar and slipped it in ahead of the other orders. Laura picked it up and took a sip. The icy gin and vermouth bit her lips and filled her mouth and throat with the warm burn of alcohol.

"You look different from this morning," Brent said.

"Same old me."

Hank lifted his wine glass. "Cheers."

Laura raised her glass over the center of the table in their general direction then put it down without drinking. She pulled out the swizzle stick and sucked off an olive. They were the jumbo kind, which she appreciated. She chewed it slowly and watched the two men watch her.

Deliberately, Brent turned toward Hank and asked how he liked working for QualData. From there, he peppered Hank with questions about the culture and what the company's play was going to be in cloud computing. Laura sipped her drink and made occasional staccato comments when there was a break in the flow of words, but mostly she waited. It was only a matter of time before they finished their drinks and would be faced with the decision of whether to extend the evening.

The waitress made the decision for them. She returned before Brent had finished his beer. Hank's wine glass was empty. He ordered another Cabernet. Brent nodded for a second beer. Laura said, "I'm not ready yet. I don't want to drink this too fast."

When the second round of drinks came, Brent took two quick hits from his beer and then gripped it between both hands. "So when do you start poaching at Avalon to build out your new team?"

Hank grinned. "No plans yet."

"None?" Laura took a sip of her drink. She really didn't want to finish it. The alcohol had a clear and calming effect now, but a few more swallows and that feeling could turn quickly. She pulled out the stick and worked the second olive into her mouth.

Hank waited while she chewed the olive, then said, "How is Margaret doing?"

Hank was looking at Laura, but Brent spoke. "Great. Really great."

"Glad to hear it. She's a good gal. Smart."

The gin burned inside Laura's skull, whipping like a wildfire across her brain at Hank's dismissal of Margaret. He probably thought he'd offered a compliment. While Brent and Hank talked about the changes — non changes, really, just a variation in style, otherwise following the re-packaged strategy Hank had set out eighteen months earlier — Laura sucked the pimento out of the final olive. She swallowed it and ate the olive, holding it between her fingertips, taking tiny bites of the firm flesh. It was tart and salty and soaked with gin. She licked her fingers and moved to the edge of her chair. "I'd love to catch up more, but I need to get going."

She stood.

"Already?" Hank said.

She pulled a twenty out of her purse and dropped it on the table.

"It's not that much," Hank said. He pushed the bill in her direction.

"You just got here," Brent said. "I thought you wanted to enjoy a few drinks?"

"One martini is enough, don't you think?" She lifted her glass and put the bill underneath the base.

"That's too much cash," Hank said.

"No worries." She put her purse carefully over her shoulder, gave them a half wave, and walked purposefully toward the door, suggesting she had somewhere important to go. And she did.

The back lot where Hank had parked was twenty or thirty yards from the eight-lane 101 highway. BMWs and Mercedes, the Porches and the Lexuses of the privileged high tech workers raced alongside Hondas and Camrys and Fords. Another feature of Highway 101 was the sixteen-wheelers traveling up and down the state of California, banned from the scenic 280 Freeway closer to the foothills. The highway created a mind-splitting din twenty hours a day. She got in her car and settled down. She pulled out a pair of thin cotton gloves and put them on, then reached up and angled the rearview mirror so she'd be able to see anyone approach. She removed the gun from her purse and laid it on her lap. There was one other car besides Hank's on this side of the building — another Mercedes, older, beige. That owner of that car was the only risk. But what were the odds of two people walking out to this part of the lot at exactly the same time? Slim to none.

Less than twenty minutes after she'd settled down she saw a man striding across the parking lot. Hank's pace and rigid posture were distinctive. She climbed out of the car, leaving the door open behind her. A truck lumbered by on the freeway, as if to reassure her she wouldn't be heard. No one from the rooms high above would be able to recognize her or even see her car, parked too close to the building to be seen from that angle. She held the gun in her right hand, letting her arms hang naturally so he wouldn't notice it before she was ready. "Hank."

He stopped. Too far away. Twenty feet, at least. She'd never fired a gun. To ensure she didn't miss, she needed him close. Just like that truism her former manager used far too often — *keep your friends close and your enemies closer.* She smiled and took a few steps toward him, hoping her casual stance would draw him nearer.

"I thought you left."

It was a ridiculous thing to say, meaningless. "I deserved the Ops Director job."

"Are you going to rehash all that again?"

"No, I've moved on."

"Good." He walked toward his car.

She took a few steps forward. "There was one thing I wanted to tell you."

He stopped and pulled his key ring out of his pocket. "What's that?"

It was impossible to see his eyes, but she could feel his attention. Was that how it was for Vanessa? He was good looking, but not gorgeous, so it wasn't an attraction to physical perfection. It was that power thing. What she'd felt in herself. It made her want him. And Vanessa had been right about that, although it pissed her off that Vanessa recognized it. She wanted to be around him, to have him notice her, and she noticed her body responding to his presence. She edged closer until she felt his breath on her, warming her skin, the musky scent of wine.

He took a few steps back. She moved closer and put her hand on his belt buckle.

He tried to wrench away, but she had a firm grip.

He grabbed her hand, squeezing her forearm until it ached, trying to pry loose her fingers at the same time. "What are you doing?"

She laughed.

"I found out why your former team all left the company at once," he said.

"You don't know a fucking thing."

"It was exactly this kind of behavior. Bringing sex into the workplace."

"Like your admin? Is that why you're leaving? Men want

sex and then they run from an aggressive female."

"You're very screwed up, you know that?"

"Besides, all I did was tease them a little, act like one of the boys."

"Talking about your sex life, grabbing at them."

"It's an exaggeration. If it was that bad, they would have reported me. It was blown way out of proportion. Just an excuse. They left because they heard there was going to be a RIF."

He was still trying to pry her hand off his belt, but he wasn't trying very hard. They remained locked together in an awkward stance. "Either way, your career's over," he said.

"Wrong. Remember that man who was stalking me? I killed him." She laughed. "I'm not some weak, gossiping, emotional female." She lifted her right hand and pressed the gun into his stomach. "*Your* career is over, mine's just getting started." She pulled the trigger. The explosion was shattering. Louder than she'd imagined, and louder than the traffic on the freeway. At least in her ears. From further away, she was sure it would be lost in other sounds.

He doubled over. She let go of his belt and let him fall. He collapsed on his knees and groaned. "This was a big mistake." His voice was faint, almost female sounding.

She pressed the gun deeper into the soft part of his belly and pressed on the trigger three more times. He collapsed on his side. His head slammed onto the pavement. The rumble of trucks covered the sound of the impact, but the weight of his fall pulled at her body, filling her stomach with waves of nausea. Before the queasiness could overtake her completely, she shoved her hand in his pocket and pulled out the money clip full of cash. She unclipped his phone from his belt and powered it down. She returned to her car, dropped the gun, phone, and money clip into a waiting garbage bag and got inside. After she'd peeled off her gloves, she shoved them into a second bag, both of them to be discarded miles away. A drive to Marin County, maybe Santa Rosa, would be nice. The darkness and lights of passing cars would clear her head.

She started the car and headed toward the freeway. She'd known she was smarter than most of them, but getting to the top had nothing to do with brains. It was all about being in the right place at the right time, playing your cards with skill, and more importantly, cunning. Success required a willingness to take risks. It was time to start over at a new company. Now that she knew she needed to be ruthless, she'd climb up much faster. And her fortieth birthday was still three months away.

Twenty-seven

VANESSA SAT AT the kitchen table. Hank's Montblanc pen was lying in front of her — rich, shimmering red on the pale pine. All the lights in the house were out except the one over the table that she'd dimmed to the lowest possible setting. It cast a faint glow around the pen, making the red appear like a dark streak of blood.

It was difficult to believe Hank was gone. She hadn't even cried. Yet. The text message from Janelle had been so terse, so shocking, she hadn't believed it. She'd called Janelle and listened to her whispered confirmation. At first she'd thought the gunshots into Hank's body had blown a hole in the center of her life, but maybe not. Maybe the hole was already there. It wasn't as if Hank would grant her access to his office ever again. Even if he hadn't figured out she'd taken the pen. His dismissal had been final. She'd been right — they'd never see each other again.

The Four Seasons was a hotel out of place — five-star

elegance and ultra sleek decor built on the edge of crime-ridden East Palo Alto. She'd never understood why they put it there. It was a pricey hotel that did nothing but incite envy. He'd been robbed. Oddly enough his car wasn't stolen. Possibly the mugger, the killer, thought it was better to play it safe, take what you could get and not burden yourself with something that advertised what you'd done. She understood the thinking.

She turned the pen so the tip pointed at her. She picked up her wine glass and took a sip. Smooth, oaky Cabernet. Matt would be disappointed she hadn't waited for him, especially since it was such a nice bottle, but she needed to steel herself. It was only a small amount, less than half a glass. She took another sip. Their relationship was about to change. This could be the end, although maybe she'd already pushed him to the end. She felt she'd been asleep for years, ignoring all the great parts of her life, frantically chasing things she couldn't have. She couldn't explain, even to herself, why she wanted those things. Excitement, whatever that was. It wasn't happiness, that was for sure. She loved Matt. Why had she put all her energy into flirting with Hank? It wasn't as if she'd ever wanted him as a person. It would be hard to live with a guy who loved his career more than anything, a guy who loved his job so much, he moved out of his house to live close to his office, like a man moving into an upscale condo with his mistress. A man who was remote and confusing.

She held the stem of her glass with both hands and lifted it up to the light. The ID bracelet slid down her arm. She thought about the hidden word — princess. She laughed. What was she — ten years old, wishing she were a princess, admired and doted on? The flip side of being a princess was no one really liked you for who you were. Yet, for some reason, Matt did like her for who she was. Although he seemed to have a better idea of who that was than she did. She put down the glass and opened the clasp on the bracelet. The metal was heavy in the palm of her hand. She turned and pulled open the junk drawer. She dropped the bracelet on top of a stack of takeout menus.

The sound of Matt's car in the driveway pressed on her heart like she was walking down the aisle of a store, about to slip something into her purse. She touched the stem of the glass then pulled her hand away. There was only one sip left. The garage door opened, Matt's Mustang pulled into his space. The door closed, followed a few seconds later by the sound of the knob turning on the pantry door. She moved the pen so it was near the edge of the circle of light, dark and ominous. Did the size create that impression, or was it all in her mind, knowing what it cost? Hank must have noticed it was gone. He must have known she'd taken it. But he hadn't bothered to ask about it. He figured he could let a seven hundred dollar pen go without putting any effort into tracking it down.

Matt was in the doorway. "Did you pour me a glass?"

She pushed out her chair and stood. She finished her wine,

carried the glass to the counter, and set it next to the clean one. She poured wine into both. His glass was cold on her fingertips, the wine cooler than it should be, stored in the garage where it was too hot in the summer, too cold in winter, so their red wine was never quite right. "We should get a wine cabinet for inside the house," she said.

"What brought that up?"

She shrugged and handed the glass to him.

"Where'd you get that pen?"

"Let's go sit down in the living room and I'll tell you about it."

"I thought we were going to eat. It's almost seven."

"I'll make something quick. Mac and cheese, after we talk."

"About a pen?"

She picked up the pen and walked into the living room. She put the pen on the glass top of the coffee table, kicked off her shoes, and settled near the center of the couch. She pulled her feet up and sat curled like a cat. She took another drink of wine. Matt sat next to her and put his hand on her knee.

"What's the big secret? It looks expensive."

"Seven hundred bucks, at least. Some are as much twelve hundred, or more."

"What the hell?"

"It's Hank's."

He took his hand off her knee. "He gave it to you?"

"No."

"Then how did you get it?"

"Can you put your hand on my leg, it felt good."

"What's going on?" He put his hand on her knee again but his touch was tentative.

"I took it."

"You took it?"

"Stole it."

"Why?"

"Because."

She sipped her wine, waiting for another question, but none came. "He's dead, so it won't matter."

He put his glass on the table and turned toward her.

"He's dead!? Hank?"

"He was shot last night . . . at the Four Seasons in East Palo Alto. I guess he met Brent and Laura for drinks. He parked in a deserted back lot and someone shot him."

"Was he robbed?"

"Sort of. His cash was gone, and his phone. But his car was still there."

"Are you okay?" He squeezed her leg.

"I guess." She still didn't feel any hint of tears, and she wasn't sure why.

"You don't think taking his pen will . . . why did you take it?"

"I take a lot of things."

"What?"

"All the nail polish? The make-up? The clothes I haven't

worn. Other stuff. I take things."

"What do you mean, you *take* things?"

She swallowed some wine. "I shoplift. I've been doing it since I was fifteen."

"No shit?"

"Are you disgusted?"

"Not the word I'd choose." He stroked her leg for a moment. He pushed his hand between her knees. The pressure felt good on her bones, warm and secure, as if he had her firmly in his grasp.

"What word would you choose?"

"Surprised. Curious." He laughed. "What makes you do something like that?"

"It's exciting." She'd thought a lot about it, and that really was the truth. The compulsion was a need she had to satisfy, but the need wasn't just about proving she was smarter than other people. The main thing was the excitement. Not knowing what would happen, adrenaline pounding through her heart, quickening her brain like she'd had a double espresso.

"Interesting."

"I thought you'd be mad. That you'd want me to confess to the police or something." She sipped her wine. The glass was almost empty. She wished she'd brought the bottle into the living room. "I thought you might want . . ."

He looked at her, his hand still firmly planted between her knees. God it felt good. She relaxed her shoulders.

"You thought I might what?"

"That you'd want to split up."

He slid his fingers up her leg. "Hell no. I'm crazy about you."

"Really?"

"Especially now."

She put her glass on the table. "Especially now?"

He put his glass next to hers. He put his other hand on her waist and worked his fingers down her side, probing at the fabric until he reached underneath and touched her skin. Heat shot through her. He put his face close to hers and bit gently on her earlobe. "You have a lot of secrets. The way you attacked me in the dining room a few weeks ago . . ."

"You didn't seem very excited then."

He turned his head so she couldn't see his face. "I thought I was a stand-in for your boss."

Her throat tightened. She tried to swallow. "Never." Her voice was thin, barely audible with only a dribble of oxygen to support it. She'd come much closer to losing him than she'd realized.

"I think I see that. Now."

"You still want me? Even though I'm a thief?"

"Why would I give you up? You're the most exciting woman on the planet."

She laughed. "Don't be stupid."

"I'm not bullshitting." He pulled his hand out from between her legs and put his palm on her face, turning her head toward him, sliding his other hand up to the edge of her bra. He kissed her, long and slow. After a few minutes, he moved his head back a few inches. "I can't let go of you. You're gorgeous. And funny. You're smart. How many people can shoplift and get away with it for all that time?" He laughed again.

She tried to shrug her shoulders. It was difficult to move, the way he'd pinned her to the couch from all angles. Maybe she'd misjudged him. Maybe she didn't know him either. Maybe he did want more, whatever that meant.

"Let's get married," he said. "Now. This summer. And then . . . we need to figure out something else for you to do. Obviously you have a lot more talent than you've let on." He put his mouth on hers. It was soft and warm. Her lip gloss had worn off when she was at Bloomingdales, possibly licking her lips too much without noticing what she was doing. Feeling his skin on hers without anything between them was nice. Lip gloss looked great, but maybe it didn't make her lips any more kissable. She let herself melt into him. She had no idea where things were headed. It was so exciting she could hardly breathe.

THE END

About the Author

CATHRYN GRANT IS the author of Suburban Noir novels, ghost story novellas, and short fiction. Her writing has been described as "making the mundane menacing".

Her fiction has appeared in Alfred Hitchcock and Ellery Queen Mystery Magazines, and been anthologized in The Best of Every Day Fiction. Her short story, "I Was Young Once" received an honorable mention in the 2007 Zoetrope All-story Short Fiction contest.

When she's not writing, Cathryn reads fiction, eavesdrops, and plays very high handicap golf. She lives on the Central California coast with her husband and two cats. Contact Cathryn through her website at SuburbanNoir.com or sign up for her quarterly newsletter to receive updates when new books are released.